Seeing
in the
Dark

Seeing
in the
Dark

Short Stories by
R. Chudamani

Translated from Tamil by
Prabha Sridevan

Edited by
Mini Krishnan

OXFORD
UNIVERSITY PRESS

OXFORD
UNIVERSITY PRESS

Oxford University Press is a department of the University of Oxford.
It furthers the University's objective of excellence in research, scholarship,
and education by publishing worldwide. Oxford is a registered trademark of
Oxford University Press in the UK and in certain other countries

Published in India by
Oxford University Press
YMCA Library Building, 1 Jai Singh Road, New Delhi 110 001, India

© Oxford University Press 2015

The moral rights of the authors have been asserted

First Edition published in 2015

ISBN-13: 978-0-19-945967-4
ISBN-10: 0-19-945967-3

Typeset in 12/14 Garamond 3 LT Std
by Excellent Laser Typesetters, Pitampura, Delhi 110 034
Printed in India by Rakmo Press, New Delhi 110 020

To my tapestry of friends

Contents

Translator's Note / ix

Introduction: Unfolding Wings of Thought in the Inner Air ...
by Prema Nandakumar / xvii

Kinship Terms / xxxiii

A Trace of Envy / 1

We Don't Know / 3

That Fragile World / 8

Bhuvana and the Star Sign / 18

The Nagalinga Tree / 29

Who Could Have Told Them? / 40

Seeing in the Dark / 46

Ascent to the Shrine / 59

After Three Years / 69

Growing Up, Growing Apart / 77

A State of Mind / 88

He Is Not in Town / 95

The Downpour Outside / 106

Nothing Ever Happens / 117

Doctoramma's Room / 124

TV Aunty / 131

Heat and Rain / 140

A Rainbow in Her Hands / 149

Does Anyone Care? / 157

Woman in the Dark / 170

The Visitor / 177

Doors Closed Forever / 187

Neelayathakshi at Sixty / 196

The Couple / 208

The Fourth Stage of Life / 219

Loss of a Crest Jewel by Ambai / 233

About the Author and the Translator / 238

Translator's Note

Why did I start translating the book *Nagalinga Maram*?

Did Chudamani herself prod me?

No, this is not a vain statement. I will explain.

Chudamani bequeathed almost all her possessions to three institutions, and appointed my friend Bharathi as the executor of her will. Bharathi and Justice Chandru invited me to the function when the first instalment of the bequests was given away. It was then that the book *Nagalinga Maram*—a short-story collection—was released.

I read the stories in a single sitting. When I came to the end, I just wanted to talk to someone about it. Just then, my friend Chitra Mahesh called me, and I bubbled over with the stories that 'touched' me. She said, 'Such a pity I can't read Tamil.' I decided then that I would translate the stories. In fact, it was something I wanted to do for myself, really. I had no plans to get them published. A day or two later, Bharathi mentioned that there might be a demand for an English translation. I asked her if I could do it. She was thrilled and said it must be Chudamani's own decision. Both Justice Chandru and Bharathi were very encouraging and we vaguely discussed what should be done. Justice Chandru even started planning its release!

When I started writing in a thick diary, I felt a gentle presence near me, encouraging me, sometimes nodding assent, sometimes saying no, but always present, always gentle. I finished translating all the stories and informed Bharathi and Justice Chandru. I was unsure of the quality because this was my first attempt at translating a whole book. I had earlier translated Mahabharatam slokas into English for Prasanna Ramaswamy's play *Karna*. But this was different; it was an entire book. Bharathi took a few of the translated stories and showed it to Dr K.S. Subramanian. He told me they worked. Then we began wondering who should publish them. We considered several options but somehow could not make up our minds.

'It will happen, just see,' Bharathi said. 'Chudamani will make it happen.'

And one day, I happened to meet Mini Krishnan at the Delhi airport, waiting to board the same flight. She asked if I was a judge. I said yes and also that I knew who she was. Waiting for our flight, we discussed various things.

'Do you publish translations?' I asked her.

'Do I?'

'I have translated a collection of Chudamani's short stories. Will you look at them?'

And that is how this work stands here before you.

Now am I right in saying Chudamani prodded me?

This is my first attempt and I know I could not have chosen a better subject.

Chudamani looked at the world through a window, and there stood a Nagalinga tree. In her stories, she has seen the woman from different angles. A bored woman at home wishing for some excitement; a liberated woman who lived life on her terms; a young woman who is jealous of her schoolboy son's crush; the ordinary wife of a straying husband; a woman who frowns at a younger man's attraction for her but in her heart smiles; two sisters grown totally apart; a woman tired of being pregnant for the seventh time; a village girl who identifies the landlord who raped her—the underlying theme in each story is the woman as herself. There are stories where the woman is both absent and present—the soulmate mourned by her husband of many years; the girl who ages as she waits to get married; the unmarried woman and her blind father; the woman in a coma and her penitent son. Chudamani speaks of woman's sexuality, a taboo subject, in an oh-so-gentle tone. You wouldn't call her a feminist but what do you call a woman who firmly felt that a woman should be the master of her body, captain of her soul? Chudamani is never judgemental, she just sees.

She is equally wonderful in bringing children to life. Her perception, her insight, her understanding of the child's psyche is amazing. Whether it is the young boy and his crush on the 'TV aunty', the little girl who is possessive about her young woman friend, the proud little boy refusing the *murukku* offered by strangers, or the wicked glee of two boys torturing a maid-servant's son ... all facets of a child—the tender, the violent, the cruel, the loyal—are drawn with complete control of form and content. The story about the two boys disturbed me, and when I translated it, the vulnerability of the poor child in the face of unabashed cruelty of the rich children upset me deeply. So in our edit session, I postponed it to the end! It was an unsettling finish.

The firm strokes with which Chudamani paints human nature and behaviour; the formal words of condolence that we offer which are meaningless; the lascivious interest that the world has in 'the other woman'; the smug hypocrisy of the pious; the uneven scales on which man and woman stand; the children on the street fantasizing that they are film stars; the reluctance with which we welcome the inevitable old age and ... I could go on and on.

Chudamani is universal and for all time in some ways, but she is also *of* her time and her space. She is like Jane Austen, you cannot modernize her stories: the Ambassador car, the bell-bottom pants, the blue terylene shirt, the baby food booked in ration shops, and even considering sixty as very old(!) are essential to her stories. So the stories can only be of that time. Emily Bronte can be 'made over' to the twenty-first century, not Jane Austen. But both are universal.

Chudamani wrote in English too under the name of Chudamani Raghavan. It is interesting that sometimes, in these stories, I felt she was translating from her own English versions. But I was left perplexed when, at times, she used typically Tamil phrases. How does one translate *Vai pulichudo, manga pulichudo?* Was it the mango which tasted sour or the mouth? No, this does not work. So instead of translating directly I tried to capture the meaning. Chudamani was born into an Iyengar family. She has experimented in some stories to employ a tone and an accent which is not a Brahmin one. But there she slips and we know. I wonder why she tried it ... were the compulsions external or internal? We will never know but I feel she is best as she is ... as herself.

Chudamani chooses her words with care; nothing appears by default. In 'The Nagalinga Tree', it is a bargain over Brinda, so the object alone is named, not the others. It rains in many of her stories, not incidentally but because it *must* rain. She describes the scene so vividly that one can see the clouds, the streets, the leaves, the sunrays leaping like fierce beasts, the falling rain. Her women are wheatish in complexion ... such a change from our obsession with fair skin! I salute you, C! And how can we forget sweat? Yes, she mentions perspiration so frequently ... did the smell assault her delicate sensibility? The foods that she writes about are not chosen arbitrarily. Bournvita and the little boy; chips coated with sugared curds and the sisters; idlis in the leaf parcel and Ulaganathan—they all belong together.

Chudamani is a 'citizen' of Madras. Purasawakkam, Chintadripet, Kasturba Nagar, the route through Walajah Road to the beach, the Adyar bridge—these are all mentioned and we clearly see the map of Madras before the 1990s. She needs just two lines to etch the scene in our minds.

Where a catch-all 'aunt' serves in English, in Tamil (and in other Indian languages), we have specific words like *chithi*, *athai*, and so on. *Appa* and *amma* are used not only to address parents but are also terms of tenderness or respect. Then we have words like *pennudaya amma* (girl's mother) or *paiyanudaya amma* (boy's mother), when the 'boy' is a young man really, who has come to 'see' the young woman as part of the structure of an 'arranged marriage'. Perhaps it harks back to a time when it really was the girl who married the boy. Here, the words 'boy' and 'girl' have been used. Even the names of the characters indicate the caste, and even the class; a person familiar with the milieu will know. In that regard, this was an eye-opener.

She has 'seen' these stories wearing the skin of the characters. Nowhere do we feel 'This is not how that person would have spoken, no one will react like this'. She also 'sees' the settings of her stories. Bustling Luz, wet crowded Egmore, traffic-laden Mount Road, and the project township near Simhachalam come alive before your eyes. Sometimes Mini and I would stop our editing and say to each other, 'It's like being there, *illey?* And just in two sentences ...!' But enough now, I want you to savour it for yourself.

The edit sessions were joyful hours. Mini knows that I went there as much for the editing as for the lovely coffee, and so I will not dissemble! I thought translation meant 'Not a word more, not a word less'. But Mini said, 'No, Prabha must be seen through the words of Chudamani.' She made sure that I was seen. Each of our sessions was just like a *cutcheri*, a music concert. I would go to her room and we would talk of this and that, quite like the singer warming up. Then the editing itself would be the *ragam tanam pallavi*, the main piece in a Carnatic music concert. After it was over, we would wind down with some interesting thing that happened or share a joke like the end pieces of a concert. The way we searched for the right word, tasting it on our tongues, hearing the sound ... and bingo! Just before we wrapped up our editing, we usually plunged into doubt again. Had we got all the nuances that Chudamani had so skilfully woven into her language? We did not know how to assure ourselves. Then I had an idea. 'Mini, Chudamani also wrote in English. I will see if Bharathi has something in English by Chudamani. If we sound like her, then we are on the right track.' I approached Bharathi. Incredibly, that story was 'My Daughter Shobana' which Mini and I titled 'Seeing in the Dark'. This was from *Glimpses: The Modern Indian Short Story* (Affiliated East-West Press Pvt. Ltd, edited by Aruna Sitesh). As I read on, I could not believe that even the rise and fall of the words were similar. The book said 'Translated by the author'. My eyes welled. The gentle spirit had not left my side. I called Mini and said, 'Mini, we have done it right. Chudamani approves!'

Sometimes when we came to the end of the story, I with my Tamil and Mini with my draft, we would be in tears. Bhuvana's story was one, and 'The Nagalinga Tree' was another. 'The Downpour Outside' too. Sometimes we would be silent, like when we had finished 'The Visitor' or 'Doors Closed Forever'. Chudamani presided over the birth of my friendship with my editor.

Translating the titles was another battle. Some titles worked in Tamil but sadly 'died' in English. So we went through torturous moments. As soon as I returned home, I would send Mini a fresh suggestion, and within a few minutes, I would get a counter suggestion. Sometimes Mini would send me a title. And I wondered, for me it is my only work but for her it is one among many, so why should she labour as I did? That is Mini. And that is why I think Chudamani intended that Mini should do it. And let us remember it was Mini who brought out

Chudamani's first work in translation, *Yamini*, in 1996. Mini did a final round of honing which I would like to acknowledge, studying every line to further improve my final draft to our mutual satisfaction.

That is why the meeting at the Delhi airport happened.

Chudamani guided us all the way. We wanted Ambai to write the foreword to this collection. Then we toyed with the idea of translating her 'Manadhukkiniya Oru Thozhi' (A Dear Friend) which is appended to the *Nagalinga Maram* collection. Should Ambai translate it or should I? Mini spoke to Ambai, and she was fine with me translating it. After a while, she mailed Mini 'Loss of a Crest Jewel' written by her immediately after Chudamani had passed away, which appeared in *The Hindu*. Should we use this or the translation of 'Manadhukkiniya Oru Thozhi'? Ambai had written more in the Tamil piece, but both articles were essentially the same. Mini felt 'Loss of a Crest Jewel' had a valuable sharpness and urgency. I agreed. I am sure Chudamani wanted *this* to be there in our book! A crest jewel ... how apt!

As for the title of the book! So crucial that we catch the reader's eye! 'Chudamani: A Collection', 'The Nagalinga Tree', and some others were chosen. Both of us liked 'A Rainbow in Her Hands' at first. Then we thought 'Heat and Rain' was better. Or 'Seeing in the Dark'. Finally, we settled on the last.

My parents instilled the love of reading in me, my children thankfully inherited it. They share my joy now. Sridevan will be smiling too, I'm sure.

To Justice Chandru and Bharathi, thanks are not enough. They dreamt of making this work. And even when I had my doubts, they did not, and encouraged me!

To Mini, of course. We laughed, wept, raised our eyebrows, and marvelled together. My first editor—even if I do not write anything else, she will always remain that!

To Chitra Mahesh, but for whose remark I would not have embarked on this exciting and moving adventure of mapping the Chudamani Country.

I thank Dr K.S. Subramanian for his encouraging comments, and Mrs Raghu and Mr Srinivasan who typed the rough drafts.

I thank the reviewers of my final draft, for their enthusiasm, patience, and valuable suggestions, and Prema Nandakumar who very warmly contributed the Introduction.

And to my tapestry of friends!

Chennai
21 February 2014

PRABHA SRIDEVAN

Introduction

Unfolding Wings of Thought
in the Inner Air ...

R. Chudamani's first story was published exactly sixty years ago. She was not yet twenty-five but this beginning would become her spiritual support for half a century and more. The 2010 collection *Nagalinga Maram* came with Chudamani's autobiographical reminiscence (1999) about her first story that was published in 1954, 'Parisu Vimarsanam'. She was twenty-three, and she was excited. Parental encouragement lit up her world. Her father had patted her and made an illuminative comment, 'Not bad at all. Relativity theory of a different kind! Write a lot!' He was certainly an intuitive critic. Going through Chudamani's five hundred stories, as also her dramas and novels, one recognizes her effortless art of connectivity. All problems can be solved if only we know how to *connect*. Oh, these barriers raised by customs, by preconceived notions regarding social barriers, class, and the ubiquitous sense of caste!

In 1958, my mother-in-law, the legendary writer Kumudini, took me to meet her, for they were distant relatives. Being a young bride, I was shy but sat fascinated when they discussed one of her recent stories. Prompted by my mother-in-law, I went forward and gave Chudamani my first book which had been published just then. She smiled in an angelic way and was happy to know that I had not given up my doctoral studies after marriage. 'You have a mother-in-law who will encourage you no end,' she said. She stood up when we took leave of her. Only then did I realize that she had a problem with her feet and that she was unusually short. Suddenly, I felt a wave of strength in me. One must face life with a heroic smile like this writer! I never met her again but she has remained an inspiration, an image of 'the courage never to submit or yield'.

She was a tireless writer who handled several genres like novels, plays, and novellas. Even poetry. All that she wrote could be termed as a sincere recordation of life as she knew it with just that shadow behind, which the artistic imagination tried to seize and convey as a meaningful experience. She would never give into any primitive cry of hatred nor weave gossamer romances of idealistic utopias. She has given us her view of social culture in independent India, warts and all.

What then was her base when she could not become a part of the hurly-burly of life, of travelling in crowded buses, of having to struggle as a worker in the world or a housewife at home? Where should we look for that experiential reality which gives an utter naturalness to the flow of Chudamani's storytelling?

A prefatorial remark in a reprint of a collection of her stories reads:

> Her stories written in an uncomplicated style, opened in the fifties with simple thoughts. Her writing slowly acquired an inner strength as the decades passed by. In the sixties she had mastered the art of story-telling. By the seventies she could make the critic sit up with wonder. As the rest of the century moved forward, one could notice how effortlessly she could touch high spires in creativity.[1]

[1] Sita Ravi and K. Bharati, *Thanimai Thalir*, tr. Prema Nandakumar (Nagercoil: Kalachuvadu Publications, 2013), p. 14.

A fair-enough approximation to Chudamani's creative fire which burnt steadily, marking a subtle progression but never rising to a self-destructive blaze. Chudamani remained herself upto the end. Not for her 'the fumes of scorching flesh and smoking blood'. Her subject was the home, and her prime inspiration came from herself, her family, and immediate circle of friends and household servants, as though she was watching the events with half-shut eyes, ready to forgive, and, of course, forget.

Naturally, the subterranean grottos of human emotions that format the stage in these tales call for conversations that are not heard in the physical. They rise in the mind and subside there. 'Nothing Ever Happens' (Nigazchi) is a sliver of stream of consciousness like Chudamani's style, which is one long exploration of human behaviour. There are occasional exceptions but generally external action is consigned to the minimum when the author proceeds to analyse her characters caught in varied situations.

Women and children are predominant in these fictional structures. A sensitive woman who had not allowed resentment to enter her heart, Chudamani uses three approaches to get at the truth that determines patterns of behaviour. The woman seen by herself (as in 'Neelayathakshi Ammal: Arupathu Vayadhu' [Neelayathakshi at Sixty]); the woman scrutinized by other women (as discovered in short stories like 'Iruttil Irundhaval' [Woman in the Dark]); and the woman analysed by men (as found in 'Sobhanavin Vazhvu' [Seeing in the Dark]). In this world generally crenellated by women, we have children observed with acute perception by Chudamani. Though each story is independent, together, they form a vast tapestry of clearly defined paintings (she was herself a painter) that leave no ambiguous endings. Not for her sententious elegances or romantic claptrap. She saw the world of human affairs more as a vile mix of ignorance and cupidity and was amazed that men and women could not count their blessings but remained slaves to their body—hankering after adulation, affection, admiration, pomp, and pride. Which is perhaps a reason for the frequent theme of marital infidelity in the stories, for example, 'Dhandanai' (He Is Not in Town) and 'Iruttil Irundhaval' (Woman in the Dark).

Chudamani does not take sides. Mostly, it is the woman who often becomes a hurdle to herself and her family, and finally has to bear the brunt of societal abhorrence. She has to be subservient to maintain peace at home. She has to conform to the received tradition. And the received tradition in Tamil Nadu has been inimical to women from times immemorial. Consider the inequalities based on gender in the Sangam Age. For instance, the concept of chastity (*karpu*) was associated only with female chastity. Interestingly enough, there is no instance of a woman giving in to adultery in Sangam literature. But a man could spend his time with *parathai*s with abandon, as the community of courtesans was institutionalized. As for the treatment of widows, it is a tragedy too deep for tears. Here is a young lady pleading with the potter in the ancient Tamil anthology *Purananooru*, for a bigger burial urn, so that she can join her dead husband to reach the unknown:

> Oh potter! Oh potter!
> Like the tiny white lizard
> Attached to the spokes of a wheel
> I have accompanied him all these days
> Through many hurdles.
> O potter who makes pots in this old city,
> Make the burial pot wider to yield me also
> Kindly space within.[2]

---

[2] *Purananooru*, verse 256. Translated by Prema Nandakumar.

How is one to overcome this attitude deeply ingrained in a woman's psyche? Even if she dares to remarry, provided someone is prepared to marry a widow, there are other shackles that condemn her to lifelong loneliness. The sheerly brilliant 'Iruga Moodiya Kadhavugal' (Doors Closed Forever) says it all. The stream of consciousness from Kesav inundates the spaces around. The innocent villain of the piece is an eight-year-old boy who reacts emotionally to his mother's decision:

'Do you like Chellappa uncle, Kesav?'
'Oh! I like him very much.'
'I ... I too like him very much, Kanna!'
'He is a nice uncle.'
'Shall I make that nice uncle your father?'
An uncomprehending expression on the boy's face—like a hurdle—and a hesitation on Amma's face.
'What, Amma?'
'Shall I marry him?'
The son had now turned into a figure of shock.
'Mmmhmm. No. It is wrong.'

So mother had tightly shut the doors to her new life. Now the grown-up Kesav, married and a father, is buffeted by the stream which engulfs him with feelings of guilt as he looks on at the still figure of his mother whose life is ebbing. Chudamani's story is taut to the point of snapping as Kesav's thoughts loudly bang at our psyche:

Why did you listen to that child's words, Amma? Why did you listen to that child who could not think of anything beyond his mother? Why did you listen to the child who was a product of a traditional society which thinks that widow remarriage is wrong?

Though she touches life at very few points, Chudamani's intense explorations get piled up as in an investigative agency's filing cabinet. The man–woman relationship has many facets, and all of them usually hinge on chastity. The institution of marriage established by our ancients was no doubt meant to curb loose morals and make parentage fairly definite for the children. During a casual conversation, a lawyer friend told me wryly, 'I often think that marriage is a contrived institution, to make sure one's progeny inherits one's wealth.' We have no clue to the original impulsions, but physical chastity is considered the ideal for the human being, a mark of civilized behaviour. Marriage, perhaps, is a help to define cultural parameters.

But the human being, in the course of evolution, has not yet shed his animal origins entirely! We accept this human condition too. What galls Chudamani are the double standards adopted by society when it enforces the diktat of marriage. Again, it has been this way for as long as we can remember. Obviously, it is the man's right to seek pleasures of the flesh, but the wife must not look at another man, must not even complain against the husband's ways. A group of elderly women in the ancient Tamil poem *Paripadal*, advise a wronged wife:

> To the aggrieved wife thus they appealed:
> 'How can a wife keep her husband back,
> Preventing him from going to his paramours
> Who offer him delights of infinite variety?
> Can you mount guard o'er your man all the time?
> Of course, you cannot! For chaste wives noble
> Are superior e'en to elders wise:
> Such will cherish their husbands ever,
> Even when they ignore 'em and go astray.'[3]

So it is the man who has all the advantage. The wife can never 'swear she'll avoid his broad chest for good'. It is the man's right

[3] K.G. Seshadri (tr.), *Paripadal* (Chennai: Institute of Asian Studies, 1996), pp. 209–10.

to cast his wife away but the woman cannot do the same. Such societal norms naturally led to a very narrow view of 'chastity'; one that was limited to the woman and gave rise to the iconic character of Kannaki of Silappadhikaram. How strong is this structure today in the context of education, empowerment, and feminist stances of rebellion and freedom? Are any cracks appearing in this seemingly cemented sarcophagus of Indian culture? 'Dhandanai' has a male chauvinist pig as its hero who flaunts his maleness to his subservient wife and even tries to justify his affair. She need not worry because he wanted to experience it to assure himself that he was not getting old, after all! Till his wife's soft words cut him down:

> Can this insensitivity to another's pain go unpunished? Anjali's face quivered for a moment and then became calm. There was a new expression in those eyes which were looking at him ... as if floating in a dream, an elusive expression.
>
> 'That's not it. I'm thinking ...' she said softly.
>
> 'Thinking of what?' he asked bending over to light the cigarette with his lighter.
>
> 'The thought that though I felt the same way as you, I never realized that there was this solution to it—until you told me.'
>
> 'See.' And she smiled.
>
> He looked up sharply and stared at her.
>
> Suddenly, he went pale.

But the tone of Chudamani whether in this story or elsewhere is not raspy. Shanmugam's behaviour does not get justified by Anjali's insinuation of adulterous longings for herself. Nor is Shanmugam's own adultery hotly criticized. Our author is not prepared to be a judge. She is a witness of her times, and thus presents reality as it is—the pleasant and the unpleasant rubbing shoulders all the time. It is the reader who has to meditate upon the problem and set down his/her own solution. The author's job is done in having hinted that it is time women are not taken for granted. Infidelity apart, male insensitivity is spread all over the marital structure, as we note in the manner in which another Shanmugam treats his wife in 'Doctoramma Arai' (Doctoramma's Room). What is a wife but a child-bearing machine? A machine that creaks occasionally and one fine morning gives up its ghost.

Not all women-centric stories are overtly feminist. The villain is often a blind tradition or a nameless fear of the unknown. Fate takes a hand, coming as death or a disability. 'Nagalinga Maram' (The Nagalinga Tree) is literally a statement of harsh reality, as if seen through a glass, darkly. A maimed body does not stand in the way of a young man if he wants to marry a beautiful, healthy girl. Who cares for her feelings, especially if this marriage could educate her brother in the bargain?

Chudamani rarely went for complicated crafting, but this story is an exception. The art of cauterizing one's feelings is learnt naturally by those who feel fenced-in and helpless and know that they cannot afford to react as they should, if they want to survive. Life becomes a concentration camp for the uneducated young girls from poor families, and their only way out is to forget the reality and move around holding on to something else, recording other scenes and other voices in their mind. 'The Nagalinga Tree' is a single long conversation between the parents of the boy and the father of the girl. A marriage broker has fixed this meeting, so that the boy can meet the girl. They haggle over the money the impoverished father of the bride has to spend on the marriage. All the time, the girl reacts mechanically to the orders of her father, but is staring through the window at the Nagalinga tree which is in full bloom. She too is a flower in full bloom:

> ... Wheatish colour, but a sculpture of that hue. Her face and form challenged each other in beauty; of more than average height, with a dignity that glowed forth pushing aside the poverty with ease like one would swat a fly.

Brinda looks as though she is an alien in the group and keeps looking at the rich flowers hugging the tree. When the prospective mother-in-law wants her to speak to them, she speaks about the tree with unselfconscious ease:

> ... Do you know this tree sheds its leaves at least thrice in a year? The dried leaves will keep falling for four or five days. They gather in a heap ... impossible to sweep them away. But even as we look at them, they wither, and in the next few days, green leaves sprout and cover the tree fully. You will wonder if this is the tree which was so bald a few days ago. Do you know how beautiful it is to watch the tiny green leaves sprouting alongside the dried ones shaking and falling down? Almost as if the new tree is emerging, sloughing off the skin of the old one.

The whole story is punctuated by Brinda's counting the flowers to herself. The sheer contrast between the ugliness of the human beings haggling inside the room and the glorious beauty of the cannon-ball flowers outside leaves in us an unforgettable impression. Chudamani also draws our attention to the foul smell that assaults us once the Nagalinga flowers begin to fade. The boy is not interested in the bartering, but the mother will not leave it at that. When the father pointedly looks at the boy's leg, the mother is incensed and comes out with the words uttered a million times in our society:

> ... All said and done he is a man. It does not matter how a man looks. Is he not educated? Is he not employed? But considering everything we asked only for 7,000 instead of 20,000 or 30,000. If you bargain even harder ...

Chudamani was writing in 1979. We have to convert these amounts to lakhs today, but the bargaining continues! And the profound statement: All said and done he is a man. Brinda is a wise girl. She should not be a burden any more to her natal home. She should be able to get her brother educated. She should not allow her emotions to get out of hand. How to do it? How to do it? She tells herself silently:

> … Must count the flowers carefully and correctly … 9, 10, 11, 12, 13, 14 … Surely there will be three dozen. 25, 26, 27, 28.
> As she continued counting, suddenly the flowers on the tree vanished and she saw instead three dozen lame legs.

Though there are dark shadows in this story, Chudamani has left a redeeming streak of hope. To go by the lives of many Brindas in our society that I have observed during half a century, our heroine may actually make a success of her married life. The ugliness might intrude, but the flowers could win the day for her. And as far as the mind of the hero is not maimed as his legs, all should be well.

Since the author preferred to see humanity as a whole, while noting its varied samples, there are plenty of sharp-tongued, unfeeling women too who almost frighten us by their presence. Chudamani had a special connect with children. She had watched them closely and also imagined the currents of thoughts that swirled within them, seeking clues from their external reactions to adult behaviour. By sheer application, she had mastered the distinctive and convoluted child psychology which could be predictable and equally unpredictable. There is only one term that rules the world of children and that is love. Love alone can help an adult to connect with a child; this is the message that comes across when we come face to face with Devaki and Leela in 'Arumbu Ulagam' (That Fragile World).

The Nagalinga tree is almost a rare symbol-presence in Chudamani's stories. There are some recurrent themes like sibling love, a mother on her deathbed, the painful shades of adolescence, young boys falling in 'love' with women in their prime, husbands who are unfaithful to their wives, the final journey of a dear departed, and maternal love that is possessive. She probes the secret of what constitutes gratitude, what makes tradition so impregnable, and the defining moment when a person breaks the fetters and sails into freedom. Since there are no complicated symbol worlds, usage of metaphors, recourse to allegory, and antimetabole or poetic passages bordering on pathetic fallacy, translating Chudamani ought not to be too difficult. She is engaged in telling a straightforward story in the current idiom. The second half of the twentieth century was also the time when English entered conversational Tamil diction in a big way. The story is the thing! An English-educated author has told a story in Tamil. Now the same story is recounted in English. So where is the problem?

Aye, there lies the rub, to borrow a phrase from Prince Hamlet. It is probably much easier to translate a heavy text from ancient Tamil literature than to receive in English the easy-flowing content of a Chudamani story. What sounds utterly natural in Tamil could become banal when transcribed into English. Of course, each language has its own unique élan that helps a person convey a good deal by just a word or two. Fortunately, English continues to be a pliable medium and one can always come up with an eminently readable and occasionally elevating translation that does not reject the original's vibrancy. After all, eternal verities like love, honour, and patriotism are common to the whole of humanity. Besides, Chudamani consciously avoids the heavy diction of Indian heritage that has seeped into every-day conversation except where a reminiscence or pun calls for it. The juvenile mispronunciation of *sindhoora varna* (saffron-complexioned) as *Sindhu Ravana* and the child justifying the mistake with loveable pomposity has been effortlessly settled in English in 'Oru Mananilai'.

'Why not? Sindhu means the sea. Do you know? That is Samskritam, and next door Sastri Maama said so. Then wasn't

Ravana the king of Lanka which is in the middle of the sea? And so Sindhu Ravana.' Seven-year-old Radha was amazed at her elder sister's knowledge of Samskritam at age ten. To this date, whenever she heard 'Sri Gananatha', the words 'Sindhu Ravana' would flow into her mind before she corrected it to 'Sindhoora varna'.

No words are wasted in this translation and we come face to face repeatedly with Chudamani's brief brush strokes that produce an image, create a mood, or assure us of an inward reality.

My eyes dimmed.

Is this not a pilgrimage?

Rain or shine, they climb up, moved only by their love. Is not this exertion a holy service?

Yes, and not only that. Because these devotees come, this place has become a temple.

I looked at the crooked steps going down. I looked at my feet. The vision of the small tender feet that had become red moved my heart. Suddenly, I felt ashamed and felt humbled. My arrogance and self-conceit vanished without a trace.

From indoors came the train song.

This tremendous story, 'Padikal' (Ascent to the Shrine), could almost be Chudamani's fictional explication of a profound poem of William Wordsworth. She was indeed a voracious reader and was herself a writer in English:

My heart leaps up when I behold
A rainbow in the sky:
So was it when my life began;
So is it now I am a man;
So be it when I shall grow old,
Or let me die!
The Child is father of the Man;

I could wish my days to be
Bound each to each by natural piety.

The old man convalescing near the Simhachalam hill learns
how to appreciate nature and the love that is in the spontaneous
gestures of working-class children.

Hesitatingly, the shy, timid one came close to Vaidehi and
handed her a white-rayed cotton flower plucked from the wayside bushes.
    'For you!'

Now the old man can learn to appreciate nature, natural
wonders, and the immanent divinity within nature with a
child's heart.

The stories that appear in this welcome package represent
hardly five per cent of Chudamani's short fiction. Admittedly,
it is a difficult job to choose, but Prabha Sridevan has wisely
depended upon an earlier collection, *Nagalinga Maram*, edited
by Dilip Kumar. She had found it unputdownable. Soon she
was deep into the job of translating the stories. There is a charm
about one's first book of translation which calls for a continuous dialogue with the author. Living in Chennai in almost the
same cultural atmosphere of upper-middle-class families, it is
not surprising that Prabha was able to find the stories familiar
enough. With her family background and her own attainments,
she has marked a fine beginning as a translator for herself; also,
this book is an indicator, a beginning for transcribing all the
writings of Chudamani into English.
    It is a rather disturbing truth that the new generation of edu-
cated Indians are losing touch with their rich mother tongue,
and Tamilians are no exceptions. Even when born and brought
up in Tamil Nadu, one finds the younger age group aliens

to the multifoliate efflorescence of modern Tamil literature. Unfortunately, this means becoming strangers to their own culture, foreigners in their own homes, a reality darkly hinted at by Chudamani in a couple of her tales. So, English, which has been hailed as the language of opportunity, must become the receptacle of various cultures. These translations would then make the coming generations aware of the adventures, agonies, ecstasies, and immortal creations of Tamil literature.

As for the translation itself: How much of Chudamani do we get in an alien language, and how would she react if she were around? The precise answer comes from a close friend of Chudamani. Ambai says of her own stories translated by Lakshmi Holmström:

> It is a strange feeling confronting a translation of one's stories. The characters seem different; the images are sketched differently; the colours are not what one imagined and the words sound different. And then when one slowly gets into the mood of the translated language, one sees one's stories bound in a certain way, and take wings, traversing the distance between the two languages. The magic of a story taking shape in another language can happen only if, like pushing a fishing boat into the sea, a translation gently nudges a story into the vast ocean of another language.[4]

I can say that this translocation in English has been done with affection and expertise by Prabha Sridevan who has drawn the Tamil original into a global readership. Perhaps her career as a judge has helped her too. If Chudamani saw the world of the maimed and the helpless with sympathy from her armchair at home, Prabha has watched, from her elevated seat, people

---

[4] Ambai, *In a Forest, A Deer*, tr. Lakshmi Holmström (New Delhi: Oxford University Press, 2006), p. viii.

who are caught in the dark side of our society, the marginalized, the sick, the helpless seeking attention silently, pleading for humanitarian justice.

The present volume gives an organized insight into the works of Chudamani—women and children. Women who do live life on their own terms (Shankari), avenge the assault on their womanhood (Abhirami), and have their own code of honesty (Thangam). Next to women, children occupy a considerable space in this collection. Poverty dehumanizes, but not always. Children of the poorest households seem to be capable of extreme self-control (Ulaganathan), while not always does an English education and a rich lifestyle produce ideal children. We do notice often how the ability to sympathize with the marginalized is siphoned out of many children by isolating them from stark reality. 'Veliye Nalla Mazhai' (The Downpour Outside) is a warning.

Reading magazines, playing Rummy, word-building for Scrabble—everything becomes 'boring', so Ramesh and Suresh enjoy torturing their servant Nagamma's son, Mani. There is violence in the diction, in the stance of the rich children, in their behaviour, when they set their dog Tiger upon the shivering boy who runs away outside, which is dark, preferring to face the pouring rain. The story is proof enough that Chudamani was a silent social reformer. She did not write with a deliberate purpose, but such was her vibrant sympathy that the stories were no idle jottings. With an uncanny ability to spot the essentials of character, she made them come alive in her words. And never did she despise anyone, not even the sinner. She just smiled. Men have a way of blundering, don't they? She smiled again. Ah, the boundless generosity of women! And now her smile was bordered by a slightly wet cheek as she saw the children, most of them quite dark. These divine creatures come to show us heaven on earth! Heaven lies about our sick bed when their presence weaves a fairy gauze as do pixies, sprites, and elves. As the narrator says in 'Ascent to the Shrine':

> ... I am unable to say with which yarn they did it. Impossible to hold the magic wires of joy. All I could feel was the light that radiated from them. If a lotus bloomed in your heart, how do you describe the fragrance? The only way to honour that emotion is to be brimful with silence while the fragrance spread through your entire being.

17 April 2014   PREMA NANDAKUMAR

Kinship Terms

akka	elder sister
anna	elder brother
annachi	elder brother
appa	literally, 'father', but used as a term of endearment in addressing a child and also an exclamation indicating relief
athai	father's sister, who is often also one's mother-in-law
avan	third-person singular male used to indicate persons equal or lower in age or status, or even familiarity as contrasted to *avar*, a term of respect
ayya	a term of respect used for men
chinna muthalaliyamma	junior boss/employer/master's wife
chinna paatti	junior grandmother
chithi	junior aunt
doctoramma	a term of respect for the lady doctor
ejamaniamma	the mistress of the house
kanna	an endearment
maama	uncle
maami	literally, 'aunt', but used as a term of respect for an older woman

mausi	Hindi for aunt
paatti	grandmother
periya muthalali	senior boss/employer/master
sambandhi	parents-in-law of one's son or daughter; used also when they are the prospective parents-in-law
thaatha	grandfather or term of respect for an elderly ma
thambi	younger brother or, in this context, a younger man, a stranger

A Trace of Envy*

*I*t is very appropriate that I should write in *Dinamani Kadir*[1] about the publication of my first story. It is an unexpected coincidence because it was in *Dinamani Kadir* that my first story was published.

The title of the first story which was published in 1954 was 'A Prize Review'. A schoolgirl wins a book as prize for her academic proficiency. The story is about the different perspectives from which her family members and her neighbours view it. You cannot even say it was a story. It was a sketch. Whatever it was, it was my first creation to be published.

That moment of joy was unparalleled. Though many stories were published later, seeing my writing in print for the first time was a unique experience. The doors of the writers' world opened for us, the fruition of new emotions, that our imagination is being transported and unfolded before many unknown faces. At the same time, there is the eagerness to know what others think of the story, and a rush of enthusiasm to write the next one.

---

* Originally titled 'Thuli Poraamaiyagavum Irukirathu', the story was published in *Dinamani Kadir* on 9 May 1999, and later appeared in the collection *Nagalinga Maram* in 2010 (pp. 13–14).

[1] A popular Tamil weekly magazine.

My mother went on a tour of the neighbourhood, with the issue of *Dinamani Kadir*, in which my story was published, in her hand. 'My daughter's story has been published in this. Do read it!'

The reader had to praise it. If not, she would come home and tell me, 'S/he is envious of you!'

When I think of that now, I am filled with laughter and tears. I think the greatest compliment paid to my story was this love.

After reading the story, my father said, 'Not bad at all. Relativity theory of a different kind! Write a lot!' He patted me happily.

Beside my parents, it was Thiru K.R. Kalyanaraman (Makaram), our family friend and our writer-friend, who rejoiced most on my writing being published. The encouragement and enthusiasm he bestowed on me deserve my eternal gratitude.

Today, whenever I attempt to write anything, a thousand questions arise: Will this come out well? Does this deserve to be written? Self assessments. But in the thrill that ran through me that day when I held my first published story left no room for any dissatisfaction. Though I am older and so much more mature now, sometimes—just sometimes—I am slightly envious of that twenty-three-year-old woman.

We Don't Know*

*I*t was decided by the panchayat[1] that Velappan was not guilty.

'He was the one, he is the one!'

Abhirami had declared loudly. Before the members of the panchayat, the elders, and all the villagers, she had pointed to Velappan and accused him with her fiery eyes.

They had questioned her again and again.

Are you sure?

Could she have made a mistake in some confusion?

She had said she was taken by force, could it be true?

If that was so, had it been dusk?

Could she have made a mistake because of that …?

Every angry shiver that ran through Abhirami's body identified him.

'*He* was the one, he *is* the one.'

Was she the only one who could have identified the man? Fifteen other low castes, like Abhirami, both men and women,

* Originally titled 'Enakku Theriyadhu', the story was published in *India Today* in 1996, and later appeared in *Nagalinga Maram* in 2010 (pp. 294–8).

[1] The village elders who adjudicate complaints and by whose verdict the villagers abide.

were working in the fields at that time, anyone of whom could have identified him.

They did not.

On the day it happened, two men from the rice mill armed with thick staffs had set off from the rice millowner's house and had headed for Abhirami.

'Did you go to the Periya Muthalali's house yesterday to take care of his grandson?'

'Yes ... so?' Looking up from her transplanting work, Abhirami pushed back strands of hair from her forehead.

'It seems the gold chain the child was wearing is missing.'

'What? Chain?'

'They suspect you. So Chinna Muthalaliyamma has sent us to bring you to the house to make enquiries.'

'What a baseless accusation! The child wore no chain. Have you come here simply to create a scene?'

'You come with us now and say whatever you want there. These are Chinna Muthalaliyamma's orders.'

'Chinna Muthalaliyamma would never have said such a thing. As her maid was not well, she sent for me to look after the child in between my field work. That is why I went. She knows I am honest. Moreover, the child was not wearing any jewellery. Please go away.'

Abhirami bent down to resume her work.

Chinna Muthaliyamma *did* know that Abhirami was honest. The trouble arose because Chinna Muthalali had seen how beautiful she was.

Chinna Muthalali Velappan, who had followed his two men, grasped her hair and yanked her up straight.

'Thieving slut, what impertinence! You won't obey if we send for you? You will, only if we drag you.'

Velappan dragged her away as she shouted and screamed, while the fifteen witnesses stood like stone, petrified by his autocratic strength and the power of the two henchmen. Used as they were to living in servile fear, the grass bundles and sickles dead weight in their hands, they watched mutely while the three men disappeared with Abhirami.

The next day Abhirami's complaint echoed throughout the village. She did not conceal what had happened to her. She did not shrink with shame. She did not drown herself in a pond. Though she was tossed by grief, humiliation, and rage, she stood up straight, looked Velappan in the face, and pointed accusingly at him, 'He is the one who ruined me.'

There was no alternative. The panchayat had to be convened.

Four days before the panchayat met, Velappan's father, the rice millowner, met the village head who was the president of the panchayat; he gently hinted to him that they shared the same ancestors and left after some cordial conversation. One of his kinsmen had called all the fifteen workers who were witness to what had happened to Abhirami in the field and conveyed a message. The crux of the message was that if at the panchayat any of them gave evidence against Velappan, the women witnesses and the womenfolk of the male witnesses among the fifteen would meet the same fate as Abhirami.

The panchayat met and questioned Velappan.

Velappan said he was innocent.

Abhirami said he was guilty.

Velappan had political leanings. His father and his men stated on oath that on the date of the occurrence, Velappan had gone on party work to Chennai and that he had not been in the village. The fifteen persons who appeared as Abhirami's witnesses were questioned.

'Tell us what happened.'

Each of them had answered 'I don't know.' 'I don't know.' 'I don't know.'

In the end, the village head gave his verdict.

'In the majority of rape cases, the men are not to be blamed. They do not approach the women on their own. It is the *women* who provoke men to rape them by their behaviour, the way they dress, and their expressions. But in this case even that did not happen. It is proved that Abhirami's charge is utterly baseless. She could not produce even one witness to support her case. The evidence only shows Velappan's innocence.

'Velappan is young and from a wealthy family. He belongs to the ruling party. So he could not have committed any wrong. Yet, Abhirami has again and again accused him of raping her. Above all, there is one more very strong, indisputable reason why her charge is false. Velappan is a high-caste man. Would he have stooped to touch the low-caste Abhirami? Is it probable? It is impossible. Therefore, this panchayat is of the opinion that Velappan is innocent.'

A month went by ...

Velappan went to Chennai with four lorry loads of people for a mammoth political gathering. Having earned the praise of the local secretary, and dreaming of contesting the next election, Velappan then returned happily to the village for some rest. The next morning, under the tamarind tree on the outskirts of the village, lay Velappan's blood-soaked body.

On it were fifteen sickle gashes.

Velappan's father was enraged. Grief-stricken at the loss of his son, he vowed to burn down the whole village.

The police came to investigate the matter.

When asked about the murder, the villagers had only one answer. 'I don't know.'

'How can there be a murder without *anyone's* knowledge? Tell me what happened,' shouted the police inspector.

'I don't know.'

'I don't know.'

'I don't know.'

'This is an unnatural death. There are numerous sickle gashes. There is no house in the village without a sickle. Do you have any idea who could have done it?'

Amidst the crowd, there stood a cluster of fifteen persons, men and women, and a woman among them said innocently, 'I can make a guess.'

'What is it?'

'See this tamarind tree here? A demon lives there. We call it the Sickle Demon. Last night it must have attacked Chinna Muthalali. If it attacks, there will be marks like this on the body.'

Calmly she looked into the inspector's eyes as she spoke.

And calmly the fourteen persons who stood beside her looked at the inspector.

The entire crowd standing behind them also looked at the inspector calmly without blinking.

A chill of fear pierced the inspector's guts.

He stepped back.

His report to the higher authorities read: 'The simple villagers believe that the tamarind tree demon has done this. In any event, they do not know anything else. It is possible that someone belonging to the rival political party from a neighbouring village may have come here. Out of spite and unable to bear the rising popularity of the ruling party, they might have committed the murder.'

That Fragile World[*]

'Can you draw a lion?'

'Oh!'

'Let me see.'

'Let me see, eh? Where and how at *this* age did you learn to speak like an adult?' Devaki pinched the child's cheek with rough affection.

'Don't pinch me, Akka. It hurts!'

'You cheat! I just touched you and you say it hurts? Dupes!' Her arms went around the child. Leela rested her whole weight on her. The tender body throbbed with an inexplicable emotion. She raised her eyes. What is this yearning in the kohl-rimmed eyes?

'Akka, I love you.' The child thought a bit, and corrected herself, 'I love you very, very much!'

'I love Leela kutti too!'

'I love you more than you love me. I love you thiiiiiis much.' The child stretched her arms without stirring from the embrace in which the two were locked.

* Originally titled 'Arumbu Ulagam', the story was published in 1971, and later appeared in the *Nagalinga Maram* in 2010 (pp. 61–9).

Devaki laughed. 'Is that so? Good. Now get down. Don't you want me to draw a lion?'

The child got off her lap. Devaki started sketching in the drawing notebook, with her head inclined, the tip of her tongue peeping out of her lips, the wrinkled forehead indicating her concentration; and the pencil drew the strokes on the white paper from which a lion slowly emerged.

'Sssssh, don't fall on me. If my hand shakes, the drawing will get spoilt.'

The child moved away, but only for a short while. She moved again to rest on Devaki's back, and peeped over her shoulders at the notebook. It looked as if two heads had sprung from one neck, two flowers blooming from one stalk; one was a young woman's face and the other a little girl's.

'Only the eyes remain ... ah ... finished! See how fiercely it frowns! Is the lion nice?'

Leela clapped her hands with joy. 'It is super. Akka is soooo clever!' The tender hands went around her neck. Wet lips pressed on the cheek.

'Hey, hey, no more kisses! How many? You are tickling me. Are you going to stop now or not? Take your hands off now, Leela. You are throttling me!'

Panting and laughing, she slowly moved Leela's tiny arms and hugged her from the front. Smiling, they rocked to and fro.

'Hmm, hmm, I've laughed so hard, my eyes are streaming! Stop laughing, my little one. Otherwise your tummy will hurt!'

'Akka, I like you so much. Will you come and stay with me, or shall I stay here?'

Devaki removed the soft hands which held her face and gently kissed them, 'Leela, you come here every day anyway. We play for a long time. Just keep doing this. If you stay here, won't your Appa, Amma, Thaatha, and Paatti miss you and cry? Look, there's not even a little brother or sister there.'

The child was quiet and pensive and her face was downcast. 'Athai used to be there, but not now.'

Devaki stroked the girl's short hair. She removed the loosened hair slide, gathered the locks that had fallen on Leela's forehead and fixed the slide again.

'Leela kutti, you must not talk like this. Doesn't your Athai visit you every now and then? See, I have completed this lion. The notebook is full of animals. Shall I draw a little girl for you now?'

'Little girl? Who? Me?' In a moment, the child's dull eyes brightened.

'I won't tell you. You see for yourself.' A little girl appeared on the white paper, by the magic of the pencil.

'Who is this, Akka?'

'Hey, hey, don't press your elbow on my thighs so hard. It hurts. This is a princess, a very beautiful one.'

A beautiful girl with curly hair, a long frilled dress, and rosebud lips was lying on a bed.

'Why is she lying down?'

'She is sleeping.'

'Is it night in the picture?'

'This girl sleeps day and night, sleeps always. Her name is Sleeping Beauty.'

'But why is she sleeping? Is she lazy?'

'No, silly! Poor thing, she has been cursed.'

'What is a curse?'

'Curse means ... your head. Curse means ... a curse. Don't rishis like Viswamithrar or Durvasar[1] curse people in our stories? Oh, okay. I should not have talked about this to you forgetting that you are only a baby.'

'I'm not a baby. I'm five years old.'

---

[1] There are mythological stories about the curses cast by these two famous sages.

'All right. Do you know when this girl will wake up?'

'Didn't you tell me that she will always be sleeping?'

'She slept like that for many years. Then she woke up. Do you know how?'

'How?'

The pencil scraped on the paper ... another figure.

'Who is he?'

'He is the prince ... because she is a princess, right? So he is the prince. Prince Charming. See how smartly he stands!'

'And then?'

'He is about to wake her up!' Devaki hesitated for a moment. Should she narrate all the details to this little child?

'He is going to wake her up. Do you know what will happen after that? They will get married!'

The child's eyes widened, 'Married?'

'Yes, isn't the story nice?'

Devaki's eyes melted in her feelings; she was of an age when dreams flower with fragrance. Her dream had a form, a face, a voice, and a name. But he had misunderstood some casual argument of hers, and blown it out of proportion and snapped the ties. Anyway, neither could she ever forget him, nor would she marry anyone else. It was futile to think of that.

'Isn't the story nice?'

'So, this is the bridegroom?' Leela was still staring at her.

'Yes, the groom.'

Leela's face suddenly turned fierce, her eyes reddened with rage. 'I don't want this picture. I don't like it. I don't like the bridegroom. I don't want him!' The tiny fingers turned into tongues of flame and scored the second figure with venom. 'No bridegroom ... no, no, no!' The tiny figure trembled with the intensity of rage. The pencil drawing was mutilated. How many stabs, punches. 'No bridegroom, I don't like him.'

'Hey, Leela. Why did you scratch like this? You wait and see.'

'I don't want the bridegroom. I don't like him. He is bad, I don't like him, I don't like her. She is bad, too.'

With clenched teeth and angry tears, she tore, punched, and scratched the paper.

'Leela, Leela.'

'Akka.' The tiny figure sprang up and curled into her arms. Devaki felt the intensity behind the sobs that shook the tender body.

A tiny little heart, it is a separate world; though it has beauty and depth, it is a nascent purity, like the secret of dawn. The fragrance of a child's heart will pour out like the perfume from a tiny vial. It held so many emotions yet unfurled, all so delicate.

To a meaningless question, 'Do you like Appa or Amma?' would come the quick response, 'Neither of them ... I like Athai!' The love which suffused these words and filled the tiny heart would be reflected in the shining eyes, the hugging arms, and in the melting snuggle against her body. This was the life-throb of a young world.

'Athai alone must feed me.'

'I'll sleep only with Athai. I don't want Appa or Amma.'

'Athai, tell me a story.'

'Athai, I learnt A, B, C, D at school today. Shall I repeat it?'

'All of you see how Athai has written my name. L-E-E-L-A. That is my name from now on. No one must call me Leela. Only L-E-E-L-A.'

'Athai, I kissed you only on one cheek. Did the other cheek cry?'

'Athai I like it only if *you* comb my hair. Amma and Paatti don't know how.'

'I love you very much, Athai!'

Then one day, Athai was seated with a garland around her neck wearing a beautiful new saree. Next to her sat a Maama, also wearing a garland. An indescribable jealousy sprang within Leela. She asked him, 'Why are you sitting here?' The Maama

smiled gently. Her mother took her away saying, 'Stupid questions!' and whacked her. Leela screamed and ran back and
tightly hugged her aunt. The pandal[2] was filled with jokes and
laughter, 'When you send her to her in-laws' house, send the
niece too!' Her father pulled apart the arms that were tightly
wound round Athai's neck and carried her away.

'Athai ... Athai ... Athai.'

She burst into tears. Then one day, her Athai went away,
leaving Leela weeping and heartbroken, 'Shall I go, darling?'

The grief that bubbled from the depths of her being and
made her sob, 'Athai, Athai', the yearning in search of the aunt,
staring at the emptiness in every corner of the house, the abject
suffering of the tiny heart and its inexplicable, orphaned pain,
were tremors that shook her little world.

It was not as if Athai would never come back. She lived in the
same city. But the child gradually understood that Athai had
moved away from *her*. She understood the connection between
the love and care that was showered on her and the words,
'Amma, he will pick me up on his way from the office.' Though
she hugged her Athai, asked her to look at her school book,
and shared 'Teacher said today ...', she was aware that there
was something new between them now: A boundary line. The
embracing love which said 'Come, my little Leela' and kept her
close day and night had changed to 'Leela, I have to go now, will
you let go of my hand?' and a hasty withdrawal of her finger
from the grasp of the little hand. She knew marriage meant
bridegroom, and bridegroom meant separation.

Though she felt a sly pleasure in throwing a book or ball
on that Maama and pretending it was by accident, she realized
that the final triumph was his, when Athai got into the car with
him, leaving her with the warmth and wetness of her tears.

---

[2] The decorated space where the wedding is performed.

The little sprout wilted in loneliness. Appa, Amma, Thaatha, and Paatti had their own worlds. They did not have the eyes to look into the empty world of the child who sat with wide, sad eyes.

Then suddenly a change, a breeze, blew from the next street. When did she first see Devaki, how did she get to know her, how did she grow to love her were questions that had become unnecessary at this stage when she was soaking in this joy. Devaki was a young woman, just like Athai, the same liveliness, the same embracing affection, the same 'Leela kutti', the infectious enthusiasm, and the comfort of friendship.

The gentle breeze transformed the drooping sprout, which now danced with joy. There was new meaning to the language of the heart. There was once again the old joy of rushing back after school, to repeat what the teacher said, to explain a game, to describe how Asha blinked unable to recite '*Paarukkulle nalla nadu*'[3] and so much more. There was again the eagerness to remember all this. There was a soulmate whom she could hug, against whose face she could press her face, in whose lap she could bury herself, and confidently pester, 'Draw a picture!' 'Tell me a story!' And to trail behind, gripping the saree *munthanai*.[4]

'Akka, did you see my frock?'

'Akka, will you listen to my new rhyme?'

'Akka, Amma gave me two sweets. I brought one for you.'

'Akka, you read your library book. I won't trouble you. I will just sit here.'

'Akka, I will just kiss you and go. Amma does not know I've come from school. I came straight to you. Now I must rush home.'

'Akka, surely you like me?'

---

[3] A patriotic song composed by Subramania Bharatiar.

[4] Pallu, or the end of a saree.

She trailed Devaki all day long. Once, when Amma said 'You must not pester them', her face fell.

'Akka, am I pestering you?'

Devaki hugged her in reply.

Leela trembled with joy.

'Amma says so.'

'Forget Amma. Can I be without seeing Leela kutti?'

Those were happy days ... That day Leela held two roses.

'What is this flower?'

'They planted a new one, no? It flowered today. Amma plucked a few, and I told her I wanted some for you. Wear it in your hair.'

'How about you?'

'I have short hair, not lovely long hair like yours.'

Devaki pulled out one petal gently and fixed it with the hair slide on Leela's hair, and then wore the flowers herself. The child's face blushed with pride. Pursing the joy in her lips, she kept touching that single petal on her hair.

'Akka, will you draw an elephant in my notebook today?'

'Oh!'

'Akka, you are so beautiful, your eyes are lovely, your nose is lovely, the saree is lovely.'

'Leela kutti's speech is very lovely.'

'Our holidays are starting in two days ... you know that? Akka, school reopens only in June. Yesterday Appa and Amma went to a movie. Paatti was angry and said, after they left, that they go out every day. There is a new maid. I don't like the very look of her. Today Amma made *dosai* for tiffin.'

'Stop, take your breath! Why this speeding train? My God, so much news in half a minute,' Devaki laughed. 'How many dosais did you eat?'

'I have not eaten yet. Before that I wanted to give you these flowers. Do you like them, Akka?'

'Very much, my darling. Now go home right now, have your tiffin and come. Or else, your mother,' Devaki said lightly tapping her back, 'will make dosais here.'

'Elephant picture?'

'Come over after tiffin, I will draw it for you.'

Leela ran home. Devaki picked up the half-read novel, smiling to herself.

'Post!'

She got up and received the letter and opened it.

My dearest Devaki.

Isn't this letter, the echo of the voice she heard unceasingly in her heart? Not just the voice, even the name, face, and form of her dreams appeared in the written words.

Forgive me, Devaki. I lost my temper in haste. I realized how stupid I was. I feel very sorry for it. My darling, will you forgive me? Next Sunday, I will explain everything to you and seek your forgiveness. I am confident that I will regain your love. I am sure very soon we will get married and I am coming there with that hope.

Is this true, really true? Or is it a dream?

Time passed. She was transported to the peak of a world of joy.

'Akka, I'm back.'

'Come, Leela kutti.'

Leela hugged her. 'Sweet Akka, soft Akka, golden Akka.'

'Oh!'

'I like you very much, Akka.' Leela clung to her with joy. Then she remembered the elephant picture. 'Will you draw that elephant now?'

Devaki picked up the drawing notebook, but in her intoxication of joy, she could not focus on anything else. 'Not now, Leela.'

'But you said you would.' The little lips quivered.

'Not today. Tomorrow, okay? Leela is a good girl. Oh! Oh! I didn't write your name on the notebook ... what if someone takes it? I'll write that now. Picture tomorrow. Mmm?' The pencil was poised on the first page. 'Your initial is V, right? V. L-I-L-A.'

'No, no.' Old memories exploded. 'L-E-E-L-A. That's how you should write. That is my name.'

'Why are you crying, my little one?'

'You must write my name like that.' The face blurred with pain. Moist lips trembled. The child who hid herself in the embrace did not speak for a long time. Sobs alone were heard.

'No, kanna don't cry. Why are you crying? You are a big girl. Will big girls cry? Won't people laugh?' Devaki wiped her tears. 'What has happened? You want an elephant picture, right? Come. I'll draw it for you. Should you cry for that?'

'Akka ... Akka,' the child's voice broke. 'You ... you too won't go away with a bridegroom will you?'

Bhuvana and the Star Sign*

A sudden impulse prompted me to give him a lift. It was exactly when I had received the bill at the Mount Road petrol bunk and was waiting for the cars ahead of me to move, that I saw him at the bus stop on the other side of the road.

Would he be fifty?

Perspiration had evidently altered the shade of his *veshti*[1] and shirt. His wide forehead shone in the sunlight. He stood shifting his weight from this slipper to the other, wiping his face every now and then and often adjusting the black bag tucked under his armpit, his eyes fixed far away, his appearance eloquently saying that he had been waiting for a long time. There was no one else at the bus stop. He stood all alone like an orphan in the blazing heat.

When the two cars ahead moved on, I drove my Ambassador forward and had it filled, then drove out of the bunk slowly and stopped in front of him. I stuck my head out of the window and asked, 'Excuse me, where does sir want to go?'

---

* Originally titled 'Bhuvanavum Viyara Kiragamum', the story was published in *Puthiya Paarvai* in September 1992, and later appeared in *Nagalinga Maram* in 2010 (pp. 271–80).

[1] A dhoti.

His face clearly showed shock. Baffled, because it was a stranger who had stopped to ask, and a little disturbed because of that, he stepped backwards, as one would in reflex to a raised hand.

'Who? Who … are you, sir?'

'Ah! I don't know you either. From the petrol bunk on the opposite side, I saw you standing here. I thought I could give you a lift if we're going in the same direction. That's all.'

He looked at me, confused. He may have wondered if I had a screw loose.[2] At close quarters, his face didn't show the signs of fifty years. The premature baldness and the lean tired appearance were not the marks of age.

'My name is Rajasekhar. S.T. Rajasekhar. Accounts Manager at Saravana Exports.'

I took out my wallet from my bushshirt pocket and handed it to him.

'Why all this?'

'You must know that I can be trusted isn't it? Suppose you think I'm a kidnapper.'

When he laughed aloud, his teeth shone.

'Why would anyone want to kidnap me? Am I a millionaire, a politician, or a young girl? I'm an invisible daily wage-earning man.'

It hurt me to see that smile.

'You have been waiting for a bus for a long while, isn't it?'

'I'm used to it.'

'Where do you want to go?'

'T. Nagar, Tirumalai Street.'

'Get into the car,' I said, opening the front door.

'No need, sir. Your direction may be different.' His eyes scanned the distance.

'I'm going to Bazullah Road. I'll drop you and go.'

'Unnecessary trouble.'

---

[2] Meaning, mentally imbalanced.

'No trouble at all. I too will have some company. How long will you stand in the sun and suffer?'

'I forgot to bring my umbrella. My mistake.'

Once again he looked up and down the road. No sign of a bus.

'No point waiting for a bus. It could be a sudden strike. Just get in.'

'Are you really going to Bazullah Road?'

'Just get in, sir. We'll talk about everything in the car.'

He was still hesitant. But his legs, tired of standing, had decided to say yes before he did.

'My name is Mahalingam. I'm a clerk in a private company,' he said before getting in.

Then he got into the car and sat next to me as if by the introduction he had given himself some reality. I shut the door, went round to the driver's seat, and started the car.

'Must be a very important bag,' I said casually.

'Yes.' He hugged it tighter.

'May I know what is inside?'

'Horoscope, my daughter's horoscope.' A sudden sharp laugh. 'For an average lower-income family man, what could be more precious?'

In spite of the breeze that blew into the moving car, his face shone with drops of sweat which broadcast that he was a 'girl's father'.

My thoughts jerked to a stop. I too am a girl's father. But I'm not standing in the sun, and instead of the odour of sweat, there came from me the fragrance of aftershave lotion; next to his handloom veshti, my terene trousers, and my shiny black shoes juxtaposed with his slippers which were slipping off because he had stretched his feet.

'I too have a daughter. Name is Niranjani. What is your daughter's name?'

'Bhuvaneswari. We call her Bhuvana.'

I didn't tell him we call Niranjani, Nikki Tikki.

'I am going to a house on Tirumalai Street to hand over Bhuvana's horoscope,' he continued.

'Somebody you know?'

'No. I heard about it through someone in the office. He said they won't expect much dowry. So I thought let me give Bhuvana's horoscope and if it is destined to happen, let it.'

'Do you know the door number?'

'Mmh.' He unzipped the bag and turned over some sheets of paper. I could see the horoscope with its four corners stained yellow.[3] There were other papers too. Maybe the address was written over or a letter from a friend, or details of other matters.

I drove on.

I stopped at a red light.

'Take a look?'

I turned to look at a passport-size photograph that he had pulled out of a small cover to show me.

'This is Bhuvana.'

Couldn't call her a beauty, but there was an attractive innocence in that face. Big eyes. Dark hair tightly plaited as if gummed to the head. Small single-stone earrings. Since it was a black-and-white photograph, the earrings looked black, so they could be red stoned, but they were certainly not diamonds. The pottu[4] on the forehead was slightly large for the innocent face. A little make-up would have enhanced her beauty. But in those wide eyes, which looked at the world with wonder, there was the radiance of youth.

'This is Bhuvana,' Mahalingam said again, with a bright smile and looked at my face.

'She looks very nice. How old is she?'

---

[3] It is customary to stain the four corners of the horoscope with turmeric, which is auspicious.

[4] The traditional dot on the forehead worn by Hindu women.

'She completed nineteen last December.'

'Just nineteen! What's the hurry for her wedding?'

I thought of my Nikki Tikki at twenty saying, 'Appa, after my MBA and computer science, I want to get a degree abroad.'

'You say what's the hurry? You think the marriage will be fixed as soon as I start looking? Once Bhuvana completed eighteen, I started my rounds with her horoscope. Till date, no luck.' He put back the photograph in the cover and replaced it in the leather bag.

'Just eighteen? At eighteen, a girl is still a child, sir.'

'That depends on the kind of family she is born into.'

His words fell like a hammer on my head. I did not answer. The light turned green. I started the car. We drove past the Kalaivanar statue.

'I educated her up to Plus Two which was all I could do. We have a boy and a girl younger to her. My wife earns something by tailoring at home. Even so, is it easy to get a girl married? Sons-in-law cost the earth. I don't know what I'm going to do. But because of that can I keep the girl unmarried at home?'

As he spoke, it was as if fatigue had wrapped itself around him, in spite of the comfortable drive.

He got out of the car on Tirumalai Street two doors ahead.

'Let them not see me stepping out of a car. They will raise the rate thinking I'm rich. Okay, shall I go? Thank you very much for the lift. It was a stroke of good fortune that I got a car ride today.'

He stroked the car with his hand for a second. 'Bye, sir.'

He brought his palms together in *namaskaram*. I returned the salute. He walked away rapidly, his slippers flapping.

I turned my car towards Mylapore to meet a businessman friend: If one's daughter is to achieve her ambition, besides praying, is it not also necessary to cultivate people?

I had no work in Bazullah Road.

God has showered his grace on me abundantly. Nikki Tikki
secured high grades in the management course. Then she earned
a computer diploma in my friend's business organization. She
got her student visa, went to the USA, got a degree in computer
science, and worked there for a year before returning to India.
She is now an executive in a big company in Bangalore. Her
husband is equally qualified, an engineer with a foreign degree.
A son-in-law I had secured with four lakhs. Nikki Tikki and
her husband have one child—a planned family. The only heir
to her parents' love and wealth, little Nikki is today lisping
English in a convent.

That God did not let me down is apparent. By due diligence,
I rose to be the GM of my company. Then I became a director. I
was recognized as a financial wizard. At fifty-eight, I retired and
started my own business, Nikki Finance, and am now rolling
in wealth.

Even when the sun blazes, my wife does not wear anything
but silks. Her favourite jewellery: China jade and Amsterdam-
cut Blue Jaeger diamonds. We live in Bombay and visit Chennai
once in three years. Our relatives are here. Moreover, we want to
breathe the air where Tamil is commonly spoken. And a visit to
the Marina[5] is a must. Though on a diabetic diet and my grey
hair stained with Godrej dye, can one resist the magic sites of
childhood? Another reason is that I have to visit Kanchipuram[6]
to buy silks for my wife.

Today the Chennai breeze blows over me again.

I was in the car at the petrol bunk. After my Ambassador,
came a Maruti. And now in its place I bought a Contessa, just
here in Chennai last week. I must send it to Bombay.

[5] The beach at Chennai.
[6] The town in Tamil Nadu renowned for its silk weaving.

We wanted the first long-distance trip in the car to be a temple run. So we had planned to visit Mangadu[7] the next day with my wife and my daughter's family, which is why I was here to fill it up.

It looked as if it would take some time. I got out of the car. In its milling crowds, the many-toned noises, the huge number of cars, the tall buildings, Madras was really competing with the other premier cities. If you looked around, every house had a dish antenna on its roof, the twenty-four hour deafening cacophony of Cable TV, Star TV ... do all cities have the same face?

But the sound of a driver shouting at a pedestrian, 'Hey you. Decided to kill yourself? Inviting death. Move away, you *kasmalam*[8]...' and those sweet words in pure Madras *tamizh*,[9] indicated that I was indeed in Madras.

The buses, taxis, autos, and cars moved with a swishing sound this way and that, weaving a fabric of sounds. Then, in a single moment, a scene tripped in my memory and stuck to my consciousness.

It was him.

He stood there. Chithirai[10] perspiration had altered the colour of his veshti and shirt. The same black bag tucked under his arm. The same bus stop. His hand shading the eyes which were searching the distance. He was surely waiting for his bus.

I removed my dark glasses hastily and peered at him. My vision was quite sharp after the cataract surgery. Without a doubt it was him. What was his name? Chockalingam? Ramalingam? His spectacles were an addition. He was almost completely bald, but the features were the same.

---

[7] A temple in Tamil Nadu where Goddess Kamakshi is said to have done penance standing on one foot.

[8] A swear word.

[9] Tamil.

[10] The Tamil month corresponding to 14 April–14 May.

My head swam for a moment. Had a mischievous brat turned the clock back deliberately? I, on this side of the road at the petrol bunk; him, on the other side waiting for the bus. The same scene. How long ago? 197 ... yes almost fifteen years ago. Fifteen years!

The calendar had changed fifteen times. A whole Mamaangam[11] had come and gone. Our country had seen six prime ministers. A super power had been knocked out of the world arena. A freedom fighter had got his freedom after twenty-eight years in prison. The American *Voyager* had circled Jupiter and travelled several billion kilometres in space.

But he still stood in the same place.

I shook my head. I brought time back into perspective. After filling my car with petrol, I drove straight up to him. I raised my hands in a namaskaram and said, 'How are you, sir? Do you remember me?'

His start was also something I had seen before. His eyebrows rose in confusion. There was a grey hair in those eyebrows. There was baldness and several wrinkles on the face.

'I am Rajasekhar. S.T. Rajasekhar. Fifteen years ago, I gave you a lift at a bus stand just like this, do you remember?'

I could see from his blank expression that he did not remember me immediately. The hands gripped the leather bag more tightly. That gesture suddenly jogged and cleared my memory and I asked, 'You are Mahalingam, right?'

'Yes.'

'Last time, I took you in the car when you had to go to Tirumalai Street with your daughter's horoscope. Come now, I'll drop you wherever you want.'

'I now remember faintly. You said you had to go to Bazullah Road, right?'

'Yes.'

'Did you go?'

[11] A cycle of twelve years.

I laughed. 'You are really priceless! Get in, please. We'll talk as we drive.' I opened the front door.

'What did you say your name was?'

'S.T. Rajasekhar, get in please.'

'Why do you take the trouble?'

'No trouble.'

'I have to go to a place in Chintadripet.'

'I am going that side too.'

This time, he laughed. The teeth did not shine as before. They looked dull as if they too had aged.

'You are too good sir ... but ... my bus will come any moment.'

'Let it come. Consider that you are keeping an old friend company, a friend whom you are meeting after a long time.'

His tired face wanted to accept my invitation, but politeness made him search in the distance. The wrong bus rumbled up, stopped, and left.

'Forget the bus, Mr Mahalingam. Get into the car. Cars couldn't stop here. Wrong side. The police will catch us. Get in ... quick!'

'Thanks.' He got into the front seat. He removed his spectacles and wiped them and the sweat on his face with his shirt, and he replaced his spectacles.

'I should have brought my umbrella when I came out in the sun, I forgot.'

I shut the door, came round, and sat down in the driver's seat and asked, 'Where should we go?'

'Turn at Periyar Road and go over the bridge.' I drove the car. The air conditioner was pleasant behind the darkened window glasses. For a while, neither of us spoke.

I thought he had gone off to sleep when he said, 'I've retired.'

'Yes, you would have, it's been fifteen years, isn't it?'

'My wife died three years ago.'

'Oh, oh! I'm very sorry.'

'Her time had come. But in a way, she is very lucky. After my retirement, I am now a clerk to a school correspondent. I know the headmaster ... and on his recommendation ...'

I didn't answer. A bitterness trickled down my heart as if I had bit into a neem fruit. For a moment, the air-conditioned chillness scorched like fire.

He opened the leather bag, took out a dull paper parcel, and checked some papers and other things. He put them back again.

'You see? Today is Saturday, so no school.'

'Then you should have just relaxed at home. You look very tired.'

'Can I stay at home because of that? Once my work is over, I'll go home, have a glass of cold buttermilk, and lie down.'

Again silence. The car went past people, houses, streets, shops, cinema posters, political cutouts. We reached Periyar Road.

'Where are you, now?'

'Bombay.'

'I suppose you visit Madras occasionally.'

'Once in three years.'

'Madras must be insipid after Bombay.'

'But it is still my place of birth.'

'Yes. This seems like a new car. Very nice ... with air conditioning.'

'Thanks.' I turned the car at a bend. 'My daughter, son-in-law, and my granddaughter have also come from Bangalore. The whole family is planning to go to Mangadu Temple by car tomorrow.'

'Very good. Do go. Please pray to Kamakshiamman that my Bhuvana should get married soon.'

When I turned suddenly to look at him, my attention scattered and I very nearly hit a taxi. The taxi driver's voice said, 'Sir, be careful. You look like an educated man. But you drive like ...' and faded away.

'For Bhuvana? You mean the Bhuvaneswari you mentioned back then? For her?'

'Yes. Guru[12] has not glanced at her yet. Even now, I'm going with her horoscope to Chintadripet.'

I could not speak. I felt as if my body was aflame. My head reeled, it was quite surprising how I reached the street without causing an accident.

'The car cannot enter the street. Drop me here. I'll walk.'

Like a machine, I stopped, went round the car and opened the door. He got down.

'Okay thanks, sir. I'll take your leave now.'

In his haste a paper packet fell out of the bag he had forgotten to zip up.

I bent down. The packet had opened slightly. Without him noticing I closed it at once, replacing the object that peeped out and returned the packet to him.

'Thanks, sir, Bhuvana had asked me to get something. If I had left it behind, I would have had to rush to the shop again.'

He put it back into the bag and zipped it firmly this time.

'Let me go now. I have given you a lot of trouble. Sorry. Goodbye.'

The weary slippered feet walked slowly into the street.

I got into the driver's seat. I stared down sightlessly at my expensive Gucci shoes. I rested my head on the steering wheel.

That paper packet had held a bottle. Godrej Hair Dye.

---

[12] According to Hindu astrology, Jupiter's favourable position in one's horoscope improves prospects of marriage.

The Nagalinga Tree^{*,1}

'Brinda, fetch the coffee, Amma.'

Brinda brought the coffee into the room.

'Here is Brinda for you to see.' Indicated his tone.

And as for the visitors ... well ... they looked at her.

The girl was not very fair skinned. Wheatish colour, but a sculpture of that hue. Her face and form challenged each other in beauty; of more than average height, with a dignity that glowed forth pushing aside the poverty with ease like one would swat a fly.

'Do *namaskaram* to everyone,' ordered the girl's father.

Brinda did namaskaram to everyone.

'Sit down, Amma,' said the boy's father. Brinda sat down and looked through the window at the Nagalinga tree.

The boy's mother frowned at her husband covertly. Who did he think he was to ask the girl to sit down, when she, the boy's mother, was present? And as for that girl, she too had sat down promptly.

'Please, drink your coffee,' requested the girl's father.

---

* Originally titled 'Nagalinga Maram', the story was published in 1979, and later appeared in *Nagalinga Maram* in 2010 (pp. 132–41).

[1] *Couroupita guianensis* is the botanical name, whereas cannonball tree is the common name.

'We will.' Then turning to Brinda, the boy's mother asked, 'What have you studied?'

The girl's father was taken aback. Were these not details that the marriage broker had conveyed to them?

'We stopped her studies after the eighth stan ...'

'Why? Was she unable to study?'

Brinda focused more fiercely on the tree.

High up, the fresh green leaves were lush, starting with the lower branch, covering the entire trunk, and the flowers had blossomed on their slender stems reaching downwards, like falling drops. The flowers, their blossoms shaped like *naga*[2] and *linga*[3] looked as if they were crying out 'Call me Nagalinga'. These flowers did have a special beauty of their own, with those pale yellow and rose-red petals with the hooded naga and the tiny linga in the centre.

'No, she was very good at her studies. She too had wanted to study. Only that we lacked the facility.'

'What facility do you need? Isn't education free?'

'When I say "facility", I mean that the family situation did not permit it. My wife's health is not very good. I'm a travelling pharmaceutical salesman. So Brinda had to discontinue school and look after both the home and her mother.'

'That's all right. Is it so necessary to go to school?' said the boy.

Everyone's eyes, except Brinda's, turned at the entirely unexpected remark. The mother's face flushed angrily, even the father looked at him in some distress as if to say 'You idiot!' and asked his son, 'When even a BA is so common nowadays, isn't it surprising that she has not finished even school?'

'I had asked the broker to tell you all the details about us. He did, didn't he?' the girl's father asked anxiously.

[2] A snake.
[3] The symbol of Siva.

'Mmmh, he did, he did.'

For the first time the girl's mother looked at the boy's mother as if to ask, then why the question 'Was she unable to study'? Was it for just the pleasure of asking?

'The coffee is getting cold,' said the girl's father to others who were holding the coffee.

'The coffee is excellent,' said the boy's father, thinking it must have been made specially for them.

'Made by our Brinda. Even the *bondas*[4] and the *rava kesari*[5] have been prepared by her. She is very intelligent and can manage everything,' said the girl's father with a shopkeeper's pride.

The girl's mother sat without looking at her daughter who was barely visible at the corner of her vision. She feared that if she saw her, she would break down.

Just look at the flowers! Brinda started counting the flowers as far as she could see. 1, 2, 3, 4, 5. By the time she could count up to a dozen, the flowers merged into one another. Had she finished counting the flowers on the upper branch? Perhaps two dozen flowers in all. A floral, visual fluid, soft and colourful. Some flowers would have also fallen at the foot of the tree.

But she could not see them because the wall under the window frame hid her view. If she stood up, she could see them.

'Why is the girl silent? What is it you are staring at there?' the boy's mother asked Brinda.

'I'm looking at the Nagalinga tree,' answered Brinda without turning her eyes away.

'Why look at that? Turn this side and talk to us.'

'What is there to talk about?' she said, her eyes fixed on the tree. Suddenly she spoke up, 'Do you know this tree sheds its leaves at least thrice in a year? The dried leaves will keep falling

[4] A popular snack where vegetables are dipped in batter and fried.
[5] A sweet made with semolina.

for four or five days. They gather in a heap ... impossible to sweep them away. But even as we look at them, they wither, and in the next few days, green leaves sprout and cover the tree fully. You will wonder if this is the tree which was so bald a few days ago. Do you know how beautiful it is to watch the tiny green leaves sprouting alongside the dried ones, shaking and falling down? Almost as if the new tree is emerging, sloughing off the skin of the old one.'

The boy was looking at the girl joyfully. The girl's father and the boy's mother noticed this.

The wretched fellow doesn't know how to restrain himself. Look out. Your eyes may drop off! The boy's mother, suppressing her anger and wanting to divert attention, turned urgently towards Brinda and asked, 'Why Brinda, your father said you have made these snacks. Can you cook too?'

Now she could not see the two dozen flowers, may be four or five less. Because the petals had spread wide, it created an impression that there were more flowers, that's all.

'Hey, Brinda, can't you hear what Maami asked? Why are you silent? Turn around and answer,' reprimanded Brinda's father.

Brinda turned around and responded, 'Maami what did you ask?'

'I asked if you can cook.'

'I can.'

'Didn't I tell you that Brinda is good at these things?' said Brinda's father.

'Mm, mm.'

'Of our sons, the older one Seenu is a really brilliant boy. He will do well if he joins college. If you can do the good deed,' smiled the girl's father ingratiatingly. He was emboldened by the broker's advice, 'Why don't you ask? It would be good for you if they agree.'

The boy's parents took time to get over the shock. Then ... 'A fine story indeed! Have you ever heard of something like this? We thought that we were being considerate, in view of your circumstances, and agreed to your spending only 7,000 rupees including the dowry. Now you want us to undertake your son's educational expenses. Has anyone heard of something like this?' The boy's mother exploded.

'If he asks, are we going to say yes? He is expressing his wish, let him,' said the boy's father.

'Not wish, more like greed. He can't say anything that trips on his tongue,' said the boy's mother.

'I'm not asking for anything improper. I'm asking you to help me. We are not strangers. We will soon become *sambandhi*s,' said the girl's father.

'It is common for the boy's parents to ask for even 10,000 rupees and 20,000 rupees. We thought we'd agree to 7,000 rupees. You didn't think of that. This is unheard of.'

'That 7,000 rupees is like 70,000 rupees for us, Amma ... we are that poor. Yet we want to do what we can for our daughter. Please think of that and if you help our son's edu ...'

'You are doing your duty. How can you think you are justified in asking anything in return for that? If you take back what you are going to give us, what are we left with?'

Brinda again started looking at the Nagalinga tree.

'What will you be left with? ... An excellent girl,' said the girl's father.

'An uneducated girl. For that alone you must give 3,000 rupees extra,' said the boy's mother.

'But what about her accomplishments? For that you can reduce 2,000 rupees.'

'What accomplishments? Bonda was too spicy, coffee smelt of grit. Can there be a marriage without 10,000 rupees? We thought we would relax ...'

'Such a beautiful girl is worth several thousands.'

'Don't say this too loudly. Everyone will laugh their heads off. We agreed to this low rate only because the broker said the girl would be somewhat nice looking. Otherwise won't the boy's side expect at least 20,000 rupees?'

The girl's father looked at the boy.

'For this boy?' were words he did not utter. The boy reddened and tried to hide his right leg with his veshti, and his parents also fell silent.

Smiling, the girl's father said, 'Why these arguments between us? The broker had explained all the details to both of us, right?'

'Then why not conclude the matter instead of raising the subject of your boy's education?' interjected the boy's father.

'It is not such an unacceptable matter.'

'What is this trick? Have you ever heard of the boy's parents educating the girl's brother?'

'The broker said that many alliances did not materialize for your boy,' said the girl's father softly.

The boy's father wiped his perspiration. After a moment's silence, the boy's mother said, 'Okay, give us 10,000 rupees. We will help with your son's education.'

'If we had so much money, wouldn't we ourselves have educated him?'

'Then let's not talk about that subject.'

'Why should you not get the credit of educating a very intelligent poor boy? I'm giving you 7,000 rupees and a beautiful girl. In return, a small help. You are not going to suffer because of that.'

'You want this marriage to happen, right? Are you interested or not?'

At this flash of anger, the girl's mother's eyes lit up with hope and she turned confidently to her daughter.

Brinda had mentally counted the Nagalinga flowers umpteen times ... 16, 17, 18, and so on right from the beginning again and again, and at this moment had stopped at 18.

'*Che che che*, what kind of talk is this? Had we not been interested, would we have proceeded this far? I think you have mistaken me.' The girl's father gave a worried smile. 'It's okay if you don't want to help with my son's education. Leave it. The marriage proposal need not break because of that.'

18, 19, 20, 21, 22. No. Only 21. The next one is just a bud. 1, 2, 3, 4 ...

'That's right. Why should we educate someone else's child?'

'I told you to leave it.'

'Then the matter is over.'

'Now ...'

'What now?'

'I told you about my condition. If you, on your own, mag-nanimously reduced it to say 3,000 rupees from 7,000 rupees, it would be a great help.'

'Oh wonderful! 7,000 rupees is just *sundakkai*![6] Remember, we are the boy's people. We can ask so much more from the girl's side just to make up for what we have spent for our son's education.'

'I don't disagree. But considering her beauty, you can reduce 3,000 rupees.'

'There are beauties in this world before whom this is nothing.'

'Do you agree she is beautiful?'

'So-so ... where is the great beauty? And her complexion ...'

'Is complexion the only thing? Mahabharatam describes Draupadi as a beauty without equal. What was she like? Really dark. What is there in the colour of the skin? Our Brinda's every feature is so chiselled. At least if you reduce 2,500 rupees.'

'Do you know how beautiful the Nagalinga flower is?' Brinda's voice cut in. 'Everyone walking along the street looks

---

[6] A berry used in south-Indian cooking, but here it refers to some-thing that is insignificant.

only at this house. At least one in ten comes in and asks, "Can you give us Nagalinga flowers for our pooja?" It seems it is very appropriate for Siva poojai. This itself is a lingam. We can do pooja with it. My mother does it daily. Do you know? No, Amma? Not only to Siva, Amma will place the flowers on all the pictures. The whole room turns fragrant. It must have hit you as soon as you passed through the gate. But when it fades the smell turns unbearable. At a touch the petals will fall off. But when it is fresh it is beautiful. A flower fit for the gods. The kind of flower that makes every passer-by enter the house to ask for flowers for pooja. There are so many other flowers appropriate for pooja, like jasmine, rose, *sampangi*,[7] are they not? But the Nagalinga flower is special.'

The girl's mother did not look up even once.

'We can stare all day at her eyes and hair. You must actually marry her for her looks, good nature, and accomplishments, without demanding any money. I don't go that far. All I ask is to reduce at least 2,500 out of 7,000 rupees. Or at least 2,000 ...' The girl's father looked at the boy's leg.

The boy was staring at the girl deaf to this speech.

The girl was looking at the Nagalinga tree. She could see clusters of buds at the tips of the branches. Blossoms of the future, flowers in the making.

The boy's mother asked sharply, 'All said and done he is a man. It does not matter how a man looks. Is he not educated? Is he not employed? But considering everything, we asked only for 7,000 instead of 20,000 or 30,000. If you bargain even harder ...'

The girl's father looked at his daughter, 'Brinda why are you wearing this thick saree? Didn't your friend Meenakshi give you a georgette saree last week? Go wear it and show us. Let Maami see it all.'

---

[7] *Magnolia champaca.*

Brinda sat unmoving.

'I asked you to go ... go.'

Brinda shut her eyes for a moment and opened them. Then she stood up and went inside.

'Our Brinda has a very close friend. A *chettiar*[8] girl named Meenakshi. They have been inseparable since childhood. Whenever she goes to Singapore or some other place, she will never return without a gift for Brinda. Her father is a millionaire. Do you know how many georgette and nylex sarees Meenakshi has bought for Brinda!'

Brinda entered wearing the georgette saree. The diaphanous, figure-hugging saree revealed her beauty very clearly. The boy's eyes widened. Noticing that from the corner of his eye, the girl's father told the boy's parents, 'See how beautiful the saree is. Meenakshi loves her. Such a good heart. She brings such lovely, expensive sarees and insists that Brinda should take ...'

Brinda prepared to sit down.

'Brinda, go get the betel-nut packet placed on the table,' said her father.

Brinda walked right across the room to the other end and returned. The boy's eyes followed her.

'There is no betel-nut packet here, Appa.'

'O ... I suppose I ate it. I forgot. It's all right, do sit down.'

Brinda sat down.

The boy's eyes sat with her.

'Though she has such a rich friend, we are very poor. I want to get the children married. A big family, a sickly wife. Seven thousand is beyond my capacity. I feel sick in my stomach just to think of how I'm going to repay the debt. Even if you sell me, you won't get that much. Show some pity. I will follow tradition and perform the marriage without reducing the

---

[8] A wealthy community in Tamil Nadu traditionally engaged in trade or commerce.

rituals. But if you reduce at least 2,000 rupees, it will be a great help,' said the girl's father.

'You are speaking as if it is a matter of lakhs. Why should we reduce 2,000 from the paltry 7,000 agreed upon? If this is the case, then we have to call off ...' the boy's mother had not completed her sentence.

'What is wrong if we reduce a bit, Amma? It's okay, sir, 5,000 is enough,' said the boy.

The parents stared at him angrily.

Brinda started looking harder at the Nagalinga once more.

'What are you blabbering?'

'No blabber. The poor man has pleaded so much. Can we sit like stones?' said the boy.

'Big Mr Magnanimity. Hey fool ...' began the father, but he was restrained by a touch.

'I am the one who is going to marry her. If I don't object, why should you care?'

The boy's father was dumbstruck.

Brinda started counting the flowers with greater concentration. 1, 2, 3, 4.

There was a mutual agreement on how to reduce the 2,000 rupees, and then they left after asking the girl's father to fix the date for the wedding.

As they left, for formality, the girl's mother saw them to the door and a moment later turned to look at her husband.

He turned away. 'Don't look at me like that. I know that the horrible *Rourava*[9] hell awaits me. I will walk up to the park.' He wore his slippers and rushed away as if he was escaping from himself.

The girl's mother turned towards the daughter, then looked away. She staggered weakly and sat down.

---

[9] A particular grade of hell described in Hindu mythology.

'Today there are numerous flowers on the Nagalinga tree. Above and below. I am going to count them all. There must be at least three dozen.' Brinda looked keenly at the tree. Must count the flowers. Nothing else. Must count the flowers carefully and correctly ... 9, 10, 11, 12, 13, 14 ... Surely there will be three dozen. 25, 26, 27, 28.'

As she continued counting, suddenly the flowers on the tree vanished and she saw instead three dozen lame legs.

Who Could Have Told Them?*

*T*he elders at home seethed with rage.

'How can they behave like this? Don't they have daughters?' Amma fumed.

'Oh! They noticed that the horoscopes don't match only now? After seeing the girl and after saying yes, is it? Even if they want to bluff, shouldn't they do so plausibly?' Appa attacked the obvious falsity of the lie.

'They care so little for our feelings that they don't even bother whether the lie is believable!'

Thaatha and Paatti were silent, their hearts simmering. Will this child Kamali ever get married? Soon to be twenty-five and working as a reader in a college, this was the third time a marriage proposal had failed.

Thaatha could read horoscopes, and he saw nothing in Kamali's horoscope to indicate that she was unlikely to get married. Even so, not just relying on his amateur knowledge, he had consulted two or three horoscope experts. They had also said that the horoscope clearly indicated that Kamali would get married.

---

* Originally titled 'Madiyil Poonai', the story was published in 1992, and later appeared in *Nagalinga Maram* in 2010 (pp. 281–6).

Strenghtened by that assurance, Thaatha said raising his head and addressing his son, 'Forget it. If not this boy, we will get another. It's not as if Kamali's partner is yet to be born, considering her beauty, good nature, and intelligence ... the boy who marries her must indeed be fortunate.'

'But the parents of these boys obviously don't see that,' said Appa.

'Appa, I won't die if I don't get married. Just leave it.' Kamali's pride was stung, but she knew that the problem was not whether she would die or not, it was about her self-esteem that was hurt by repeated rejections.

On three occasions, the proposal had progressed to the stage of engagement, and had been cancelled ... then ...?

On the first occasion, the parents had suddenly said that the seer[1] was not enough. The parents who came next had said, 'Our boy has just got a chance to go abroad, so he doesn't want to get married now. Please look elsewhere for your daughter.' Now, this last and third time, 'When we said yes, we had not checked the horoscopes. But now our family josiar[2] has definitely said the horoscopes do not match. That is why ...'

'To hell with everybody!' Kamali exploded. 'What do they think of themselves?'

Her aunt Parimala patted her hand, 'Calm yourself, Kamali.' Parimala was her Athai, very intelligent and an efficient officer in a bank. 'If these people say no, so what? As my Appa said, will you never find a partner? Don't worry, just wait you will get someone ten times better.'

'Yes, Parimala, you talk to her, she will listen to you,' Paatti sighed. 'Hmmm, in our community, getting a girl married is quite a problem.'

---

[1] The gifts to be given by the girl's parents at the time of marriage.
[2] The astrologer.

Parimala accompanied Kamali upstairs, with her arm around her and speaking to her comfortingly.

'I didn't want to say this in front of Kamali.' Appa drew his parents and his wife near him and said in a low voice, 'Appa ... the broker told me the real reason for those people saying no to Kamali. They somehow seem to have got wind of the fact that Kamali had tuberculosis some years ago. They are not convinced that she is fully cured. Further, she is quite thin, so it appears that they said they did not want a sickly girl. The broker in fact started quarrelling with me for not telling him that Kamali is a TB patient.'

Everyone was taken aback.

'My God! It was so long ago. How did that come out after so many years?' Thaatha's eyes looked even larger behind the cataract glasses.

'Don't these educated people know that TB is wholly curable today?' Amma gnashed her teeth.

'That's not the point. This was something known only to us, the family. How did this information slip out?' This was Paatti.

'Maybe the doctor ...' Thaatha dragged and Appa cut him short, 'No, no, Appa, nothing of that sort. Doctors have professional etiquette, and every case is confidential. They will not betray that trust.'

'Then ...'

'My guess is this. You know Murugesan who works with me? He even visited us at home once. When Kamali was unwell, both of us were very close. And when I was very worried, I had confided in him.'

'Ayyayyo!'

'Wwwhaat?'

'Then?'

'After that, Murugesan and I had some misunderstanding because I got a promotion and he did not, and he was very bitter with me. I suspect that because of his jealousy he might have given this information to the sambandhis to stop the marriage.'

'Why did you go and tell him of all people?' asked Amma.

'I was very close to him then.'

'So what? However close you may be, can you share such family matters with strangers?' Thaatha reprimanded.

'It was a mistake, a real mistake. I never thought that something like this would crop up. I am kicking myself now.'

'Maybe it was he who spoilt the match on all the three occasions. That wretched fellow! So much jealousy! But how can he take it out on our child and wreck a young life so unfairly?' Paatti fumed.

But Amma was reminded of something else. 'Maybe it was not him. You know what? My father's distant relative lives in K.K. Nagar. He has always hated our family. You remember that Sornam who used to work here when Kamali was unwell? I saw her the other day near the market. She made enquiries about me and asked if Kamali was well. Of course she knew about it because she was working for us then. I learnt then that she is now working for that relative of ours. They are quite capable of creating problems for us and spoiling Kamali's life. If Sornam had told them about Kamali's TB ... *Appappa*[3] ... how terrible, how wicked ... will such people who harm others ever prosper in their lives?' Amma said angrily, gesturing her disgust, but with moist eyes.

'There is no point in regretting the past.' Thaatha turned to his son, 'You meet those people again and tell them that Kamali is completely cured. You explain to them that it happened a long time ago and ask them to reconsider their decision.'

Kamali was coming down for her bath. It was time for college. She saw the heads of the elders huddled together and their whispers.

[3] An exclamation to indicate that it is unbearable.

'What's the matter?'

'Nothing, my child, we were just discussing how to revive this alliance.'

'Paatti, even if they say yes now, I won't agree!'

'Rubbish! You are very young, you just don't know what you are saying.'

'I don't need to know anything, just forget this alliance.'

'My dear child, you don't know the truth of it. The fact is ...' Amma looked at her husband, not knowing if she should continue.

'I know the truth is something else, Amma. Otherwise will they say the horoscopes do not match after the marriage was fixed? Whatever the reason is, it is not necessary to go and plead with anyone who has rejected me. If they say yes after such persuasion, I will not marry that boy. If they come home, I will drive them away. Don't think this is an idle threat.' Kamali walked towards the bathroom.

The elders looked at each other not knowing what to do. They turned helplessly to Parimala who stood at the staircase. Kamali was stubborn. She was very sensitive and would not hesitate to do as she threatened.

Their hearts sank. Muruga![4] Will this girl ever get married?

Amma got up and went about her household chores. Paatti was lost in thought. Thaatha cast aside his worries and opened his *Tiruvachakam*.[5] Appa, Parimala, and Kamali left for work.

When they returned home in the evening, the atmosphere was still heavy.

The house was sunk in a deep silence. Though Kamali opened a novel, her gaze was fixed on the wall, and her heart was simmering with anger, humiliation, sorrow, and disgust.

---

[4] Muruga is the name of the god Karthikeya/Subrahmanya. This is an exclamation equivalent to 'Dear God!'

[5] The religious work of the Saiva saint Manickavasagar.

At dinner time too she was not hungry, she just picked at her food. The others understood why. Parimala, who had been complaining of a lack of appetite and headache the last few days, was feeling better and ate well. They had been worried if it was the flu prevailing in the city. Thank God she looked better today.

After dinner, the elders sat listlessly wondering who would have revealed this TB news. Was it Murugesan, or the distant relative—on the basis of Sornam's words—or had any one of them let slip the information accidentally to someone? They wondered and wondered, but none of them could recall any such thing.

What was the guarantee that this would not happen again even if an alliance did get fixed? It had already happened thrice.

Upstairs, Kamali wished Parimala goodnight and went to her room. She switched off the light and stared at the whirring fan, sleep eluding her.

Parimala wished her good night in return and went to the next room. As soon as she switched the light off, she fell asleep.

Parimala is forty years old and still unmarried.

Seeing in the Dark*

*T*hunder sounded in my chest.

'Go, go, go,' I shouted.

It took me a while to realize that there was utter silence around me.

Muthu must have left a long while ago.

I sat down shattered. And stood up again. I took four steps forward, stopped, went to the front verandah. I stared at the darkness that was mine. I came back to the room. Sat down. Went to my bed and lay down.

My familiar house, where I can walk without any hesitation. Familiarity gives an ease, a freedom … is it this familiarity that had gradually bred the kind of contempt in Shobana for her to behave as she pleases.

Could Muthu have spoken the truth? Shobana … with her a strange man! Both of them walking out of the hotel together. Muthu, who had gone to order drinks for a party, had seen them. Without indicating that he knew Shobana, he had asked the manager about them. 'A couple … checked into a room upstairs two days ago … Mr and Mrs …' was his reply.

* Originally titled 'Sobhanavin Vazhvu', the story was published in *Deepam* in 1978, and later appeared in *Nagalinga Maram* in 2010 (pp. 120–31).

Shobi!

My hands throbbed to grip her throat ... *Chee* ... *my* daughter?

Perhaps Muthu had lied. My God, let it be so. But why should this young man from a family I've known for a long time lie to me? Had I been able to see, maybe I would have seen Muthu's face filling with sorrow while he told me this.

Wretched ... wretched girl! *My* daughter? I'd rather you had died instead. If this is what you wanted, you could have married. So many proposals came for you.

'Saar ... here is the tea.'

I heard the cook Iyer's soft voice and sat up. He cooled it to the right temperature and handed it to me.

In those days, when the prospective grooms came to 'see' Shobana, she herself would make the *sojji* and *bajji*,[1] as my wife had died many years ago. At that time, she was in a low-level job, so there was not much income and no servants. Shobana herself would do the housework, the outside chores, attend on me, and then go to office—a daughter and son rolled into one.

When I finished my tea, the cook took the cup away from my outstretched hand instantly, Shobana having trained him so well. Whether she was in town or away, whether at home or away, she had arranged for me to be taken care of well. Apart from the cook, there was a live-in attendant who took care of me. Besides them, a young boy came in for two hours in the morning to read aloud to me. Then I had a pocket-size transistor radio so that I could listen to music at any time. All these comforts Shobana had gradually provided for me. Usually, it is the parents who say to the children 'We gave you no cause for complaint'. But here, in my peaceful life, it is in my daughter's voice you hear the words, 'Appa, have I given you any cause for

---

[1] These are the traditional sweet and savoury when the prospective bridegroom visits the girl in arranged marriages.

complaint?' So ...? Does that mean she can go off and stay with some man in a hotel? What about our culture, our values? That too a girl! Shouldn't a girl control her instincts?

Perhaps it was a mistake? Perhaps it was some other girl Muthu saw?

I stood up and walked to the verandah again. Stepping carefully, I found my way to the easychair and sat down. The breeze on my face. The gentle fragrance it carried told me that the jasmine bushes were in bloom. I had had my tea, so it must be 4:30. The sky would still be a blinding white. There was still time for the white to change into a fusion of many colours. At least then would Shobana come home?

She had told me that she would return that evening ... an official tour out of town.

How many times might she have lied to me that she was going away on official duty?

Who was he?

A colleague?

A stranger?

Where had she met him?

How long had she been in this relationship?

You wretched girl ... you could have married instead!

'Appa, if I get married and go away, who will take care of you, what will happen to you?' How many times had she asked this question? Each time a proposal was about to fructify and I asked her to say yes, her response was always this question, 'Appa, if I get married and go away, who will take care of you, what will happen to you?'

'This way ... your whole life ...'

'I don't dislike marriage. I am ready to get married. But I can only marry a man who agrees to my condition. Appa, you come first. I will not accept a person who cannot accept you.'

It was not enough to like the girl. It was not enough to marry the girl. The bridegroom should agree that the father-in-law would live with them ... because the father-in-law, who had lost his job and his eyes, was dependent on his only child, his daughter. The son-in-law need not support him. The daughter would continue to work and take care of her father. The son-in-law had to agree to all this.

No one agreed.

But whenever a marriage proposal failed, what did I really feel? Whenever I told her to get married, it was said sincerely. I did not want her to live alone. Whenever she asked 'What will you do, Appa?' I readily answered that I would go to some old-age home. Even so my heart would go thud-thud. In that one moment before she replied, I would suffer the pangs of hell.

Will she agree?

Will she abandon me?

Such thoughts and feelings would descend on my head like a ton. The question 'Why didn't I lose my life instead of my eyes in the accident?' would rage like a storm in my heart. The moment I heard her calm response 'I don't want a married life which orphans you', relief would spring forth as perspiration and I would suffer deep pangs of shame, and shrink and die inside.

'Shobi ... don't ruin your life like this for me.'

'What ruin, Appa? If I don't get married, does it mean I am ruining my life? I regret nothing. Had I been a son, would I not have taken care of you? I have the same duty.'

I accepted her as my son.

There was gossip going round that I selfishly let my daughter remain unmarried. It reached my ears too. What could I do? Did I not look out for her? If she said 'no' to every proposal, was it my fault? I am not a bad man. I am not selfish.

Raising my head, I called out, 'Look here, Iyer!'

I could hear Iyer rushing to me.

'What is it, saar?'

'What do you think of me?'

The question—out of the blue—must have surprised him. His silence said so.

'You have known me this last seven–eight years ... so you would have formed an impression.'

'Saar ... what impression? What do you mean by impression?'

'*Adada*, you would have formed some impression of me ... am I good, am I bad? Some assessment, right?'

'Oh, that way ... of course you are good. Any doubt?'

'Good man, am I not?'

'Yes.'

'Certain?'

'Certain.'

'So you say I am good, right?'

'Yes.'

'That is ...'

'You are good.'

I leant back comfortably.

'What do you think of my daughter?'

Silence.

'Iyer, why are you silent? What do you think of Shobana?'

'Shall I truly say what I think?'

'Yes.'

Apprehension flamed inside me as if a matchstick had been struck. What was he going to say? Had he noticed something wrong? Was the blind father the only person who had truly not seen anything?

'It is only because of your daughter that it rains and the sun shines in this world.'

I was taken aback. Why was he saying this? Is he saying, 'Hasn't she sacrificed her whole life for you? What magnanimity!'

'Okay, you may go. You will have work to do ... Shobi might come home now. Keep everything ready for her.'

His footsteps faded away.

What a high opinion he has of her! Everyone thinks so too. Has she sacrificed her life for me? Was that true? What does giving up one's life mean? Is marriage the be-all and end-all of life for a woman, a human being? Hadn't she herself asked, 'If I do not get married, does it mean I am ruining my life?' But was that the only thing she said? She had also said 'I don't dislike marriage, I am ready to get married.'

Then ...

Is that why ...

Should I have forced her to get married?

It's so dark, dear God!

What should I have done?

But does that mean she could go the wrong way? Hotel room ... couple ... Mr and Mrs ...

Shobi, is it really you ... like this? Is the image of you etched in my mind altering? All that the blind have are such images. Forms fabricated from dreams. If they are erased, there is nothing left. Don't you know this, Shobi? You may form many friendships. But for me, you are the only complete, undamaged form.

How long has this relationship been going on? Chee ... no ... Muthu saw someone else.

Why should I not strangle you, you wretch?

Whose neck ... that of the one who puts me first?

Shobi, Shobi, I don't know what to think. It is all so confusing. I stood up. I walked inside again. I sat in a chair. I heard the footsteps of my attendant walking to the verandah. Then the sound of the verandah light being turned on. Time to turn on the lights? I could not sit down. Stepped out again. Now the bulb will be shining right above me. The multicoloured hues in the sky would have appeared and disappeared, and now the spreading darkness. With the new chill breeze, the scent of butter being clarified in someone's house wafted in.

In all these years, not once has there been a trace of sadness or yearning in her voice or manner.

'Appa, have you eaten?'

'Appa, I've asked for the mattress maker to come home because your mattress has become very limp.'

'Why are you curling up, Appa? Is it cold? Wait, I will cover you with a blanket.'

'If you can't sleep, will you listen to a story? Shall I read aloud?'

'Appa, the Hyderabad grapes looked good. I bought some from the market. Here.'

'Appa, put on these new slippers. It seems it is made of some special leather and won't hurt your skin.'

'Appa, I bought a new tape recorder for you. You can record all your favourite programmes and listen to them when you please.'

One day, after recording two songs by a favourite singer, I said, 'Why don't you say something, Shobi? We will record that.'

'Say what?'

'Anything.'

'Aren't we talking now? Isn't that the same thing?'

'No, something special.'

'I don't know what to say.'

She who chatted enthusiastically for hours, could not think of anything to say when I asked her to say something.

'Can't think of anything of say.'

'Say whatever comes to your mind. Like you tell me about what happened in the office.'

'Yes.'

'So tell me what happened today.'

'Mmm ... nothing happened.'

A short silence. The humour of the occasion then struck us both and we laughed at the same time. When we replayed the tape, we realized that after the two songs, we had recorded this conversation and the laughter! How we had clapped our hands and laughed.

'We forgot to switch off the tape recorder. Let it be, Shobi. Let us not erase it.'

This had happened two years ago. On a sudden impulse, I went into my room. Two steps forward, then right, four steps, and the cassette was on the table.

I called my attendant.

'Please hand me the Pithukuli Murugadas[2] tape.'

The music strain started softly '*Ulagathin nayakiye*'.[3] I was not in the mood today. I pressed the button and forwarded the tape. After the recorded music stopped, the whirring sound and then ...

'Why don't you say something, Shobi? We will record that.'
'Say what?'
'Anything.'
'Aren't we are talking now? Isn't that the same thing?'
'No, something special.'
'I don't know what to say.'
'Can't think of anything to say.'
'Say whatever comes to your mind. Like you tell me what happened in the office.'
'Yes.'
'So tell me what happened today.'
'Mmm ... nothing happened.'

A short silence. Then the sound of father and daughter laughing.

I stopped the cassette.

I slid to the floor as a great weariness swamped over me.

[2] A very popular singer of Hindu devotional songs in Tamil.
[3] Literally, empress of the world.

'Ayya, what's the matter?' The voice and steps of the attendant rushed to me.

'Nothing. Go ... go ... go see if Amma is coming.'

I sensed that he had left. A concerned attendant. Just him? No. She ... the one who gave me this whole life which embraces me. She too had left.

Traces of aging in the voice on the tape. What had happened to the youthfulness of her voice? When did it disappear? This voice on the tape was laden with age. This recording was two years ago. How did I not notice it? Even now when I heard it, why had it not struck me? Is it because I hear it every day? Even now do I *see* this voice only because of the light thrown by Muthu's words?

All these years I have thought only of myself. Every 31 December an added weight presses my heart. One more year. How do I look now? Has my hair greyed? When I walk now my breath comes faster. Are there wrinkles on my face? Is my skin drier?

Such thoughts about myself. Sometimes when my attendant shaves me or helps me into my clothes, I have even asked him so. But never, not once, have I thought of how *she* looks now.

Fragments of half-submerged thoughts now floated up. The comments of visitors, uttered in casual conversation, words becoming meaningful as they rise from somewhere in the subconscious.

'What, Shobi, does all your income go into your food? Is that a spare tyre around your waist?'

'What is this? The first grey hair. Why don't you get a *tailam*[4] from a *vaidyar*?'[5]

---

[4] Herbal oil.
[5] Practitioner of traditional medicine.

'You used to chat with guests like us happily, right through midnight. Now you are yawning at 9 pm?'

She is thirty-six now.

Till today there is no change in that tenderness. Nothing in her tone that accuses me. Nothing in her behaviour to indicate any longing, complaint, or even self pity. Till today. Even now with every breath her attitude says, 'You are my priority, Appa.'

My daughter, who is becoming an old maid, serving me. I came out to the verandah and sat in the easy chair. I got up slowly. When I flapped my hands to drive away the insects that fell on my neck and face, I realized that they must be covering the light bulb.

'What a lot of insects, Ayya. They will bother you. Shall I turn off the light?'

'No. I don't want the house drowned in darkness when Amma comes home.' An insect had slipped inside my shirt. He picked it up and threw it away.

'Appa, I have not given you any room for complaint.'

True.

I sighed.

Should desires and duties always be mutually exclusive?

The sound of a car at the gate.

Maybe a taxi? Or someone may have dropped her in his car. What did he look like?

In a few minutes, the sound of flapping slippers rushed to me.

'Appa, I'm home. How are you?'

This concern, when she had been away for just three days. The same tenderness, the same care in her voice, which caressed my head and my back.

Is she my child or am I hers?

How long ago had the youthfulness left her voice?

'I am fine. How are you? Office work over?'

'Mmh. I should have reached at 5. The train was late.'

'Go, refresh yourself and have something to eat, Shobi.'

'I had coffee at the station. I don't want anything now. I
will put my suitcase away, have a wash, and join you. So many
insects. You are sitting here, doesn't it bother you? I will turn
off the light, okay?'

Following the sound of the light being turned off, I heard
the sound of her footsteps going in. In a short while, I heard the
cook saying, 'Even if you don't want tiffin, at least have some
hot coffee, Amma.'

'No, Iyer. I am full. Did Appa eat well?'

'Oh, yes. Please drink half a tumbler at least.'

'All right.'

Soon he heard her footfall. He heard her saree brushing
against the chair nearby. Now the insects did not bother him.

'Anything happened these three days? What did you do?'

When she spoke, he could smell the fragrance of coffee on
her breath.

'Nothing special.'

'Did anyone come to spend time and chat with you?'

'Muthu came home. No one else.'

'How is he? It has been a long time since he visited us, no? Is
he all right?'

'Mmh.' Poor Muthu. I need not have scolded him like that.

'Did Alagesan finish the historical novel?'

'Yes, he did. Move your chair closer, Shobi.'

The scraping sound of the chair being moved.

'Yes, Appa.'

I slowly stretched my arms to feel her hair and stroked it.
It was not soft. The roughness of grey had set in. Have I never
seen her as an individual and only and always as my protector?
There will be subtle changes on the thirty-six-year-old face.
The young girl whom I had last seen twenty years ago would
have become a stranger to this woman.

'Are you tired after your train travel? Will you rest for
a while?'

'No, Appa. If we keep talking, I will not feel tired. Appa, you told me you wanted to read the Tamil *paasurams*.[6] So I contacted a Tamil pandit. He has agreed to come home two days a week and read out the paasurams and explain them to you.'

'Oh ... very good.'

I swallowed, and stroked her hair again. I could smell the faint fragrance of a rose, but my fingers could not feel any flower on the knot at the nape of her neck. I stroked her face once, touched the neck. Is this the neck I had wanted to throttle with rage?

'Appa, why are you trembling?' She touched my forehead.

'Shobi, I feel cold in the evening. Am I not getting old? Do you have to go to office tomorrow?'

'Yes.'

'You can't take even a day's leave?'

'Um hm. Too much work in the office.'

'What colour saree are you wearing? You used to wear a lot of green. What colour do you like now?'

I heard her peals of laughter.

'Appa, Appa. Why have you suddenly become sentimental?' I could hear the softness of her affection in her voice.

My daughter.

Haven't I been fuming how my daughter—a woman—could behave like this? The echo of tradition, centuries old. If she had been a son, would I have been so devastated by what Muthu said? When I could enjoy her protection as though she had been a son—I could accept the break from tradition and societal norms—why should I not look upon her as a son in this other matter? Is she not a warm-blooded, normal human being?

'Sentimental Appa!'

'Not sentimental, Shobi. I've not asked anything about you for such a long time. I want to know who your friends are.

[6] Devotional hymns.

Why don't you bring them home ... m ... m ... even if there is a special friend? I have no objection. I will only be too happy to know that you have a life of your own besides taking care of me.'

There was no response from her a while. I could clearly hear her even and deep breathing in the silence.

Then she spoke.

'We must thank Muthu greatly. Isn't it, Appa?'

I could hear a smile in her voice.

'Why do you say that?'

'For coming to see you after so long.' Her hand fell on mine softly. 'Just now you said you would only be too happy ... that is enough. Beyond that ... I don't think there is any need to bring home any ... mmmh ... special friend.'

Ascent to the Shrine*

I stroked my feet gently. They still hurt. I think the fever had
not subsided completely. It rose in the afternoon. I am forced
to lie down in a corner with a muffler and a blanket. From the
day I arrived in this town, I have given poor Vaidehi nothing
but trouble!

'Nothing of that sort, Maama! Is it such a big trouble to be
with you and to give you medicine?' she says. What else will
she say? My friend's daughter, and like my own, after long years
of affection. A great bond.

'You like to visit temples, Maama. Simhachalam[1] is just 50
miles away. You can have darshan[2] of the deity and stay with
me for a few days. Why don't you see for yourself, how we live
in this wilderness?' She had invited me fondly. And I came here!
I went down with fever as soon as I arrived. It was the strain of
the journey or maybe the cold affected me. This is a hilly place,
but the elevation is not really much. 'Only 2,800 feet above
sea level,' said Madhavan, Vaidehi's husband. But still, it was

* Originally titled 'Padikal', the story was published in *Kathaik
Kanigal* in 1963, and later appeared in *Nagalinga Maram* in 2010
(pp. 51–60).

[1] A hill temple in Andhra.

[2] Visit to the temple, literally to 'see'.

too cold for a town-bred person. Further, this was the month of Aippasi.[3]

I had a divine darshan of the Varaha Narasimha Moorthy[4] on Simhachalam. I went up the hill by foot. When I ascended step by step, somehow, my aged feet did not feel any fatigue. It was a pilgrimage, right? So the heart flooded with a feeling of divinity.

Is this the first time that I have climbed the steps to have a darshan? Even to Tirupati, I do not go up by bus, but by climbing up the sacred hills, step by step.

That satisfies the soul. If by your physical effort you climb the hill with a sacred purpose, you feel that the ascent is the ascent of the soul. I had even climbed up the *Muzhangal mudichu*[5] without any fatigue.

This is how I climbed to see Palaniandavan,[6] Tiruttanidevan,[7] Uchipillaiyar,[8] and etched them in my heart. I feel quite proud when I look at my feet now and feel them.

Vaidehi is a lively conversationalist. I would chat with her drinking the chlorine-scented tea. They chlorinate the water for health reasons. When it was time to leave, Vaidehi will stand up and say, 'Maama, I must go down now. It is time for school. My children will be waiting.' The house is on a small hillock, so the 'colony' was down below, and in front of the house, the mountain range. 'Yes, Ma, please go.'

[3] The Tamil month of 15 October–15 November.

[4] The famous temple in Andhra Pradesh where the deity combines the iconographic features of the Varaha (the boar form of the ten *avataram*s or incarnations of Vishnu) and Narasimha (the man–lion form).

[5] The first phase of the climb up Tirumala.

[6] Lord of the Palani Hill, Subrahmanya.

[7] Lord of Tiruttani, Subrahmanya.

[8] Lord Ganesa on the top of the hill in Tiruchi.

This is a secluded town, devoid of too many modern con-veniences. There is nothing except the uncrowded forest and mountain. It is situated where Andhra and Orissa meet and the adivasis live here. This place gained some importance only after the railway project was started by blowing up the rocks using dynamite. The engineers and others who work on the project, reside here, and their houses form the colony.

The women here had started an elementary school; earlier there were no schools for the children of this colony. Vaidehi was one of the teachers. Every morning and afternoon, she would go down to the colony to teach the children.

The children were especially fond of her, and for her they were 'my children'. The sincere work of earnest and enthusias-tic persons is really an alchemy stone which turns everything to gold.

I heard a fluttering sound. Was it the sound of the temple bells ringing, or pearls rolling on the strings of the veena, or the splashing of cool rose water, or was it the singing of the early birds at dawn?

It appeared as if a colourful wave had rolled in. There were flushed pink flower-like faces, tender bud-like forms, paintings created by an amalgam of flowers, light, honey, and the cool breeze. Lovely images of beauty came in, shy and hesitant, halt-ing and swaying.

How many different children. Frocks, pavadais,[9] shirts, half-pants, and bush coats twinkled in various colours. They moved like tender fruits piled together, and then like a bunch of flowers flung open, they would rush forth noisily.

'Maami.'

'Mausi.'

'Aunty.'

[9] A long skirt.

They would approach Vaidehi eagerly. How many tiny hands stretch out to grip her open arms! Like tassels stitched on a fabric, they would cling to her.

School children! Even after class hours, they would crowd to see Vaidehi. When they visit her, they would bring along with them their tiny brother or sister who had not reached school-going age. In a moment, the whole house would buzz with their voices. This lively chatter, along with the sound of tables and chairs being dragged along and objects being dropped, why ... even the noise of a lively quarrel amongst them would form a delightful symphony.

Though it was a Telugu-speaking area, since those working on the project came from all states, there was a mixture of languages. Children's voices would be heard in Tamil and Telugu, calling Vaidehi maami in Tamil, mausi in Hindi, and aunty in English. Somehow, she would identify each voice and answer the child in a sweet and appropriate manner. As for the childish prattle! Some were still not stable on their feet. When children, who are unsteady of gait, speak in their childish lisp, half the words dissolve in dribble. When they chattered revealing a tooth here and a tooth there, it appeared as if fragments of the moon had been trapped in their rosy mouths.

'Maami, today they made *vendakai*[10] curry at home.'

'My mother knitted a new sweater. Look, I'm wearing it.'

'Mausi, the uncle who supplies milk has got a new baby.'

Vaidehi with bright surprise on her face, 'Oh! Is that so?'

'Yes, all of us went to see the baby.'

One child asked another.

'Did you also go?'

'No.'

'Why?'

'Why should we go? We don't buy milk from them.'

---

[10] The vegetable okra, or lady's finger.

What thoughts flit in the minds of children!

Lying on my bed, I would listen to them with interest.

Such visits were frequent occurrences. When they first saw me in that house, they were too shy to look at me directly and glanced at me covertly, without saying anything. But it was clear that they had registered me in their minds, and that they would seek all details about me by asking Vaidehi.

'Maami, who is that thaatha?'

'My uncle.'

'Will he always be here?'

'No, after sightseeing he will go back.'

'Aunty, where does he live?'

'Madras.'

'What are the places he has visited here, Maami?'

'Did he see our school?'

'Did he see the tunnel?'

'Did he go in the jeep?'

'He did not fall when the jeep shook, right?'

'He has not gone out at all, he has been unwell.'

'Is that why he always covers himself with a blanket?'

'Yes.'

Several glances at me, now mixed with curiosity and sympathy.

'Mausi, aren't the two annas in Madras?'

'Anna' referred to Vaidehi's two sons, who were studying in a high school as hostel students.

'Yes.'

'When will they come again?'

'Next holiday.'

'They are your children, no?'

'Yes.'

As if pierced by a nameless and subtle jealousy, the children moved nearer to her saying 'Tell us stories', and established their right over her.

How fond they are of her and she of them! She had the gentle skill of arousing enthusiasm even in children who had scant interest in studies. She and her colleagues had purchased Montessori equipment specially for them from Madras. When she described to me the happiness of the children on seeing these objects for the first time, her face was like a mirror of that joyous emotion.

'Maama, do you know how happy they were when they handled the blocks? They kept asking me with wonder if they were bought for them!'

'No praise is sufficient for this service you are all doing, Vaidehi.'

'We get our rewards, Maama. We will explain the concepts till our vocal chords hurt. The tiny faces in front of us would be looking puzzled at the new things, and suddenly when understanding dawns, the flash of joy that lights up their faces is worth all the strain.'

Really it was a mother–child bond. After school was over, some children would come with her holding her hands. Then all of them would cluster together. One would sit on her lap. 'Maami, I'm thirsty' would come a childish whisper. Another would rush to her crying 'Mausi' and lift up the gown for her to untie the panty's drawstring knot.

Another child would glance at the class book given to her, pointing out to the fish, stork, horse, elephant, lion, and bear one by one, and saying clearly, 'This has come home.'

'Even the tiger came to your house?' I would ask.

'Oh! Yes! I threw a stone, and it fell into the water and died.'

Vaidehi would serve to each child the snacks made by her in small china dishes with a spoon. Some days there would be a torrential downpour after the children had come. The clouds would hide the mountain range, the houses, and the electric poles. At those times, Vaidehi would switch on the record player for the children. They would gather around her like a bunch of flowers and would ask her to play some songs again and again.

'Now ... what shall we play next?'

'Maami ...'

'Yes, dear ...'

'That ... that one.'

'Which one?'

'The one you played just now!'

'Mausi, the rail song!'

'Yes! The one where they will sing the names of all the stations!'

'No, let me hear "*Sun sun karthi aayee chidiya*".'[11]

'No, only the rail song.'

'Be patient. I will play them all one by one, all your favourites.'

Again and again, the same songs. Sometimes they would sing under their breath. Someday when their joy hit a high, the noise level will also hit a high. It was a lovely sight to hear their chatter rising loudly, over the sound of the music, even louder than the noise of the rain drumming on the asbestos roofing.

One little girl among them, shy, wide-eyed, and chubby-cheeked, would come every day. She would not talk much nor ask for anything. She came only to be near Vaidehi, looking at her in mute worship.

If Vaidehi looked at her, she would give a faint smile. If she spoke to her, a few shy words. That was all. But the fullness of that love!

Vaidehi looked at all the children with tenderness.

'Maama, what do you think of my children?'

'You can be proud of them.'

What else can I say? She and the children wove the fabric of joy during those days. I am unable to say with which yarn they did it. Impossible to hold the magic wires of joy. All I could

[11] A popular children's song in Hindi.

feel was the light that radiated from them. If a lotus bloomed in your heart, how do you describe the fragrance? The only way to honour that emotion is to be brimful with silence while the fragrance spread through your entire being.

'I must leave now, Vaidehi. My temperature has been normal for one whole day. Let me go to Simhachalam. One more day and then I will return home.'

'What's the hurry, Maama? Get better first.'

'I am fine.'

'Your feet will still be tired because you have had fever. Now you will say you want to climb the hill. That's why I told you to stay.'

'Vaidehi, isn't climbing a *thiruppani*?[12] Can anything be compared to that sanctity? I won't feel even a bit tired.'

'Listen to me, Maama.'

'No, Amma, let me go tomorrow. I will tell Madhavan. I will never forget the affection shown by both of you.'

As the dusk drew near, I felt energized. I suddenly remembered that ever since I had come here, I had not once stood on the verandah. So I covered myself with a muffler and came out.

The chill wind stung me. The rain had stopped only a short while ago. The trees had robed themselves with splashes of green, the mountain range lay hidden behind clouds. They looked like snow, they were white, yet they were rain-bearing clouds. I had watched the clouds every day. The cluster of clouds would visit as another guest, just like the children, who came home, and other friends. The mist which was tightly covering the mountain slowly spread around, came close, entered the house, and settled down. My eyes did not have the capacity to

---

[12] A task done with religious intent.

fully experience the beautiful sight of the cotton-white path rolling out in the middle.

I felt cold, but I didn't feel like going indoors. I hugged the blanket tightly around me folding my arms and wore my slippers. I came down the verandah and stood at the road in front of the house. The road curved on both sides and went down.

The sweeper boy who cleaned the house told Vaidehi that he was going home as he had finished his work. He hastened along the downward path. Far away, some Andhra women, their hands, necks, and noses decorated with gold, were walking along.

The shower hesitatingly sported with the wind. My eyes were fixed on the distant scene. Now the edge of the mountain range looked very faint. When I saw the mountain, my thoughts went back to the temple. What a beautiful experience it is to climb up step by step to see the Lord. Devotion springs in the heart by that exercise and the body gets recharged. This body is God's gift. What can be a better act of devotion than to see Him by straining the body? I bent to look at my feet. Again my heart filled with pride. To go to Simhachalam again and climb up to the temple ...

Suddenly, something stumbled into my vision. I was now looking down. Near the main path, there was another route formed with steps that went downwards. They were rough steps hewn in a haphazard manner on the hillock. I could see the red soil.

A wave of colour was rolling up through the steps from the colony down below! What was that?

As I was looking on, the wave came up. From the height, the faces below were not clear. Like a bunch of grapes, their little black heads, the children came, jostling against each other, puffing and panting, holding their knees with the tiny palms, sweating and rushing, climbing up the rain-wet slippery steps.

How wonderful! Is this how they come up every day? Not by the straight route but by the shortcut?

When they came to the top step, the bunch of flowers scattered into separate blooms.

'Maami!'

'Mausi!'

'Aunty!'

They surrounded Vaidehi, who came out. Though their faces were flushed with the strain, their eyes glistened with joy as they looked up. One child came close and clutched her hand. Another asked, 'Shall we listen to songs?'

Golden waves of love all around.

Hesitatingly, the shy, timid one came close to Vaidehi and handed her a white-rayed cotton flower plucked from the wayside bushes.

'For you!'

'My darling, *shukriya!*'[13]

Vaidehi received the flower. That group of children entered the house, sounding like a single strum of a veena.

My eyes dimmed.

Is this not a pilgrimage?

Rain or shine, they climb up, moved only by their love. Is not this exertion a holy service?

Yes, and not only that. Because these devotees come, this place has become a temple.

I looked at the crooked steps going down. I looked at my feet. The vision of the small tender feet that had become red moved my heart. Suddenly, I felt ashamed and felt humbled. My arrogance and self-conceit vanished without a trace.

From indoors came the train song.

---

[13] Hindi for 'thank you'.

*After Three Years**

As soon as she turned the corner, she saw Amma, and deep inside her she felt a chill.

In three years—to put it accurately, three years, two months, and eleven days—Amma had become so frail, changed so much! Whenever Hema badly missed seeing her parents, she would board the bus to Mylapore on Friday evenings, since they visited the Kapaliswarar[1] temple every Friday, to watch them from a distance. Yet today Amma's fragility hit her anew.

She felt a rush of emotion, she wanted to run towards Amma, bury herself in her, and cry her heart out.

'Why have you stopped, Hema?'

She came to herself with a start at her husband's query which felt like a splash of icy water on her face.

'Look there, four shops away, it looks like my friend Mala! I will just go up and if it is her, shall I chat with her a few minutes? We studied together in school and it has been such a long time since I last saw her.'

---

* Originally titled 'Moonru Varuda Idaiveli', the story was published in 1996, and later appeared in *Nagalinga Maram* in 2010 (pp. 287–93).
[1] A famous ancient Siva temple in Mylapore.

'If two women start talking, no chance of it stopping in ten minutes!'

'Can't you be patient for my sake, even if I am away for half an hour?' she laughed. How easily she faked the smile for her mother's sake! 'It has been such a long time!'

'So you told me.'

'Please.'

Will he say no? The hell a woman goes through when there is discord between her husband and her parents!

'You just go and take a look at the shirting materials. I'll come back as soon as possible.'

She then looked sideways anxiously. Thank goodness! Amma was still standing there! Her eyes were on the opposite side, maybe she wanted to cross the road. The vehicles were rushing to and fro and Amma was waiting for the gap. Hema silently thanked the evening-hour Purasawakkam[2] traffic rush.

'Okay, Vasu?'

'Okay, but come back soon. Let Mohan be with me. He will bother you when you are chatting with your friend.' Vasu drew the three-year-old child to his side.

'No ... I want to go with Amma.' The child clung to his mother's saree.

'Let him be with me, Vasu.'

'As you please. But it is evening rush time, be careful, he is a child. Mohan Kanna, hold Amma's hand tightly, okay?'

Hema walked casually, but only until Vasu entered the shop. The moment he disappeared inside, she picked up the child and ran towards her mother, with the long-strapped handbag on her shoulder bobbing up and down.

'Amma!'

Her voice was lost in the traffic din. She moved forward and held her mother's hand.

---

[2] A neighbourhood in the city of Chennai.

Amma was taken aback. 'Who is it?' She tried to free her hands. When she saw her daughter, eyes widening with joy and the lips opening in a smile, she stuttered, 'Hemoo, Hemoo, is it really you?'

'Amma, Amma.'

Amma's aging face had shrunk into fine folds, her wide eyes grew even wider. Had her vision deteriorated? It was not like this before. In the last three years, there may have been many changes, which she, her daughter, may not know.

'Amma, do you know how happy I am to see you!' She set the child down. 'But you have lost so much weight! Amma, aren't you well?'

'When the heart aches with longing, won't one lose weight? Hemoo, Hemoo Kannu, are you really standing in front of me? I've missed you so much. I never thought I would ever see you! Are you all right?'

She hugged her daughter, unmindful of the fact that they were in the middle of the road, uncaring that the cloth bag had fallen to the ground. There was a flash of a smile amidst her tears, like sunrays shining through the rain.

Amma's smile pierced Hema like a thorn. This apparent joy was really a facade over Amma's hidden pain.

'What could be wrong with me? I am fine. I eat well, sleep well, what else is there?' She bent to pick up her bag and to control her emotions.

'This is your child, isn't he? Mohan? I last saw him when he was six months old.'

'Now he is in L.K.G.'[3]

'Kanna, come to me, will you?'

The moment she touched him, he shrank back and stepped away.

---

[3] Lower kindergarten.

He tugged at this mother's saree and said, 'Let us go back to Appa.'

'Amma, I must go back soon. Vasu and I came here to shop for clothes. When I saw you I could not keep away ... I gave him some excuse to come and see you. I can't stay long Amma. If Vasu comes out and sees us, there will be trouble.'

'Yes, yes, go quickly. Anyway, Hemoo, I am so overjoyed at seeing you.' Her trembling fingers stroked the daughter's face again and again. The passers-by on the street looked at them with curiosity.

'I have so often desperately wanted to see you. I have even considered visiting you when my son-in-law is not around, for just five minutes, only to see you. But Appa categorically said "If you step inside the house of that man who cut off all ties with us, I will never look at you again." Not that he does not want to see you, it is just that being a man, he can be strong-willed. I'm the one who suffers. You too are stone-hearted, Hema. Couldn't you have come to Mylapore to see your parents at least once?'

'I have the same problem, Amma. I am scared of what will happen if Vasu comes to know. But, Amma, please don't think I have not seen you and Appa at all! Whenever I miss you terribly, I come to Kapaliswarar *kovil*[4] on a Friday, giving Vasu some excuse or the other, and I watch you both from a distance.'

'Stupid girl, couldn't you have come and spoken to us? We would have been so happy, no?'

'How can I do that, Amma? Vasu's sister lives in that area and she is the root cause of all the problems. If she or her acquaintances see us and report to Vasu?'

'That is true too.'

---

[4] A temple.

Three years ago, Hema's father turned 60, and it was his *sashtiabdhapoorthi*.[5] Hema, Vasu, and Vasu's sister Kamalam were all present. Kamalam's husband was not in town.

Hema's mother was running hither and thither attending on her son-in-law and his sister. When it was time for them to leave, she handed over a plastic bag containing the *thamboolam*,[6] but it slipped from her hands and fell on the ground.

Kamalam said, 'So careless, what is the use of being mature in years?'

'Don't get upset, it just slipped ...'

'If you were really careful, how will it slip? Even at the time of the wedding, you treated us all with disrespect.'

Kamalam deliberately fuelled the exchange of words, which grew heated.

Unable to bear the pain on his wife's face, Hema's father intervened, 'That is enough, Kamalam. What is the lapse now, or at the wedding when we gave you no cause for complaint? My wife is older than you, you can't talk to her like this.'

'No one needs to teach me manners. Do you know who I am? I am a very rich building contractor's wife. Just remember that.'

'Oh sure, and I also know how that contractor became a rich man.'

Kamalam screeched, 'Vasooo, did you hear what he said about my husband, and you are still quiet?'

'I said only what the whole world knows.'

'Did you hear that, Vasu? Vasu, did you hear what he said?'

'Maama, I think you are overstepping your limit. Apologize to my sister now.'

---

[5] The sixtieth year celebrations accompanied by traditional rituals.

[6] It is a custom to give, as a takeaway, betel leaves, arecanut, turmeric, and coconut when visitors take leave after an auspicious function.

'I will, but before that your sister should apologize for hurting someone older than her.'

'My sister … apologize? That's not fair.'

'Don't talk of fairness. We have understood that your whole family has no idea what fairness is.'

The verbal altercation worsened and in the end Vasu said, 'It is all over now. I will never step in your house hereafter. Hema, let us leave now, you will have no connection with these people from today.' He left with his reluctant and distressed wife.

Hema's mother sighed sadly standing on the road.

'Amma, how is Appa?'

'Oh, he is not at all well.'

'Why, Amma, what is wrong?'

'The doctor says his heart is weak, there is blood pressure too. He has to take tablets every day. Now the stock is over, and I had to buy more. Our Gomathi Maami is in this hospital with a fractured hip. So I came here to see her. This medicine shop is there right opposite, so I thought that I will buy the BP tablets as well. I was just waiting to cross the road when you came.'

'You don't cross the road in this busy traffic. Give the prescription to me. I will get it for you.'

'It's all right, Hema.'

'After so many years I have this chance of doing something for you and Appa. Will you not let me do this?'

Amma was touched. She opened her bag and out wafted the fragrance of mangoes. She must have taken some for the patient.

'Here, the prescription and the money.'

'You keep the money, Amma.'

'Hema, Hema, what is this?'

Ignoring her mother's words, Hema lifted her child and crossed the road swiftly. She returned with a brown paper bag containing the tablets and gave it to her mother.

'Amma, I'll go. Give my regards to Appa. Tell him I enquired about him.'

Amma wordlessly stroked her face and nodded her head, eyes glistening in the light of the sodium-vapour lamp.

Stubbornly holding her tears back, she returned to the shop holding her child's hand.

'Who is that aunty, Amma?'

Now the tears just burst, she covered her mouth with her handkerchief, and firmly pressed again and again as if to push back the tears that refused to be controlled.

Vasu was still looking at the clothes. 'Hema, there is so much variety here, I am just not able to make up my mind. Good that you have come to help me choose.'

'You are the one who is going to wear the shirt.' Hema attempted to smile.

'And you are the one who must see it.'

After they chose the shirt for him, they bought some clothes for her and the child, and it was eight when they entered Diwan Rama Salai[7] on his Yamaha.

Hema went in and quietly attended to her chores. She put away the new clothes, fed the child, put him to bed, and then set the table and the glasses of water for herself and her husband.

'Vasu, shall we eat?'

Now it was clearly apparent that she was upset.

'You said you will be back in ten minutes, but you took so long. At the shopping place, I mean.'

She was silent.

'I realized even then that it must only have been a friend that you had met.'

'Yes ...' She said in a low voice, looking away ... 'It was only a friend.'

'What did your friend Bala say?'

'Who? ... Oh Bala ... yes ... yes ... It seems ... she is in Madras now ... it seems she has a daughter ... her husband ...'

---

[7] Salai means a road.

She stopped. Had she not said Mala? He had stumped her by saying Bala. She looked up red-faced.

'I saw your mother too.' His face was expressionless.

She turned her face away. Lips quivering, she spoke in an empty voice, 'What is my punishment?'

'Why should I punish you? In these three years I may have changed, right?' Hema turned towards him at that.

'I may have matured enough in these three years not to let my anger affect my humanity. Isn't it?'

Suddenly a feeling swamped her as though all fetters had broken loose, her lips flowered into a smile, but her chin wobbled.

'Feel like crying? Just a minute.'

He stood up and came round to sit next to her, and put his arm around her with her head resting on his shoulder.

'Now cry.'

Growing Up, Growing Apart*

'Come, come,' she said, unable to say anything more. A choking joy had silenced her. The smiling eyes spoke.

'Hello, Savi! What a pleasant surprise! I did not expect you to come to the station,' Sowmya smiled and rushed to her.

'How long is it since we met? And you didn't expect me at the station? That thought is unpardonable,' said Savita.

Sowmya laughed. 'Ha! *Now* I know I've come home!'

For two moments, the two sisters stood like two faces of silence. Moments filled with meaning that needed no words.

After loading the luggage into the taxi at Central Station till they reached Kasturba Nagar, they did not exchange words other than

How are you?

How is your husband?

How are the children?

Though there was enough space in the car, the simple fact that they sat close to each other said it all.

Savita's husband welcomed his sister-in-law, enquired about her welfare and said, 'Ever since she heard you were coming, your Akka's feet have not touched the ground.'

---

* Originally titled 'Anniyargal', the story was published in 1984, and appeared in *Nagalinga Maram* in 2010 (pp. 161–71).

Sowmya's eyes reached out to her sister ... again a bridge of silence, again the intimacy ... in the smile.

'It doesn't seem like those many years, Savi! A touch of grey ... that's all, other than that there is no change.'

'Grey hair!' Savita smiled as if to say lightly, 'Time could do only that. Poor Time!'

It was as if this meeting had erased the years of separation. When there is mutual affection, how effortlessly one picks up the threads of a relationship even though one meets the other after many years. Sowmya was right, it didn't seem like so many years at all. There was really no distance between them at heart! So the gap of eleven years disintegrated in a second. It was as if they had always been together without ever being separated.

They had last met when their widowed mother had died. That was a different set of circumstances. They had flown in from their respective places, and come together to share the grief. So the intimacy and the oneness of that occasion were aspects of the bereavement. The conversation was completely focused on Amma and about her end. After the obsequies, they had returned to their homes.

Thereafter, this was the first real intimacy. A type of anaemia had weakened Sowmya. So when Savita had invited her, Sowmya's husband sent her from Bombay to Madras for a change, promising to take care of the house and the children.

It was as if the two sisters had recaptured their lost past. Intimacy and friendship exploded in conversation after the first day's silence. Savita's husband would tease them, 'Looks like the sisters will not stop talking.' The children's smiles echoed him. This did not affect Savita. But it was not a continuous conversation, or if there was continuity, it was of a special kind. If they had been talking about something, one would continue on a different occasion, two or three days later, picking up the same thread, 'So that's why I said ...' and the other would immediately understand. The bond between the sisters seemed like an iceberg which showed only a portion of it above the water. Small flashes outside and a huge understanding beneath.

When she served the spicy dishes for the rest of the family, sharing with her sister the bland sambhar, that similarity in taste was a small sign of their deep oneness.

They liked their coffee sweetened to the same degree. Both liked sarees with broad borders. Both preferred early morning walks to walks in the evening. Both of them would wake up around 2 am, sip a little water and go back to sleep. So many similarities! These small likenesses born of the same root, each so sweet. Savita would soon turn forty. Sowmya was three-and-a-half years younger. But this sweetness was ever young because both of them were one.

The medical treatment was going on as a matter of course.

'I think your blood count is improving. You don't look so pale.'

'All your cooking! It is not as if Bombay lacked medical facilities!'

They were chatting while eating a snack of chips soaked in curds sweetened with sugar. This was something they had enjoyed in their parents' home. 'No one else likes this snack here. Only now I have someone who shares my taste!'

It was about 4:30 in the evening when Savita's eldest son Raju, a nineteen-year-old studying MSc, returned from college.

'Amma! Tomorrow we are having a break-up party for the outgoing MSc students. So I won't come home tomorrow evening. I'll stay overnight and return in the morning.'

'All right,' said Savita.

Sowmya looked at him. 'You are only a first-year student, Raju. Must you stay overnight?'

'Not a must, Chithi. But I want to stay ... many of my classmates will be there.'

'Will his father allow it?' Sowmya asked Savita after Raju had left the room.

'Yes.'

'And you don't say no?'

'Why should I?'

'This is how they learn all kinds of habits when they start staying away from home, no? Beedi,[1] drugs, drink, in addition you have co-ed, I'm not saying anything personal about Raju now.'

'I understand, Sowmy. But can we stop the passage of Time?'

'We can stop our children and protect them, can't we?'

'Our children must grow up knowing what the world is like. Thereafter their character is in their hands.'

'Are you saying that the elders should not control them at all?'

'The more you control them, the more they will rebel. That is all.'

'Children need help. What else are parents for?'

'To tell them that they can always depend on our love. How else can you help them?'

For a while neither spoke. Was there a small trip-up in something that was going smoothly? Sowmya placed her plate on the table. There were still some chips left. Savita lost her cool for a moment, but restrained herself at once and pressed her sister's hand softly.

'Don't worry about this, Sowmy. No one grows up without getting hurt. Can we always protect children in a cocoon? First of all, will they accept it? Tell me. Okay. There is a new Hindi film. Shall we go? Or have you already seen it in Bombay?'

'Not yet, we will go.'

For a long time after they had returned from the movie, the sisters discussed it. Sowmya did not like the film.

---

[1] Country cigarette.

'Must a movie be so explicit for it to be good? Nowadays, both literature and cinema are very explicit and becoming vulgar. Don't you think so?'

'Let's ignore the vulgar aspects and enjoy the art, the story value, and the good features.'

'Why pour poison in the first place? And then search for what is good in that muck, why? Why bolt the stables after the horses have gone?'

That night Sowmya took out two English magazines from her suitcase and marked the pages for Savita to read.

Savita's eyes widened. 'Hey! Your name is printed here. Story? You write stories too? Since when? You never told me?'

'Felt shy. I thought I'd tell you in time and show it to you. I've been writing for about a year. Just for fun. Read and tell me what you think.'

Savita was excited when she read it.

'So well-written, Sowmy. Every line broadcasts the fact you are an English-literature gold medalist. Great style.'

'Leave the style. What about the content?'

Savita hesitated for a minute, then said, 'Good story, but it is like a modern fairy tale.'

'My aim is to at least write something good and pure since there is so much violence and vulgarity around.'

They were silent. A silence that grated on Savita. That feeling subsided only after they went for a walk at 5 in the morning upto the Adyar bridge.

Then, thank God everything was as before!

At 9 o'clock, the library peon, brought the new books and took back the old ones. Sowmya picked up the books. Two of them were slim ones. She looked at the titles and the writers' names and said, 'Oh! This. Have you read this, Savi? Do read it. You'll like them.' And laughed.

Savita read them and sat motionless for a long time. There was neither literary value, nor insight into human nature; pure yellow pulp. Did Sowmya really think that this is what she liked? Is that all Sowmya had understood about her?

'Why are you punishing her by taking her to every Tamil movie in Eros? Are you angry with her?' Savita's husband asked.

'She can't see Tamil movies in Bombay. She likes them, that's why we go, no Sowmy?'

'*Ora*,' said Sowmya. When the others blinked uncomprehendingly, Savita alone felt happy. When they were children, they had created a secret language known only to them and not the adults. In that private lexicon, they composed their own words which had a special meaning. 'Ora' meant yes. Savita felt that by using their private language all of a sudden, Sowmya was reinforcing their bond. They winked at each other and smiled.

'We must go to the ladies club this evening. Remember?' asked Savita.

Savita had taken her sister several times to the ladies club where she was a member. Her face and eyes had brimmed with pride when she told the other members that her sister was a writer.

The club president told Savita that day about a poor boy who lived close by. He was lame and his family had abandoned him. The boy must study. But first he must be fed. He was refusing to move out of the school compound for the last four or five days. The club president was collecting funds for his immediate relief. When she said 'Give what you can', Savita gave ten rupees. When the president turned to Sowmya, and asked 'You?' after glaring at her sister and a slight hesitation, she gave five rupees.

On the way back when Savita remarked, 'Poor boy, no Sowmy?' there was no answer.

'What, Sowmy? Have you nothing to say?'

'What can I say? Do you think I don't feel bad ... but ...'

'But?'

'These are problems to be tackled by big organizations. What can you achieve personally? Our country's poverty is a bottomless pit. It can never be filled up, no matter how much you try. What is the use?'

'It is true it is a bottomless pit. It is true it cannot be filled up. But whatever you do adds up, isn't it?'

The conversation lagged suddenly. Both returned home silently. Nowadays, the silence between them was not an eloquent one. They returned to a noisy home. Savita's fourteen-year-old daughter was running, holding a magazine and her brother, two years her junior, was chasing her to snatch it from her.

'Give it to me now!'

'You idiot. Only after me!'

'What? Will your head burst if you do not see Amitabh Bachchan at once?'

They didn't stop running. When he rushed from behind the sofa, he knocked against a cupboard. The glass pane cracked and a cutglass vase kept inside fell out. Savita rushed and caught it just before it hit the floor. Her face flushed red.

'Wretch! Can't you see where you are running? What would have happened had it hit the ground?' she asked, panting with rage and staring fiercely at her son.

'Sorry, Amma.' The boy's head dropped, the excitement dimmed, and brother and sister left the room.

Savita's agitation took a while to subside.

Sowmya kept looking at her.

'Just look, Sowmy. This is something that Appa and Amma gave me and I treasure it. The children know it and yet they are so careless.'

Sowmya did not utter a word.

'I would have died if this had broken. They gave you its pair, didn't they? You too have kept it carefully ... right?'

'It is safe.'

'Have you also displayed it in the hall like this?'

'I had.'

'Meaning?'

'The girl living in the flat above liked it very much. So I gave it to her as a wedding gift.'

Savita was shocked.

'You gave it away? How did you have the heart to part with it?'

'Why not?'

'It is in memory of Appa and Amma ...'

'Do we need mementoes to remember Appa and Amma?'

Again a moment on a razor's edge. The sisters stared at each other, confused.

'I'll make coffee for us, Savi. Put the vase back carefully.'

She brought the coffee identically sweetened, which they drank. It was an act that seemed to hold back something that was slipping away.

Two months were ending so soon? That regret was seen in their eyes. 'When will we meet again?' was the question that sounded in their continuously seeking each others' company and in doing things which the other one liked. At the same time, there was a new reserve in their conversation despite the intimacy; there was a certain caution to avoid any dissonance that might arise, both when they shared nostalgic moments of the past and when they exchanged memories. There was a lurking anxiety to stay on the safe side of the boundary.

Sowmya had sent a recent photo of herself to her husband and he had written back saying, 'You've put on weight beyond recognition. Please print "I am Sowmya" on your forehead.' From their letters, she sensed that her husband and children were missing her, though on the surface they sounded carefree and happy.

Must return soon.

The sisters decided that they must meet at least once a year and never again allow such a long gap.

When Sowmya smilingly said 'This must not be like the usual New Year resolution' with misty eyes, Savita's chin wobbled. Without saying a word, she held out a cardboard box. An Adyar handloom saree. Red with a broad yellow *gopuram*[2] border.

'Why all this, Savi?'

'Don't say anything. Just take it.'

'As you please. Only for me?'

'For me too.'

Peacock blue colour, but same broad border. Again eloquent smiles.

Time faded into the last day. Sowmya was getting ready, her luggage was packed.

'Ready to leave, Sowmy,' Savita's voice broke.

'You are coming to the station, Savi?'

Expectation met expectation, 'Yes, of course.'

'Before I go anywhere, it is my custom to do *namaskaram* in the pooja room.'

Savita was silent.

Sowmya looked disturbed.

'But there is no pooja room here,' she continued.

'So what? Pray in your heart. Isn't it enough if you have faith?'

'What do you mean if you have faith? Are you saying that is your way?'

---

[2] Temple tower. The popular motif of triangular spires on the border of a saree is called gopuram border.

Suddenly Sowmya's face changed, 'Or do you mean you don't have faith?'

'I ... I've never thought about it.'

Savita's discomfort intensified, 'Why this argument, Sowmy, just when you are leaving?'

'What is this, Savi? You say you don't have any opinion on such an important issue.'

'I don't think it is important.'

Sowmya looked shocked. The devout atmosphere of their childhood ...! Amma used to do pooja everyday. Every evening she will tell them, 'Go light a lamp in the pooja room and by the *tulsi*[3] plant.' Unfailingly she would take them to the temple every Friday. She would teach them *stotram*s.[4] She would advise, 'Whenever you face difficulties in life, your only support is His name.' When *she* had followed that path, what had happened to Savi?

'Savi, what happened to you that you have lost faith in God?'

'I'm not sure if I have lost faith. But is it so important that we ourselves have the experience? Don't our eyes, ears, and heart remain open? It's all right. When there are so many problems in the world, I don't think this is a very big issue.'

'How casually spoken! As for me ... I can't live without believing in God.' Their eyes clashed, confusion and fear in them. Sowmya's shock was evident, wondering at the elder sister with the question, 'Who is this stranger?'

Then the glances unlocked.

Savita was pained and disturbed. She didn't know what to say. She felt that nothing she said would convey any meaning. It is true that they had grown up together. It is true that their thoughts, perspectives, and assessments had their roots in the

[3] Basil plant sacred to Hindus.
[4] Religious verses.

same tradition and same upbringing, but when they grew up there was such a difference.

Is every human life unique? What differences! Do the echoes raised by life depend on one's nature? How senseless then is it to say 'I know you' or 'I understand you'. However close the relationship may be, each time one must introduce oneself to the other anew.

The change that time brings in, lies not in grey hairs alone.

Love ... that is the basic warp ... throb of life. It is the reason why relationships do not die because of the differences.

Forgive me, Harold Robbins. Throughout our lives, it is strangers that we love.

'It's getting late. Shouldn't we set off for the station? The taxi is ready at the gate,' her husband said looking at them. 'Mark a "to be continued" to your conversation. You can pick it up when you meet next.'

'We'll come in a moment. Come, Sowmy.' Savita held her sister's hands. They walked to the gate without letting go of each others' hands. But they did not look at each other.

A State of Mind*

It was in a bus that a man called her 'Paatti' for the first time. He had stood up and given his seat saying, 'Poor Paatti, you have been standing this long ... please sit here.' He was a young man. He probably had a grandmother of his own, paternal or maternal, or both, for that word to roll off his tongue so smoothly.

She was amused. 'Thank you', she said and sat on the seat he had vacated. There was a faint look of surprise on the young man's face at her response in English. Amazing how so many stereotyped images are imprinted in the minds of many ... a widow, a white saree; a good man, *vibhuti*[1] on the forehead; a good woman, the back covered by the saree. Similarly, if they spoke in English, they must be young. In their assessment, if you spoke English, it indicated you were modern, and only the young were entitled to be modern. So a grey-haired person speaking in English, especially a woman, was an anomaly. It is beyond this boy's imagination that there could be old women

---

* Originally titled 'Oru Mananilai', it was published in *Thinamalar*, *Deepavali Malar*, in 1992, and later appeared in *Nagalinga Maram* in 2010 (pp. 265–70).
[1] Sacred ash.

with a Master's degree. Had she said 'Thanks' or 'Very happy' in Tamil, he would have been satisfied that his value-judgements were intact. Radha felt like laughing as she thought, 'If I had said, "My name is Radha", he would have fainted.' In his assessment, she was probably a Kamakshi or a Mangalathammal.[2]

So far, no one had called her 'Paatti'. She was no one's grandmother. She had no children. Her husband had no siblings. She herself had only one older sister, who had, until recently, lived in Kovai.

Her sister had a son, a daughter-in-law, and grandchildren. According to Tamil custom, they should have called her Paatti or Chinna Paatti. But her sister's son Gopu lives in Chicago, and in the USA, children were used to calling their father's aunt by the same term that their father did. Because Gopu called her 'Radha Chitti', the children called her 'Aunt Zhadha'. She would tease them that while even among Tamilians some could not pronounce zha, it was easy for the Americans.

It looked as if the young man also had to alight at the Kulathankarai stop, and he did along with her. Glancing at her grey hair and slight build for a moment, he asked hesitantly, 'Where do you have to go, Paatti? Do you know the way? Shall I come with you?'

'No ... Thambi, thank you very much. My house is close by. I can go.' This time she replied in Tamil in order not to disappoint him. She stood for a while looking at him walk away, and then turned towards Mada Street.

She was not upset about growing old. It was true she was shocked when an old lady had peered at her from out of the mirror the first time. It was true that her first grey hair, her

---

[2] Chudamani uses the names Kamakshi and Mangalathammal, which are old-fashioned and therefore more suited in the minds of the young people for a woman of Radha's age.

first day with spectacles, her first dentures, had given her a jolt. But she could accept it as a process of nature. If one lived long enough this is what would happen. When you bless a child saying 'May you live long!' it only meant 'May you acquire grey hair, dentures, a walking stick, and spectacles'.

But the real agony of a long life is none of these. It was something else. It was seeing so many relatives and friends die and to have to bear in one's heart ... their corpses one ... by ... one.

It was already blazing hot at 10:30 in the morning. Vaikasi's[3] fiery rays leapt down the air. She reached home and, wiping her face, opened the front gate and entered the compound. It was a two-storeyed building, and the trees nearby moved their leafy fans to and fro so that the house would not perspire.

Radha closed the gate and fastened the latch. The dead leaves of the mango tree that stood next to the compound wall had fallen, spreading a brown carpet below. She stood for a while staring at the dead leaves, and then entered the house.

Her husband was in the hall reading the newspaper. He asked without looking up, 'What did the doctor say?'

'What will he say? Lungs and stomach are okay. It seems there is no need for medicines. He says, "Nothing, Ma. There will be such minor problems when you grow old. Do some light exercise and keep your mind cheerful. There is nothing for you to worry." Just because he can wear the stethoscope ... a stripling of a chap ... with not even a proper moustache ... thinks I am making a big fuss though there is actually nothing wrong with my health. This is the general impression about old people. Born just yesterday, he talks to me condescendingly as if he is giving a lollipop to a crying child,' said Radha, looking at her husband seated opposite him on the sofa stroking her knee.

[3] The Tamil month broadly coinciding with the period of 15 May–15 June.

He was so engrossed in his newspaper that it was impossible
to say whether or not he had heard her through. His lot was
better. He had regulated his days into an easy routine. For him,
passing the day was not a problem like it was for many retired
persons. His time fitted into a schedule with the newspaper,
books, meditation, TV, Rummy at a recreation club, and other
such things; as snugly as a pillow fitted into a cover.

Radha leant back and stroked her knee again, her eyes
closed. It hurt. The pain was worse these last twenty days.
Her sister Rohini ... the pain in her knee ... her sister Rohini ...
the pain.

Rohini, three years older than her, had been brash and
opinionated even as a child. She talked as if she knew everything. Even if she said something wrong, she would insist she
was right.

A childhood memory rose inside Radha like a full moon over
waves of laughter. Even before a music teacher was engaged to
teach them music, the girls would sing to themselves what they
had heard here and there.

Once, Rohini, who had heard someone sing the geetham[4]
'Sri Gananatha',[5] taught her younger sister clearly enunciating
'Sri Gananatha Sindhu Ravana'.[6]

Radha had a doubt, 'Ravana? Here?'

'Why not? Sindhu means the sea. That is Samskritam, and
next-door Sastri Maama said so. Then wasn't Ravana the king
of Lanka which is in the middle of the sea? And so Sindhu
Ravana.' Seven-year-old Radha was amazed at her elder sister's
knowledge of Samskritam at age ten. To this date, whenever she

---

[4] A carnatic musical piece taught to beginners.
[5] Song in praise of Lord Ganesa.
[6] The demon king of Lanka in the Hindu epic, Ramayanam.

heard 'Sri Gananatha', the words 'Sindhu Ravana' would flow into her mind before she corrected it to 'Sindhoora varna'.[7]

So many memories, funny memories, moving ones, memories of angry quarrels too. But there was no venom in the anger. Once when they were young, their uncle had bought a beautifully carved sandalwood box from Mysore, and Rohini had snatched it from Radha saying, 'It is for me. I am the elder one.' But the very next week, on Radha's birthday, she gave it to her saying, 'This is for you, Radha.'

In the silence of that room, the ticking sound of the quartz clock could be heard clearly, beating rhythmically. The room's heartbeat, as if the room would die if the clock stopped.

She opened her eyes and looked at the clock. It was 11:10. No sign of her husband. When had he left ...? The newspaper lay folded neatly on the table. An advertisement for some shop was seen, with the words 'Quality Materials' in bold English letters, the 'Q' looking as if the letter 'O' had sprouted a small tail. When she saw the 'Q', she was reminded of the childhood game when blindfolded, she had drawn a tail on the picture of a cat on the blackboard.

Radha got up and limped to her room, with her knee and the pain there all part of her. She rummaged about in the old trunk placed on top of the cupboard and dug out the sandalwood box. It was now just wood. In the intervening forty years, the sandal had gone. She went to the window, held it up in the light, and looked at it. Her eyes dimmed lightly. Cataract? On the lid, there were three figures: Parvathi[8] in the centre and

---

[7] 'Sindhoora varna' means vermilion coloured, used to describe Lord Ganesa. Using a play on words, the writer is gently making fun of the way the words in the lyrics can be mispronounced, thus indicating a totally different meaning.

[8] The consort of Siva and Goddess of valour and courage, and strength in the Hindu pantheon.

Lakshmi[9] and Saraswathi[10] flanking her, carved with intricate workmanship. Parvathi's lion, Lakshmi's elephant, and Saraswathi's peacock were all of the same size.

She opened the lid. Like the genie of Aladdin's lamp, an old woman sprang at her from the discoloured mirror, fixed on the inside.

For a moment she was startled. How time had flown! Did she not comb her hair before the mirror every day? Or mark her *pottu*? But this mirror had transformed nineteen into fifty-nine.

Not at all surprising that the young man in the bus had addressed her as Paatti. What was surprising was that she had not been called so oftener.

She raised her eyes and looked out. There were more dry leaves on the concrete floor, fallen leaves, and on the tree there were leaves waiting to fall.

She looked again at the mercury-faded mirror, as if searching for something, as if wishing it would restore to her the two young girls. Not even that. It was enough if it gave back that one old lady along with this old lady. If she and her elder sister seated next to each other and singing in aged sagging voices 'Sindhu Ravana' ... could smile at the two old ladies in this magic mirror ... But Rohini will never stand next to her again. Rohini was no more. It is twenty days today. Cancer. Another synonym for Time. She had returned from Coimbatore only two days ago after the final rites.

As a huge perspiring feeling engulfed her, Radha closed her eyes and leant on the window bars. Her knees hurt badly. Time was dying slowly second by second between the hands of the clock on the table.

She heard the sound of lively laughter. She opened her eyes and looked out. The dried leaves had gathered in heaps along

[9] The Goddess of prosperity and wealth.
[10] The Goddess of learning and the arts.

the compound wall. When had the fallen leaves turned into heaps?

The heap moved. From the womb of the dried leaves a small curly head slowly emerged. A five-year-old boy. The neighbour's child. Two more boys appeared near the gate. This one shouted triumphantly, 'You didn't find me!' and the three ran out laughing and disappeared.

How come they are here now? Oh! Vacation time! In their 'thermostat' years, they will not feel the heat.

From far off she could again hear the sound of children laughing.

The old lady straightened up. It was as if the pain in her had suddenly faded. She sensed that from here she was joining in their laughter. 'Monkeys! They have come in again and run away without closing the gate!' She came out scolding them as if striking them with flowers.

As she waited to hear those sounds of laughter again, she felt she need not have criticized that poor young doctor so harshly.

He Is Not in Town*

She put the phone down and held her head in her hands.

How many phone calls?

How many times had she replied to all the callers who asked for Mr Shanmugam that he was not in town?

If the callers were office friends, the answer was, 'He has left for his village quite suddenly on some personal work.' If the callers were family members, her answer was, 'He's gone to Ahmedabad on some urgent official work.' If it was not Ahmedabad, it was Delhi, Bombay, Mysore, or whatever slipped from her tongue. If you mentioned a specific place, the lie was dressed in truth. The listener believed you.

But she had to lie even to Veena!

Now again the telephone shrilled.

She raised her head from her hands and picked up the receiver.

'Hello, Mrs Shanmugam here.'

'Amma, it's me.'

'Veena? What's the matter?'

'I feel like talking to Appa.'

'Appa has not returned yet.'

'Not yet? How many days has it been?'

* Originally titled 'Dhandanai', the story was published in 1986, and later appeared in *Nagalinga Maram* in 2010 (pp. 183–93).

'What can *I* do, Veena? If it is office work, doesn't he have to finish it before returning? There's also trouble because of the Indian Airlines lockout. And it is two days from Delhi by train.'

'Delhi? The other day you said he had gone to Kurnool.'

'Aaah ... yes yes. But Veena, you're pining only for Appa. Amma is right here talking to you and I don't see you being happy about that.'

'Don't fib. I've spoken to you. It's Appa I've not spoken to.'

'Appa, Appa! I'm sure your husband is going to tease you.'

'Yeah. He is standing right here and making fun of me.'

'See? Didn't I say so? You're a wife now, you must behave like one. As soon as Appa returns, I will ask him to call you. Don't you call me again before that!'

Anjali put the phone down on its hook. Henceforth, she must remember which town she had mentioned to whom.

Sorrow burst in her, and her hands now held her sobs and not her head.

She would never have imagined he would change so suddenly. He had not even looked at a woman other than his wife till he was forty-six ... if *his* fidelity could crumble in a second, how could one trust anyone or anything again?

Shanmugam had told her that he was going to Madurai on behalf of the insurance company where he worked. That same night her brother had conveyed to her the message that Shanmugam had not travelled alone. Her brother had gone to the station to see his friend off and had seen Shanmugam and his companion. But they did not see him. He had left the next day, having come from the north to attend Veena's wedding.

Veena's wedding had been celebrated grandly two weeks ago. Shanmugam was all right then. Veena, their first child, was his darling. She too was very fond of her father. How emotional he had become when he gave his daughter away in marriage! How many boys had he considered for her before this one? How picky he had been in choosing the bridegroom. 'He must deserve my child!' Four days after the wedding, he had gone with Anjali to escort Veena to her husband's house.

Then ... *he* had set off on *his* 'honeymoon'. A sob burst from her covered mouth. After crying for a while, she gathered herself and fell limply on the sofa.

The vestiges of the wedding celebration were still evident. The mango-leaf *toranam*[1] on the door had not been removed. The wedding album lay there. Still fresh in her memory was the image of both of them laughing and watching the photos with the children.

What had happened to him suddenly?

After so many years?

A weakness he had not shown in his younger days surfacing now? And this after their daughter's wedding?

How shameful if it became public? What will the *sambandhi*s think?

The phone rang once again.

'Hello, Mrs Shanmugam here.'

'Can I not talk to Mr Shanmugam? I am his billiards friend.'

'He is not in town.'

'Where has he gone?'

'He's gone to Nagpur on office work. It is ten days now.'

'When will he return?'

'I don't know. Please give me your name. I'll ask him to call you when he returns.'

She put down the receiver. In two seconds the phone rang again.

'Hello, Mrs Shanmugam here.'

'*Vanakkam*,[2] Veena's father-in-law speaking.'

[1] A string of mango leaves hung in front of the house on festive occasions.

[2] A greeting.

'Vanakkam. Everyone fine at home?'

'Of course. We took some colour pictures during the wedding, remember? They are ready now. If you and Mr Shanmugam are at home, I'll bring them now.'

'I'll be home. But he's not in town.'

'Is it so? Where has he gone?'

'On office work ...' she quickly recalled, what had she told Veena? Yes. '... To Kurnool.'

'When did he go?'

'Ten days ago.'

'When he applied for leave for the wedding, he should have taken a month's leave. Poor man, in four days he's gone back to work.'

'That is true. He used up all his leave for the wedding preparations.'

'That's also correct. Do you know when he will return?'

'I don't know. Shall I ask him to call you as soon as he returns?'

'Why trouble you? I'll call after two days.'

'Such good people!' she thought while putting the phone down. If one loses face before such people? Won't they find fault with the daughter for her father's immoral character? Shanmugam hadn't even thought of that.

She stood up and walked back and forth. She stared at the wall. She came to the door and stared blankly at the passers-by.

Why had he betrayed her now? Was it because she was growing old?

She had completed forty. She could not deny that this milestone had bothered her. She thought that she was bidding farewell to youth and felt the same pangs as one would when one parts from a friend of many years.

She walked slowly to her room and stood looking at herself in the full-length mirror of her wardrobe.

Medium height, fair complexion, a slim figure, and natural grace. But this was not what Anjali saw. She saw the faint lines on her face, forehead, at the corners of her eyes, and lips. She could see the veins on her petal-soft skin on the back of her hand between her bangles and the ring. The white smiles of age shone here and there in her thick black hair.

Grief stabbed her sharply. She did not hide the lines on her face, she had not coloured her hair. She hated anything false. She didn't run away from old age because of these thoughts, nor did she drown in permanent sorrow. She was prepared for every stage of life. But it was true that these thoughts troubled her occasionally. She realized that step by step she was moving away from youth. Perhaps he too noticed what she was losing. Is that why he was chasing a young girl, turning away from her? Her brother had said that the girl was young.

She moved from the forty-year-old mother-in-law in the mirror staring at her, and stood before the big photograph on the wall looking at it.

'How can you betray me? Am I not your wife? Do you know how much you've hurt me?'

He did not know. He had lied to her that he was going away on official work only because he didn't want her to know.

'But your heart will know. It is deliberate betrayal. Is it fair? Can you do this? Am I not your wife?'

She pressed her head against the picture. Try as she might she could not stop the welling tears.

The telephone rang. She collected herself and rushed to the phone.

Now who? Veena again? How many times a day will she call?

'Hello, Mrs Shanmugam here.'

'Mr Shanmugam here, madam.'

She breathed rapidly.

'You?' A stupid question. But she couldn't think of anything else to say.

'Yes, it's me. I'm calling from the station. I got off the train just a short while ago. How's everything at home?'

'Anjali. Are you there?'

She started as if she had just woken up. 'Ah ... aah. I'm here. What did you ask?'

'Come on! I asked you how everything is at home.'

'Mmm fine.'

'Are the children fine?'

'Mmm ... Veena has called at least twenty times in these ten days to talk to you.'

'Yes, she told me.'

'She told you!'

'Yes, I called you only after talking to her.'

'Oh!'

'It seems you told her that I had gone to Andhra Pradesh.'

'Yes.'

'But I told you I was going to Madurai.'

'That's what you said.'

'Meaning?'

'Nothing. Are you coming home now?'

'Where else would I go?'

'How do I know?'

For a minute he was silent. 'Okay. I'll be home in fifteen minutes. I want something to eat.'

When he entered the house, Anjali saw that beyond the fatigue of travel, his face shone with joy and radiance. Shanmugam enquired about the children. He had something to eat. He went into the bathroom saying, 'I'll have a shower and wash the train dirt away.'

She heard him singing in a low voice. A new habit.

Soon after he came, the children left for a movie with their friends. It was 7 in the evening. Just the two of them at home. Anjali wondered if she should vent her feelings and ask him. But she didn't think she could bear to do that. What was the point in probing the wound? What has happened—happened. If he didn't think it was wrong, nothing she said would be of any use. Nor would her self-respect allow her to argue and establish her rights and demand justice.

But what was this? Seated on the sofa one leg slung over the other he said, 'Anjali, come, sit here, I want to tell you something.' Why? Was he going to talk about that?

Her heart beat quickened.

'Why discuss anything now? You must be tired after the journey. Go and take rest. We can talk later,' she said hastily, wanting to avert the danger.

'I'm not tired. Sit down.'

'But *I'm* tired. I have not yet recovered from the exertion. Moreover, all the relations who were staying with us left just yesterday and I need at least two months to recover from this fatigue.'

'You don't have to strain yourself. You just have to sit and listen to what I have to say.'

'Oh! I forgot. Veena's father-in-law called. The colour photos are ready. Shall we go and see them? First call him.'

'There's no hurry for that. Come and sit down.'

Very slowly she went to him and sat down. Her mouth went dry.

A thought flashed through her. Maybe he has a different explanation. If it's about her, will anyone voluntarily broach the subject with the wife?

With renewed hope she asked, 'Is the Madurai office work over? Do you have to go again?'

'I did not go on office work.'

The dam had broken. It was futile to try anything anymore. Whatever it was, she would have to listen. Let it be good news. Will a person who has been true to her really change after so many years?

'I went on a private trip with another person. I'm not returning from Madurai today. We went to Madurai and other places together and returned today.'

Anjali looked at his face.

'That person is a woman, a young girl. She works in my office. She has always been attracted to me. I have spent ten days with her. You understand what I'm telling you, no?'

Her eyes widened, she stared. As he continued to talk more and more about the matter, she felt her confidence draining. She was shocked at how he could talk about it so casually and so easily forgetting the thought of his betrayal.

There was neither hesitation nor embarrassment on his face. Nor were there feelings of guilt or shame when he spoke. Her astonishment grew. Then the feeling of surprise at how he could be so unmoved by her heartbreak grew and grew and filled her heart.

'I'm not saying that what I did was right, but if I tell you everything, I think you will understand my feelings.'

She sat frozen.

'Why are you silent? You are listening to me, right?'

Her lips moved, but at first no words emerged. Then moistening her throat she asked in a feeble voice, 'When you say brazenly and to my face that you've betrayed me, what's there for me to say?'

There was slight disapproval on his face. 'If you say I have betrayed you in the ordinary sense, then it means you have not understood me at all. You hear me out and then tell me. All these days, have I even looked at another woman's face?'

She shook her head as if to indicate 'no'.

'I was like anyone else, living with my wife and children. I never thought that time was rushing past but, for sometime now there's been a vague feeling, a niggling thought in my mind, that I'm growing old. I wonder if you understand … perhaps women are made differently.'

'No, I understand. I too feel the same way. A thought that I am leaving my youth behind.'

'If so, you will understand me well. When Veena stood next to her husband, I felt as if someone was saying "Hey Shammu, you've become a father-in-law. Next year you may become a grandfather. Time is passing by. You are becoming an old man."'

'I understand.'

She looked down.

Shanmugam got up and walked around the room. He went inside and fetched his cigarette packet, lighter, and the ashtray. He lit up a cigarette and slowly drew four puffs. Then looking at the smoke rings rising up he said, 'My hair has not gone grey, Anjali. But one day, do you know, when I was shaving, I saw a white hair on my chin. I felt as if the white hair was screaming in my mind at Veena's wedding. I felt a rush ... I must prove to myself before its too late that I'm not yet old, and still have youth's traces in me and comfort myself. That's why ...'

'So you chased youth, in search of your youth.' A voice came from the bowed head.

'Yes, exactly. How well you understand me, Anjali.'

The bowed head and shoulders shook slightly. Astonished, Shanmugam looked at her.

'Why are you crying? What has happened?'

She did not look up. The trembling didn't stop.

'*Chee chee*, Anjali why are you so silly?' Shanmugam lost patience and snuffed out the cigarette in the ashtray.

'You must be happy because you should know that unless I loved you deeply, I would not have told you. Instead of that you are crying? What has happened? You are the one who has the status of my wife. Not she. Moreover, I will never do this again. I have appeased my longing. It's not a problem anymore. The restlessness in my heart has ceased. I am ready to become old now. I've also unburdened my heart by telling you. There's nothing to cry about.'

She continued to sob.

'Are you going to stop crying or not?'

A life-long habit of doing what that voice ordered made her hand wipe her eyes, distancing itself from the ache in her heart.

'Ah. This is my Anjali.' He got up and patted her back. Then he stretched himself slowly.

'*Appada*!³ Whatever it is one can relax only at home. I'll call Veena. I couldn't talk to her for long from the station. Is my child happy?'

Without waiting for her answer, Shanmugam rang his daughter.

Anjali lifted her hand. Though the wetness had been wiped away from the eyes, the sorrow remained. Her breath heaved and drowned in her heart.

'Yes, oh yes. Not just Kurnool, I saw the whole of Andhra,' Shanmugam said and winked at his wife. 'The house looks empty without you, Veena. But if I say that, your husband may get angry. It seems the pictures are ready, are they good? I'm sure you look beautiful. I want to see you, Veena. If I come now, will you be home ... okay, I too thought so. I'm glad. However late it is, I'll stay awake. I don't have anything more important to do than to see you. I'm as usual ...'

How naturally, without being conscious that anything had happened without any regret or remorse, he is able to carry on a conversation. Anjali could not take her eyes off his smiling and satisfied face. His mind is clear and his heart light. As soon as he had confessed the truth to his wife, his burden rolled away. He will break faith, then without owning any responsibility, he will make his wife bear even that burden and cleanse himself easily!

After talking to Veena, Shanmugam came back and sat on the sofa before her. 'Veena and our son-in-law are going for some

³ An exclamation of relief.

dance performance. She said she'll come here after it's over. The silly girl asks me is it okay if it is past 10 o'clock.'

Anjali was silent.

'Keep some warm milk ready for them.'

She didn't move. She kept looking at him. Her lips tightened so the lines around her mouth deepened.

'What are you looking at me like that for, Anjali? Oh, are you still thinking of what I told you? You must be crazy. Didn't I tell you it won't happen again? I have revisited my youth. My problem is over. Now I'm happy we can forget the matter. What's the menu for the night? When the children come from the dance performance, can we all eat together?'

Anjali did not break her silence.

'So you won't say anything? You just said you had the same feelings. But in the end, you have not understood me. Is that it, then, finally?' Irritably, he dragged the cigarette box towards him, pulled out a cigarette, and put it to his lips.

Can this insensitivity to another's pain go unpunished? Anjali's face quivered for a moment and then became calm. There was a new expression in those eyes which looked at him ... as if floating in a dream, an elusive expression.

'That's not it. I'm thinking ...' she said softly.

'Thinking of what?' he asked bending over to light the cigarette with his lighter.

'The thought that though I felt the same way as you, I never realized that there could be a solution to it—until you told me.'

'See.' And she smiled.

He looked up sharply and stared at her.

Suddenly, he went pale.

The Downpour Outside[*]

*I*t was raining hard outside. Seen through the closed glass window, the world looked as if it had veiled itself. The vehicles moved through it like shadows.

In the hall, Ramesh was losing in the game of Scrabble. His scores did not go beyond single digits. How did Suresh always make words which scored more points and also hit the double word count?

Suddenly he shouted, 'You cheat, you pick up the tiles after sneaking a look at them!'

'I don't sneak. It's my luck that I get the high-score letters.'

'How is it that you always get the better tiles? Your score keeps on rising, but mine does not.'

'Even if you get better letters your score will not improve. You don't know big words.'

'Nothing of the sort! You are cheating!' Ramesh flung the board away angrily. The tiles scattered.

'Spoilsport! Can you ruin the game because you don't know how to play and are envious of my success?'

---

* Originally titled 'Veliye Nalla Mazhai', the story was published in *Kanaiyazhi, August Malar*, in 1985, and later appeared in *Nagalinga Maram* in 2010 (pp. 172–82).

Suresh pounced on his younger brother. Ramesh's hands and feet were no match for Suresh's strong ones. Hurt by the blows and kicks, the hair pulled and tousled, he went to his mother sobbing, 'Amma, look at this Suresh. He cheated at the game and hit me too.'

Suresh, who followed him, also had stinging marks where his brother had bitten and pinched him. '*You* are complaining only about my beating you. Amma! He beat me too. Look at this. He has bitten me. We must tie him up like a dog next to our Tiger.'

'So you should thrash your brother like this, is it?' Amma drew the younger one to her and wiped his eyes. Suresh was very upset. 'Just because he is younger can he do anything? He was losing in Scrabble because he did not know more words than I do. Does that mean he can ruin the game?'

Amma pacified him when he was about to pounce on the younger one. 'Don't play Scrabble, play some other game. Can't you play indoors without fighting even for one day when it is raining? Good boys. Go play quietly. I want to sleep.'

The boys returned to the hall and sat in different corners staring glumly at each other. They didn't play anything after putting the Scrabble box away. They didn't want to play any of the other indoor games like Rummy, Monopoly, Chinese Checkers, or Carrom. All old games and boring.

On ordinary days, they would have gone out in the evening to play cricket or some other game with friends. Or their friends would have come home. If it had been a holiday, they would have planned a nice way to spend their time in the afternoon. But this was not a regular holiday. This was an unexpected holiday due to the unprecedented rain because of which they could not visit their friends either.

Cooped up inside the house and not being friends but brothers, they quarrelled constantly.

Suresh approached the window and looked out. Now even the vehicles were not visible. The world had turned into rain.

Ramesh too came and stood next to him, not wanting to miss out on anything that his brother saw.

'There is nothing there! What are you looking at?'

'Your head!'

'If you speak like this, I will tell Amma.'

'Cry baby! You're nothing but a tale-bearer.'

'Amma!'

'Shut up! I will beat you black and blue.'

'Amma, Suresh is beating me.'

'Liar! If you lie, your tongue will be eaten up by rats in hell.'

Startled, Ramesh looked at his brother. Suresh was looking out, totally fed up. It was terribly boring to be confined in the house, just staring at the rain.

What was that figure, a movement, in the denseness of the rain?

He peered.

A movement. A blob moving in the rain.

It entered through the screeching front gate. A small white tent. It came closer.

The boys exchanged glances which said, 'What is this?' 'Who?'

In a short while, there was a knock on the door. At first, because of the roar of the rainfall, it was not even clear if it was the sound of a knock. Again a knock, a hesitant one.

'Who is it?' asked Suresh.

The knock stopped, like someone who is afraid stops crying. Then again it sounded.

'Who is that? Knocking at the door without ringing the bell?'

'Mmmee ... it's mmee.'

Suresh opened the door sharply. His eyes had to look down. A figure which came up to his chest. A boy ... maybe five years old? He had knocked because he couldn't reach the bell. The plastic sheet with which he had covered his head stretched down like a tent. The raindrops showered like splintered glass shards. Faded blue shirt, khaki shorts with frayed hems, there was a small puddle, where the rain entered the house with him. A very dark-skinned boy, so dark that it looked as if the dark colour would run in the rain. Two wide eyes looked up and out of the dark face. Seen from his height, Suresh and Ramesh assumed gigantic proportions, and their ages of thirteen and ten seemed out of reach.

'Who are you?' said Suresh.

'...'

'Speak up. '

'Mani.'

'Clock "*mani*"[1] or beads "mani"?'

The boy shrank and retreated at the brothers' laughter.

'I am asking you, isn't it?'

'I'm ... Mani.'

'Oh! Just Mani? Why have you come, Just Mani?'

'My mother ... sent me.'

'Who is your mother?'

'She works here ...'

'Oh! Nagamma's son. Don't you know servants should enter only by the rear door? Why did you knock on the front door?'

'Such impertinence!' said Ramesh.

Scared, Mani said, 'No, sir, I didn't know I had to come by the rear door.'

'Why have you come?'

'My younger sister has fever. Amma asked me to borrow ten rupees to pay the doctor for an injection. There's no money at home.'

'No money here either, get lost.'

Suresh stopped his younger brother with a look as if to say, 'You fool!' Here was new sport at hand.

[1] Mani, a name, also means the hour and beads in Tamil.

'Don't chase him away, Ramesh. He's after all a little boy. Hey, Mani! From whom did your mother want you to ask for the money?'

'From Ejamaniamma.'

'That's my mother. I'll get it from her. But first you must play with us for sometime, okay?'

The dark-skinned face lit up.

'Sure, shall I call you both Anna?'

Before he could finish, there was a sharp blow, 'Servant's son, you want to call us Anna? I will pummel you. Call us "sir" respectfully.'

Suresh's blow, Suresh's face, Suresh's voice—all three were like knives that cut through his guts. Mani held his cheek, his eyes brimming.

'I'll go ... I won't play.'

'Don't you want money?'

'Yes.'

'I'll get it from my mother only if you listen to me.'

Mani bit his lips. His cheek was still burning.

'Yes.'

'What did you say?'

'I said yes.' The frightened voice was inaudible.

'Have you forgotten you should call me "sir"?'

Ramesh was disappointed that his brother did not land another blow, so he raised his hand. But before the blow fell, 'Please don't hit me, sir, please don't hit me!'

'Rascal!' said Ramesh.

'Mmmm ... come inside.'

When Mani placed a foot forward Suresh's voice rose.

'Hey! Hey, you dirty fellow. You've made our verandah all wet. Your dirty feet too. Mmm ... first wipe all that clean and come.'

'A cloth?'

'Oh! We should give you a separate cloth, is it? You have your shirt, don't you? Remove it and wipe the floor well.'

'With my shirt?'

'Ya.'

The upturned eyes pleaded. Suresh's face was unmoved. Ramesh's right hand clenched and unclenched. With his eyes on the hand, the boy quickly moved away, removed the plastic cover, and then his shirt and wiped the floor. Something rolled up again and again up his throat and choked him.

'Have you wiped your soles as well? Good. Throw that in the corner and come here.' Mani hesitatingly came inside. His bare chest shivered in the cold. Suresh locked the door.

'Let's play ball for a while. Ramesh, bring our ball.'

A pink ball, three-fourths the size of a football, arrived. The sofas and chairs in the room were placed alongside the wall. The two tables in the middle were moved away by the brothers and Mani.

'Look here, Mani. You stand there. Ramesh will stand here. When we kick the ball to your side, you must kick it back to us, okay?'

'Yes, sir.'

'Ramesh, you begin.'

Ramesh kicked the ball towards Mani. Mani, with his tongue peeping out, focusing on the ball, was about to kick it when with lightning speed, Suresh's foot kicked the ball to another side. Mani rushed behind the ball to kick it when Ramesh butted in and kicked the ball towards his brother. Chasing the ball that was rolling away, Mani had come near ... and had now even touched the ball with his foot. Eagerness bubbling ... but why isn't the ball rolling? Suresh, who sprang from somewhere, stopped the ball from rolling and kicked it to the opposite side.

In the enthusiasm to play, Mani forgot the cold and ran behind the ball, and just when he was about to reach the ball,

Ramesh kicked it the other way. For a while, Mani ran this way and that breathlessly, and then stood looking at them, disappointment writ large on his face.

'Why have you stopped? Don't you want to play ball?' asked Suresh.

'You don't allow me to kick.'

'In any game, there will be such competition. You must run and kick.'

'Are you a moron?'

Mani said 'No' and shook his head.

'Then play.'

For a while the game continued, Mani breathless with all the running. The ball eluded him, spinning around the room.

'Mmmm ... kick the ball, you twit. You are an idiot who can't play.'

'You must kick like this,' Ramesh said, and pretending to kick the ball, landed a kick on Mani's leg.

Mani cried 'Ayyo, Amma' and sat on the floor. 'You've kicked me.'

'What did you say?' glared Suresh.

Mani got up in panic.

'You've kicked me, sir.'

'When you play, sometimes you'll get hurt. Play with care.'

'I don't want to play. I'll go. Ask your mother to give me money.'

'I'll do that only if you play and kick the ball at least once.'

'I don't want money. I'll go.' Mani moved towards the door. In a dash, Suresh stood in front of it.

'You can't go.'

Petrified, he looked up at the brothers. They stood laughing.

'I want to go, I want to go,' Mani shouted. From somewhere in the house echoed a dog's bark.

Mani froze.

'Is ... is there a dog here?'

'Are you scared of dogs?'

'Yes ... v... v ... very scared.'

'Guard this door, Ramesh. I'll come now.' Suresh went indoors.

'Just wait. We are going to let the dog bite you because you did not play properly,' said Ramesh. Mani started trembling. He opened his mouth twice or thrice, but couldn't speak. Then the words staggered in, 'Don't do it ... don't do it please.'

Suddenly his eyes widened. A demon-sized fear leapt into his eyes. The mouth forgot to close. He retreated and shrank. Suresh stood before him with a brown coloured Pomeranian tied to a leash. The dog barked and came forward to the stranger.

Mani burst into a sweat and stuck to the wall. The blood drained from his face.

'Will you play properly or shall I let the dog loose?' smiled Suresh.

Mani was speechless. His body was paralysed, the hands alone moved indicating a No. His eyes froze on the dog as if a spell had been cast on them.

Suresh stroked the dog's neck. 'Tiger, I'll let you free if the boy misbehaves. Till then be quiet.'

The dog growled softly.

Fear blinded Mani.

The rain did not lose its intensity. Lightning flung its searchlight even in the daylight, followed by thunder.

'Hey, Mani. Now I won't play. I'll just stand holding the dog. You and Ramesh play. Ramesh will kick the ball, you must stop it with your hand. Okay?'

Mani stood like stone.

'I am talking to you, do you hear? Answer me. See, I'll let the dog on you.'

The dog came forward. Mani sprang to life 'I'll do it, I'll do it, sir, don't let the dog loose, sir, don't let the dog loose.'

'That's better.' Suresh drew back the leash. 'Tiger, shut up. Now play both of you.'

Ramesh kicked. Mani did not move. He stood, stuck to the wall staring at the dog.

'Hey, Mani. Are you going to play or not?'

'I'll play!'

The dark limbs darted. The dark arms attempted to grasp the ball, when Ramesh kicked it away. Mani ran behind the ball. The heart thudded. The breath stopped. Frozen with fear, tears did not flow. Fear of the dog ... running feet ... flailing arms ... eluding ball. There was no other world, no other truth.

'You fool, can't you pick the ball even once? Laziness is it, dog ...?'

With deeper anxiety and more speed, the dark legs and hands worked, but the back hurt with bending again and again trying to grasp the ball. He did not hear the rain, conscious only of the dog's light growl from behind.

Ramesh kicked, he reached, Ramesh kicked again, he reached for the dodging, deceiving ball.

'You are not running fast. Mani, you are lazy. You'll pick up only if Tiger joins you. Tiger, chase the boy?'

'Ayyo! Don't, don't.'

Suresh slackened the leash. He slackened it so that the dog could move freely. Tiger pounced towards Mani. Mani jumped and darted, jumped and darted away from the dog. Mani ran from corner to corner, eyes bulging as the dog chased him.

'Tiger, chase him hard,' Mani ran faster. The dark limbs became indistinct because of the rapid movement and looked like a black moving line. Saliva drooled from his mouth. There was one thought, one focus, and that was to escape the dog.

'The runt runs well. Let's see you run faster. Tiger catch him.'

Mani ran faster than ever before. The legs and shorts becoming wet, he moved like lightning. Round and round he ran, he sprang and jumped and he ran, until Mani dissolved into the running movement.

Suresh and Ramesh laughed. 'Good, good, you are a clever boy. You run well. Why don't you run a little faster? Just a little more, mmmm, Tiger?'

'Hey boys! What is the racket? You won't let me sleep peacefully? Why is Tiger barking?'

The brothers' mother came out.

Suresh immediately reined in the leash and controlled the dog. The barking reduced to a low growl. Ramesh stood as if nothing happened. The ball stood there under the sofa. A dark five-year-old boy lurked near the wall panting with fear-drenched eyes. The body was shuddering. The lips and chin throbbed. He kept looking towards Tiger with widened eyes and shrunken body.

The woman looked at him and then turned towards her sons.

'Who is this boy?'

'Nagamma's son, I guess.' Suresh mumbled looking down.

'Why did he come?'

'His mother urgently wanted ten rupees. Because it seems his sister is sick.'

'What did the two of you do to him?'

'Nothing.'

She looked at them. She looked at the dog straining at the leash. She saw the strange boy hiding himself trembling.

'*Chee*! Aren't you ashamed of yourself? Go inside right now— let Appa return. You'll get a lashing with the belt.'

The brothers went inside, heads down, and disappeared with Tiger.

She knelt down near Mani and smoothed his hair.

'Scared are you, little one? The dog won't do anything. I'll see to it.'

He looked at her with fear-filled eyes. His mouth trembled. Sobs choked his throat. Next moment, he burst into tears.

'Don't cry, Appa. Will you have a biscuit? You are not wearing a shirt. Wait, I'll get you one.'

'I want to go. Open the door. I'll go home ... to my mother.'

He did not wait for the money. As soon as the door opened, without even pausing to collect his plastic cover, or his shirt which looked like a rag, he darted into the rain.

After he left, the mother returned and scolded her sons. They listened to it as though it was a ritual with their heads down. They came and sat in the hall. They tried reading *Ambuli Mama*.[2] They didn't like it, it was boring. They tried playing Rummy. They didn't like it, it was boring. For some time they just sat silently without doing anything.

Then Suresh's eyes gleamed at an interesting thought, a vision. 'Hey, Ramesh, that fellow pissed in his pants, *da*.'

Both of them laughed hands over their mouths, out of their mother's earshot.

Outside, it rained quietly.

<hr />

[2] A popular Tamil magazine for children.

Nothing Ever Happens*

Nothing ever happens! When the heart grows listless with boredom, even the eyes feel tired. She thought it would be good just to look at four or five tender faces. It might liven up this lassitude. But where would she find tiny ones? Ramesh, her younger child, was in the higher secondary school, and the other, Anita, had completed her BA. Only after Anita gets married would there be grandchildren to brighten life.

Shalini dwelt in her imagination happily for some time. There was variety only in her imagination ... in reality? It was the same routine every day, an uneventful life at home, her daily duties to her husband and her children, but otherwise there was nothing they had in common to even discuss. Cook, eat, sleep, or read library books; listen to a play or a music concert on the radio twice a week; a visit to the ladies club for an hour in the afternoon, without interfering with her housework; visit some park or the beach in the evening with the family; and a movie once a month with everyone.

That was all.

* Originally titled 'Nigazchi', the story was published in *Thinamani Kathir* in 1960, and later appeared in *Nagalinga Maram* in 2010 (pp. 29–34).

SHORT STORIES BY R. CHUDAMANI

She did not even have to think about the tiffin to be made in the evening. There was a fixed menu for each day of the week. The lunch menu too was fixed. If she made brinjal *koottu* instead of brinjal *poriyal*,[1] her flustered husband would ask, 'Why the change today?' As if it was a catastrophe. He was a slave to habit. He would drive to the beach only by the same route, turning near Anna statue and proceeding through Walajah Road. If she suggested that they should go via the South Beach Road, he might even faint.

Life had become mechanical. There was no change, no excitement, nothing ever happened. An uneventful life. Just like the mass-made goods stacked in a factory, one day was exactly like another.

Bored, Shalini got up from the balcony and went inside. It was 1 o'clock in the afternoon and nap time. Suddenly, she remembered the library books that had been delivered the previous day. Usually, the library peon would deliver the weekly lot of books in the morning. But yesterday morning he had gone to the Karumariamman[2] temple for some function. He turned up with the books just as they were setting off to go to the beach in the evening.

'Hey, Ramesh, fetch last week's books from the room upstairs. Return them to the peon and take the new lot. Hurry!'

'Go on, Amma, why always me? Why don't you ask Akka to do it?' grumbled the son.

Her husband hastened the children saying, 'One of you do it and hurry up. It is already half-past 5. Shouldn't we be back by 7?'

What earth-shaking event was scheduled at 7 pm? All of them would be in the hall, Anita and Ramesh would be playing

---

[1] Koottu is a semi-solid vegetable dish using dal and vegetables; poriyal is the dry dish.

[2] The deity at Tiruverkadu, near Chennai.

Rummy, or Ramesh would be studying his lessons and Anita busy with a novel. Her husband would read every page of the newspaper. He would turn on the TV. 'Why do they repeat these programmes again and again?' he would say again and again. She would turn the pages of the library book. Her eyes would look at the clock every now and then, as if willing it to strike 8 pm, and rouse the stirrings of 'Dinner time'!

She had not looked at the library books last night because she had, unusually, joined the children in the game of Rummy. As soon as she remembered that, she picked up the books and lay down in bed. She read the small blurbs which were like the stories in brief. One was a thriller, and the other a Mills-and-Boon type of romance.

She just glanced through the latter here and there. Uninteresting. She put it back and picked up the thriller. She read the first ten pages, then page twenty-five, then a few pages after page fifty, then the end. She then returned to page eighty-three. When she turned the next page, suddenly a folded paper fell on her chest. For a moment she panicked thinking it was an insect. (The cockroach menace at home was unbearable.) Calming down, she opened the piece of paper casually. The moment she read the first words 'My darling', she closed the book and started reading it further with excitement, as if a third novel had come alive in her hands.

It was a brief love letter. Undated. The person who had written 'My darling' had distilled in just ten lines all the sweetness in his heart. He had signed off with 'Your own, S'.

It was not unusual to find bits of paper in library books. There were occasions when after she had returned the books to the library peon, he had handed over some note saying, 'Amma, there is some chit here.' It was nearly always some unimportant postcard. Till now, the evidence of others' forgetfulness had been only of that kind. She had found a postcard, a subscription receipt, a bus ticket, a programme card, etc. This was the first time she had found something so juicy. Which idiot had been so careless and forgetful with his love letter?

She ran her eyes avidly over the list of names on the library record stuck on the inner cover of the book. The last name was hers since the book had been delivered to her now. Who was the previous borrower? Ah! Dr V.M. Sharma! Doubtless Sharma was the 'S'. What is this, Dr Sharma? Sir, is this how you work? Who is this girl? When did you become 'her' Dr Sharma? With a respectable name like Sharma, why do you play these love games? Chee! Sharma sounds like an old man's name, not romantic at all! It is impossible to match the youthful verve that bubbles over in this letter in this strong handwriting with a 'Sharma'. Moreover, will anyone sign an intimate letter with a surname? Won't the first name be used? But the doctor's first name does not begin with S. Sorry for my mistake. Doctor, you are acquitted with honour!

She saw the other names. One Subramaniam alone was a likely suspect. Hey! *Suppuni*![3] Who are you? Do you even have a job? Or is writing love letters your only job? You have written with so much love to a 'darling', my boy! I hope you are a bachelor at least. If not, you will surely get the slipper in this life and be skewered in the next. No doubt at all!

Another thought cropped up. It is possible that this letter had been left behind not by the one who had written it, but by the one who had received it. So she must see the women's names in the borrowers' list. There were only two names apart from her own. Mrs Pushpa Natesan. Pushpa, Pushpa, is it you? Atrocious! How can you cheat poor Natesan like this? Why have you kept this rubbish inside the book instead of pouring cow-dung over 'your very own S's' head? Shouldn't you have

[3] One of the shortened appellations of the name Subramanian.

torn up this *saniyan*?[4] 'S' for saniyan. Pushpa, I am disappointed in you.

No, no, it is not Pushpa. Let's check the next name in the list—Miss Nalini. Miss Nalini, what do you think of yourself? Is it for this that we nurture you, bring you up, and educate you? Do you think there is no one to question you? If your Appa comes to know of it, he will swing the belt. Careful!

Really! ... Today's girls are very daring. How long have you known this scoundrel 'S'? Foolish girl, did you at least find out if his intentions are honourable? You go around watching these terrible movies and then run around with a boy saying 'love-dove'. Chee! Dear Nalini, listen to me please, this is not for you, Amma!

Shalini laughed aloud. It amused her to think how she had enjoyed herself for a few moments. How this little scrap of paper had set off her imagination, riotously encountering so many persons! In her uneventful insipid life, how many events had she spun out in a few moments! After making two or three vain attempts to read the book, she closed it. It was more interesting to weave visions in the mind around that note.

Even when she was serving tea in the evening, her imagination did not let her go. Maybe 'S' is Sharma's son? Good English! Literature MA or is he the Natesans' *daughter's* sweetheart? A mother who is reading novels, oblivious to what her daughter is up to ...

'Hey, Anita, the tiffin is growing cold. Are you coming to eat or not?'

'Coming, Amma!'

No sign of Anita even after fifteen minutes. What was the girl doing?

[4] Literally means Saturn, which is supposed to be a malign planet, much feared by those who believe in astrology. Here, it means 'wretched thing'.

Anita was opening all the magazines on the table with a perturbed expression. She picked up all the magazines on the table, held them upside down, and shook them. She searched underneath the cushions. She lifted the carpet. She peered beneath the cupboards.

Shalini entered the room, 'What is it, Ani?'

Anita looked up with a start.

'Are you looking for something?'

'Nothing … Amma. So much dust under the cupboard. Maragatham does not sweep well.'

'Let it be. Now come and eat your tiffin. Your father will shout that it is getting late to go out.'

Her imagination ran on even at the beach. Would 'S' be like that boy with the sideburns? No, this one is not more than medium height. Amitabh Bachchan is the present rage among the youth. 'S' will surely be six-feet tall. He and his darling will see their love ripen into marriage. *Subam, subam.*[5] Or it will be a mis-matched love, he a Casanova and she a thirty-five-year-old frustrated old maid who did not get married at the right time. In the end, a rope, police, post-mortem … tragedy!

'What, Ani, why are you again and again looking at me and Appa sadly as if you have never seen us before?'

'Nothing, Ma,' Anita wiped her eyes. '*Appappa*, Ramesh why do you fling the sand around? Look, it has fallen in my eyes.'

'Sorry, Akka. Will you come with me? Shall we go to the waves?'

'Come, let's go.' She hugged her brother affectionately and ran with him to the waves.

They returned home. As usual all of them sat dutifully in the hall. The ritual of waiting till 8 pm for dinner.

'S' is the initial for what name? Suresh, Sekhar, Sivaraman, or maybe Salim?

[5] Literally, happy ending.

Shalini was astonished when before going to bed Anita came in and kissed her on the cheek with her arms round her. She had never done that.

'What is it, Ani Kanna?'

'Nothing, Ma.'

Everyone went to sleep.

All the lights were turned off.

There was silence in the house.

The old feeling of boredom engulfed Shalini once more. She had turned half the day eventful only by her imagination, but what was really happening in her life? There was nothing. It was a lacklustre monotonous life. This thought grated through her mind as usual before she went to sleep. Today, like yesterday, like tomorrow, like the day after ... nothing ever happened.

In the next room, Anita slowly got up from her bed and with the light from a torch, started packing her clothes in her suitcase silently.

Doctoramma's Room[*]

*I*t felt as if she had been sitting in that verandah chair for
several yugas.[1] Twice or thrice her eyelids had even drooped off
in sleep. Darting a glance at her husband fearfully, Devaki sat
up straight. Her legs hurt. She felt like stretching them.

The doctor was examining another woman. Wonder what
is wrong with her, poor thing. Perhaps it was a tumour or an
ordinary fever or just a headache? But it is taking so long. Is the
doctor doing a detailed and complete examination because she
suspects something like tuberculosis or cancer? Or is it pregnancy? Dear God ... let it not be that ... anything but that.

At that thought, Devaki felt a pang of guilt and cast a side-
long glance at her husband again. Shanmugam was sitting in
his chair and yawning for the *n*th time. Not only were his teeth
red because he chewed betel constantly, they had been ground
to half their size. He was of medium height and moderate girth.
He had a serious expression that made him look older than his
thirty-eight years. He was not handsome, but since his features

---

[*] Originally titled 'Doctoramma Arai', the story was published in
1974, and later appeared in *Nagalinga Maram* in 2010 (pp. 92–7).
[1] A time period according to Hindu belief. There are four yugas
ending in a deluge: Krta, Treta, Dvapara, and Kali. It is believed that
the current phase is the Kali yuga.

were regular, he was not ugly either. Whatever it was, Devaki did not give a thought to his looks. She couldn't remember if she had ever done so. Before she could get used to her husband as a new entrant in her life, she had a baby in her arms. Thereafter, there was no time for this research about his looks since every year meant another baby.

The first three were girls, so the problem of getting them married would loom large in a few years, but that was not Devaki's present worry. When her being a woman was itself posing a huge problem, there was no time to worry about the problem of her girls. Her legs hurt very much. She needed either to stretch them and lie down or sit on the floor with her legs folded. The very fact that her condition did not permit either made her doubly uncomfortable.

Now and then her breath was laboured. Why did she feel so exhausted? If she felt like this already, as time passed what would happen ... no! Should she conclude that it is only that? It seems it could be like this for some people even if they were anaemic. What was the hurry before the doctor even diagnosed what it was?

She raised and stretched her legs since they felt heavy. As she did so, the red plastic basket that had been resting on the leg of her chair fell over. She had brought it to carry the vegetables to be purchased on the way back home, and the tin of milk powder which she had booked in the shop for the youngest child (ah, if only that child would always be the youngest!) sleeping at home, and also the medicine which the doctor would prescribe. She bent and set it upright.

'How long should we wait? It is getting late for my work,' said Shanmugam with another yawn looking at his wrist watch.

'Soon, soon. Won't that lady come out now? Luckily there is no one else. We are the next.'

'Shall we go home? We could come another day.'

'Anyway, since we are here, we will see her and go. So difficult to come again so far another time,' she said wearily and then quickly switching to explain tactfully, 'I mean it will be difficult for you.'

'Okay, okay, we will wait for another ten minutes. We cannot wait more than that. It will get too late for me.'

Devaki was consumed with worry about whether the girl before her would come out in ten minutes. The very thought made her face damp with perspiration. As the sun rose higher and its light stretched gradually into the verandah, she moved the chair so that the sunlight did not fall on her.

Fortunately, the girl inside came out in eight minutes. Poor thing, she looked downcast. God knows what her problem was. She looked very young. Good for her if she was unmarried.

Devaki entered Doctoramma's room with her husband.

It was an antiseptic room, which looked as if it had been soaked in cleanliness. The lady, who with the necessary tools single-handedly ruled this place, was elderly and her face shone with compassion. There was no nurse around. If needed perhaps she would call for one from another room.

When they entered the room, the doctor looked up at them from her chair. At first sight, the couple looked as if they were the same height. A little later she realized that Shanmugam was an inch taller.

Doctoramma ran her experienced eyes over Devaki's lean frame which accentuated her height and saw that her patient was more fragile than elegant. Dark circles round her eyes, skin pale with anaemia. She looked as if she was so tired she would sleep for a week if she were allowed to.

'Sit down, please, what is wrong with you?' asked the doctor gently showing her to a chair.

Devaki sat down and explained to her.

'Missed two periods? Then why do you still say you have doubts?'

'This is different from the others, Doctor. I feel very tired. I don't have the usual morning sickness.'

Devaki fell silent unable to voice the hope that was mixed with her breath. But the wide eyes stayed focused on the doctor's face.

'Could you wait outside while I examine your wife?'

When the doctor rinsed her hands and emerged out, Devaki straightened her clothes and waited, her heart palpitating with fear and anticipation. Never mind even if it was a tumour. Why never mind? It would be a blessing. She could go to a hospital and lie down in peace.

The doctor sat down facing her.

'It is pregnancy.'

Devaki's face fell. For a minute she stared, then her chin sank and she looked down.

'What is your name?'

'Devaki.'

'Age'

'Thirty-two.'

'How many years have you been married?'

'Seventeen.'

'How many children?'

'Six.'

The doctor's lips tightened, 'Now the seventh, is it? Hmm ... and you are not illiterate persons.'

'Doctor, mmm, is it certain?' Devaki asked looking up. Her eyes fixed on the doctor's face appeared even larger than before.

'Yes.'

'But ... even if one is extremely weak or anaemic ...'

'You *are* weak and anaemic.'

'Probably the reason my periods are delayed.' The eyelids fluttered and hope flooded her face.

'No. I confirmed it only after examination. Why? You don't want it?'

Devaki's head dipped again, she walked over and sat down limply.

Doctoramma asked Shanmugam to come in.

'I have examined your wife. It is pregnancy. She is very weak.'

'Is that so?' Nothing more; no anxiety, no concern, there was nothing in that voice.

'She may even miscarry. I will give her some medicine to carry it full term. I first thought I should tell you.'

'Okay.'

'It seems she has already had six children. She is very weak. If this had not happened, it would have been better. It may be even better to terminate the pregnancy considering her condition.'

Devaki looked up with sudden hope.

'But I don't think she has the strength to bear even that.'

Devaki looked down again. Dumbly, she stared at the dwarfed image of the ceiling fan circling above, reflected on the polished arms of the chair.

'Let's do this. This time we will manage by improving her strength, but during this childbirth we will do an operation. After that there will be nothing to worry about.'

A light shone in Devaki's eyes. With a throbbing smile she looked at her husband's face. Hope and anticipation strained to fill her eyes.

'No need for all that,' said Shanmugam.

'I am making this suggestion with your wife's health in mind. It would be best if she did not have any more children.'

'Leave it. You said you would prescribe some medicine.'

'Please think about it, sir. You could have done something about it yourself. But if you don't like it, it's okay. We'll do it for your wife. It's easy to do it at the time of delivery.'

Devaki fixed her eyes on her husband eagerly.

'I won't give my consent.'

'I'm telling you because of her condition.'

'You give her medicine. That's enough.'

Doctoramma reddened with rage.

'Medicines will help only a little. But if she keeps having babies afterwards, what will happen to her health? Seven children and she is just thirty-two.'

Shanmugam was quiet.

'You have a son, right?'

'Yes.'

'Then?'

'I don't wish it.'

'Will anyone have six or seven children these days?'

'We will get as many children as we are destined to have.'

'Is this an educated man speaking?'

'Look here, Doctor. This is my private affair. I am not a beggar. I earn five hundred rupees a month. I can take care of my children,' Shanmugam's voice was inflamed.

'Do you think that is why I am advising you? It is good for your wife's health if you stop at least now. Shall I perform a tubectomy?'

Devaki's eyes, which were fixed on his face, grew huge, the breath came fast. Her eyes were beseeching. She moistened her dry lips.

'No, I am not interested. If I don't want it there is nothing more to say,' said Shanmugam. His face looked as if a door had been shut and barred.

Devaki's eyes froze in that moment. The light in her eyes was extinguished. The trembling of her lips looked as if she was going to weep. But she did not cry. Her face expressionless, her head lowered, as if all the fatigue in her body balled into a heavy weight and pressed it down.

Something churned in the doctor's stomach. She had a daughter the same age as Devaki. She looked at that man; neither fair nor dark, a wheatish complexion, neither tall nor short, neither handsome nor ugly. A man ... nothing more.

All the way home, Shanmugam kept criticizing the doctor's high-handed interference in the private lives of people. Devaki said nothing. The red plastic basket overflowed with its contents: two medicine bottles, one milk powder tin, vegetables, a jackfruit because it looked good, and half a dozen mangoes. It was Shanmugam who carried it. When they entered the home, noisy with the children's voices, he put the basket down saying, '*Sss appa* ... *da* ... What a weight ... what a relief.'

And then Devaki turned to face him.

Her smile ... a saga of womanhood.

TV Aunty*

*E*agerness bubbles in the young face and it reddens. The bud-like lips are slightly open. Stars shine in the eyes.

'... Today in Parliament during the discussion on the Reservation bill, the opposition party ...'

'Hey, Raju, go to bed! It is going on 9.'

It fell on deaf ears. Raju's ears, mouth, face, and body along with his eyes were focussed on the TV screen as he sat on the edge of the sofa.

The hands twined and tucked between the knees, the legs stuck to each other, the boy himself had hardened into a straight line sat engrossed in the scene.

'The weather in Tamil Nadu ...' It was the end of the news. At last ...

The blue saree and pearl choker enhancing the beauty, the eyes fluttering, beneath flower-like lips opening in a smile that revealed shining teeth.

'*Vanakkam.*'

The figure disappeared. The scene changed to 'The programme for tomorrow ...'

* Originally titled 'Thulir', the story was published in *India Today* in April 1991 (pp. 6–20) and later in *Nagalinga Maram* in 2010 (pp. 241–9).

Raju stood up. The mouth yawned as if it had only just remembered itself.

'I'm sleepy, Amma.'

Valli could not still get over her surprise while she gently stroked his hair and made him lie down and covered him with a sheet.

'Raju Kanna.'

'Mm ...' the eyes closing, a moan in reply.

'Why are you so interested in the news? Do you understand anything?'

He did not answer. He smiled to himself. A slight spillover of some secret. The expression on the child's face scared her for a moment.

'Raju,' she said again.

But he had gone to sleep.

Valli had a wishful hope. Maybe her son was a child prodigy? Like a Gnanasambandar,[1] like a Mozart, in the future. 'Child prodigy! Political genius Rajasekhar who showed promise even as a child.'

But, these dreams were shattered by certain facts that came to her notice.

Raju did not watch the TV news every day. He ignored it on the days when the newsreader was a man or another woman.

This newsreader ... this one ... this woman. It was before her image that he sat at the edge of the sofa enraptured and open-mouthed.

The child ...

Child?

---

[1] One of the first four Saivaite saints—Appar, Sundar, Gnanasambandar, and Manickavasagar. Gnanasambandar composed and sang when yet a child.

Of course a child. When he said 'Aunty' it was only a child speaking. But in the comment 'How beautiful this aunty is?' lay the voice of someone else. Not a child.

Valli felt an inexplicable fear.

'No need to be afraid,' said Dayalan, her husband.

'Is our child not normal?'

'What is there in this that is not normal? It is quite usual for boys to feel a special attraction to a young woman older than them, a relative like a sister or sister-in-law, or a teacher or some other acquaintance, some woman,' Dayalan smiled at a memory. 'You've seen Neela Chithi, haven't you Valli? That is the one ... my mother's youngest sister?'

'Of course! Even at this age what beauty, what majesty!'

'Imagine then, what she would have looked like in her college days. She was literally an angel to my eyes when I was about four or five years old. I was very attached to her. She would also carry me about lovingly and pet me. Once when I was five years old, I told her very seriously, "Chithi when I grow up I am going to marry only you and ..."'

'*Ayyayyayyo*, what did she say to that?'

'Nothing. She just laughed.'

'What is there to laugh about? Shouldn't she have given you a slap? Didn't your Amma scold you? What did she say?'

'She laughed too. Not only that. She went and told Thaatha, "One worry off your head, Appa. My son has spared you the job of looking for a son-in-law for our Neela."' Dayalan also laughed now.

Valli did not laugh. She did not even speak. She fell silent as if she was disappointed that there was no use in talking about this family.

One evening when Raju returned from school with his shirt all torn, she was shaken again.

'What, Raju? Did you fight with anyone?' She was all agitated. She looked at her son's face anxiously, stroking the hair off his face.

'That Mahesh, he is a very bad boy. Just see what I will do to him ...'

'Who is he? What was the fight with him about? He has torn your shirt ... a big boy?'

'I too tore his shirt with my teeth, Amma. Do you know?'

'Did he beat you?'

'I beat him back.'

'You rascal. Do we send you to school to study or to fight?'

'So? Will I let him go if he says that the other aunty reads news better than my aunty?'

For a while she could not speak.

'Tonight who will read the Tamil news on TV, Amma?'

Valli stared at the boy who asked this wide eyed, forgetting even the blow he had received and the torn shirt.

'What is there for you to hear the news like a grown up? First come in and remove your torn shirt, clean up. Then you can have tiffin and milk.'

'Please tell me, Amma ... tonight ...'

'Will you shut up only after I whack you?'

But at night at 8:40, when boys his age would be going off to sleep, Raju had rushed to the TV screen as soon as he heard the voice, 'Vanakkam, today's headlines' and resumed the same edge-of-the-chair pose.

Eyes shining like eager stars, the disturbing involvement in the image in front of him, losing himself totally ...

'*Dey*, Raju, fighting in school, wasting your time in front of the TV at home, what do you think of yourself? Are you now coming to lie down or not?'

He did not move.

'Raju, Raju, Rajooooo.'

'Don't bother me, Amma.'

Words flung impatiently, not even turning to her.

'Dey, rascal. Watching TV without listening to me, right? What will happen to your eyes if you watch TV constantly? Just wait, I will sell this wretched thing tomorrow itself.'

His attention did not scatter. The adoration in his eyes did not falter.

Valli stood astonished for a few moments, not knowing how to break the bridge of light between his face (open mouthed and teeth shining) and the vision on the screen. Then her temper rose.

'Now ... you,' with clenched teeth she gripped his hand and dragged him inside.

'Let me go, Amma, let me go ... only some time more ... the news will be over ... Amma, Amma ...' pleading, with his head turning again and again towards the TV screen Raju was dragged away, the child's body clearly unable to resist her force. She pressed him down on the bed and made him lie down.

'If you sit in front of the TV tomorrow, I will skin you alive,' Valli said and sat next to him for a long time listening to his sobs as he lay face down.

This yearning ... this disappointed grief because he was denied his wish ... she shivered lightly.

That day he returned with a great deal of excitement. 'Amma, Amma, I am going to see my TV Aunty ... in person ... really!' He danced all over the house with his shoes on, without even changing his uniform after flinging his school bag away.

It seems the Aunty lived next door to his schoolmate Kannan. It seems she had come once when Kannan's mother had invited her for Navarathri.[2] It seems she sat on the carpet just like all other aunties, legs folded beneath her, though she dazzled in a

[2] An important nine-day Hindu festival for the Divine Mother.

silk saree and her jewels and flowers. It seems she even smiled at Kannan and asked him, 'Which school are you studying in?'

'She is such a good aunty, *da*? If you want to see her, I will ask my mother to find out from her and take you,' Kannan had promised him.

Now came the crux of the matter. TV Aunty had conveyed through Kannan's mother that Kannan could bring him to see her on Wednesday afternoon.

The boy's feet did not touch the ground. 'Okay, you can go. First, you wash your face, hands, and feet, and drink your milk,' Valli's reprimand fell on deaf ears.

'I am going to see Aunty, I'm going to see Aunty, I'm going to s ...'

'I'm coming too,' Dayalan teased him.

Raju's dance stopped suddenly. He looked at his father guardedly.

'Mmmhmm. That is not possible. I will not take anyone else with me, I will go alone to see ...'

In the changed expression a new ... jealousy.

'Amma, what shall I wear; that striped tery shirt is nice, isn't it? Then to match it my navy blue pants ...'

'What terene shirt, navy blue pants? Aren't you going to her house straight from school? Then the uniform ...'

'No, Amma. Can I go like that? My clothes will be dirty, my hair untidy ... How can I go like that, Amma? I will come home, have a bath and change into a nice ...'

He did just that. The next Wednesday evening, blue pants, blue polyester shirt. Powder on the soap-washed face, hair combed and springing in waves, shining black shoes, the attention with which he looked at himself repeatedly this way and that in the mirror, the radiance in the eyes ...

'Ta-ta, Amma. Ta-ta, Appa!'

Valli stood looking in the direction in which her son had got into the cycle rickshaw with Kannan and disappeared.

'What is this Dayal … I … don't like any of this. I wonder why we let him go …'

'Can you then stop him and not let him go? Can we spoil the child's wish, Valli?'

'Child?'

When Raju returned home, he was floating in a dream. A thousand new stars had blossomed in his eyes. An ecstasy in his expression as if he had seen divinity, in the low voice sounded the pulse of worship.

'Amma, that Aunty is so beautiful! She looks more beautiful in person than on TV. She spoke to me affectionately. She asked my name. She enquired about the school and all. When I told her I got ninety-eight out of a hundred in maths she said, "Very good, smart boy" and patted my cheek. She gave me biscuits and Bournvita, and that too after asking me if I liked Bournvita.

'Do you know how good she is, Amma? She laughed aloud when I said that of all the TV newsreaders I liked her the best. You know how beautiful she was then?

'She wore a rose-coloured saree. Amma, why don't you wear sarees like that? She then showed us around the garden. It seems she waters the plants with her own hands. She herself sent for a cycle rickshaw and saw me off.

'See, she gave this Children's Ramayanam book as a gift. When I left, she waved and said "Ta-ta, Rajasekhar". Amma, she said my full name Rajasekhar …!'

When did he stop for breath? The verbal shower flowed on as if that speech itself was his breath.

The eyes that grew excited on seeing just the image had become intoxicated with the wonder of the real vision. That girl would have surely shown the same affection to Kannan who had gone with him. She would have given him the Bournvita and the gift too. But in the heaven painted by Raju's radiant word strokes, there was no one else but him and that girl.

Valli did not like the way he hugged the book to his chest. She tried very slowly to take the book away from him by saying, 'Here, let me look at it and give it back.' He tightened his grip with a greater indication of ownership.

'Then, Amma, that Aunty ...'

'Okay, okay, you first go and change your clothes ...'

'Amma, Aunty liked this dress very much. She said so herself.'

'You change and come and sit down to eat.'

'Not hungry, Amma. Didn't I tell you that Aunty gave me Bournvita and biscuits ... Amma ... I must get hundred upon hundred in the next maths test.' His hand stroked his cheek. Did her touch linger still?

'Come here and I'll tell you. Ever since you came back, babbling Aunty, Aunty. Rascal. No other job? If you continue like this, that Aunty herself will stop liking you. Yes.'

'Nothing like that. Aunty will always like me. I too will always like Aunty.'

She dragged him by the hand, removed the new clothes, put other clothes on him, made him sit down for dinner, and made him lie down. But right through it all—the unchanging ecstasy in Raju's eyes and the grip on the book.

'Give me that book. Why do you need this book when it is time to sleep? I will keep it in the almirah. You can read it tomorrow.'

'Mmmhmm. Won't give it. Aunty's gift.'

He put it safely under the pillow. A smile on the face as if lost in some inner world.

When the light was switched off, the shining teeth and the smiling lips could be seen as if the darkness itself smiled for him. Valli went to her room, but came again to her son's room in a short while when she saw the light burning. Raju was lying on his tummy on the bed, engrossed in reading his Children's Ramayanam.

'Dey, Raju? Staying awake past 10 and reading books, what is this? If you don't close it now and go to sleep, I will take it away and lock it in the almirah ...' Valli shouted with rage, 'This is just a threat. Close it now or else.' She shouted like a possessed woman.

The face crumbling, the lips twisting, Raju said, 'Go, Amma, you are very bad,' and reluctantly closed the book, placed it safely again under the pillow, and put his hand on the pillow.

Valli stared at the sight for a moment and switched off the light, went back to her room, and lay down on her bed. Unable to sleep, she lay there staring at the ceiling. Dayalan, lying next to her, said in a sleep-heavy voice, 'Sleep, Vallimma. There is nothing to worry.'

She did not know when she had dozed off. When she got up startled by some sound, the luminous hands of the table clock showed 2:30 am. In the glow of the night lamp, a shadowy figure could be seen near the door. After a moment's alarm, she realized it was a small figure.

'Hey, Raju! What is this in the middle of the night? Not asleep yet?' she said getting up and switching on the light.

'I went to sleep, Amma. I woke up. A dream ... as if big big rakshasas[3] appear when Rama and Ravana are fighting. Teeth this long ... like a lion, demon-like faces ... it was so scary, Amma. Let me sleep next to you, Amma!'

Valli felt as if her heart had suddenly become light. She jumped up and ran to hug her child, and the shadowy clouds in her heart vanished as if touched by a magic wand.

[3] Demons.

Heat and Rain*

*H*e was returning from the temple. The *angavastram*[1] was tied round his waist to lend an air of humility to his shirt and dhoti. On his forehead, a spot of sandal dot with broad strokes of sacred ash above it, in his hands the *prasadam*[2] tray containing betel leaves and broken coconut halves, eyes lowered humbly, and an expression of extreme respect.

To the question what does the personification of Bhakti look like, the answer may well be that it is the image created by the greying and grand figure named Vaiyapuri.

When he walked along the street, all the friends he met on the way greeted him respectfully and he responded with a gracious nod. The rising heat singed his feet. His house was not far from the temple, so he had set out from his house barefoot. But if this slight physical pain added to his spiritual gain earned by the temple visit, then the overall accounts would be on the credit side. Just as he profited in this life from his grocery shop, this was accrued profit for the afterlife. He lengthened his stride, his soles raised, drawing themselves away from the heat.

* Originally titled 'Mazhai', the story was published in 1973, and later appeared in *Nagalinga Maram* in 2010 (pp. 84–91).

[1] The upper cloth traditionally worn by men in south India.

[2] A tray containing the offering to the deity.

A morning in the month of Aippasi, and already such heat? It would cool only if it rained, but the rains had failed this year. Then what hope for the crops or the harvest? Even human beings would shrivel in this heat. Would it rain in the southern region as it usually did at the end of the year? If it did not, there would be water scarcity in Chennai like in other parts of the country.

Aren't there a few good souls in the city? At least for their sake, will the sky not show mercy?

'Sir, how are you?'

'Mmm.' The feet begged him not to stop. But if he did not, thus breaching the line of courtesy, his image as a gentleman would suffer.

'Looks like you are returning from the temple. Everyone knows about your pooja and your devotion!'

'Look how hot it is already? The heat blows around as if it is Panguni³ and Chitirai.⁴ Shall I carry on?'

'Yes, sir. It must rain at least once, or else this place will just dry up.'

'God has not opened His eyes. They say it will rain at least to save the good amongst us; perhaps there is not a single good person here.'

'You are here, Mr Vaiyapuri, can't it rain for you?'

Though his soles burnt, his heart felt cool now and his feet stood still.

'Take the prasadam,' Vaiyapuri said. '*Che*, this wretched thing. Should I see *this thing* when I am returning from the temple?' He muttered at something else.

This thing was not an inanimate object. It was a living creature, a human being. A woman, a female, the focus of the whole world's attraction. Though they all vaguely knew that her name

³ The Tamil month of 15 March–15 April.
⁴ The Tamil month of 15 April–15 May.

was Thangam, no one knew how old she was. It was sufficient to know that she was young. To be young was her duty. That's all. Beauty? It would come rushing to serve her when she summoned it with a sideward glance, an enticing smile, the glimpse of a curve, or her walk. Her second duty was to be lovely. Everyone in that area knew her. Those who hated her, those who were drawn to her, those who hated her and yet were drawn to her, and those who were drawn to her and still despised her—all of them knew her.

She was not rich. She was a mother of two, and her income matched her expense. She too felt the financial crunch that afflicted society. Yet she had no sympathy from anyone. People had spat at her asking, 'Should you earn your livelihood like this? Che!'

Holding herself upright and without lowering her eyes, she would answer, 'This profession is like any other, that's all. How does it matter what I do? What is important is that I must do it fairly and honestly.'

'Karmam karmam.[5] The government passes so many rules. Can't they impose a ban to restrain such wretches from walking along the temple street in the morning? I don't know how many times I have to be reborn to wash away the sin of seeing this? Muruga! Muruga!'[6] Vaiyapuri implored, looking heavenward. Thangam went along the edge of the road, head down, crossing them swiftly, in the opposite direction. Vaiyapuri, looking at her covertly, spat on the road. 'Shameless hussy!'

A sarcastic voice floated over and turned the street corner. 'This is a road used by the public. Don't dirty it by spitting on it. If my work is despicable, so is this.'

[5] An exclamation of disgust, indicating that only bad karma would bring the other to this state.
[6] Another name for Subramania.

Vaiyapuri's face flushed with rage and he walked ahead forgetting even to give the prasadam to his friend.

When he went home, Kannappan, who was waiting at the door, greeted him. Vaiyapuri went in saying, 'Please sit down. I will join you in a moment.'

'Appa, my feet are scorched,' he set the plate on the table, drew out his angavastram, flicked the easy chair with it, and sat down. Just as the child returning from school in the evening feels released from the day's discipline and control, he too felt a sense of liberation on his return from the temple. Further, he had done his good deed for the day. Now that would take care of his lapses and faults committed during the day. This was a daily routine. He had a feeling of security as if he had deposited money in the bank.

When he saw his wife, he asked, 'Meena, is breakfast ready? I'm hungry.'

'That can wait. Kannappan has been waiting for a long time.'

'I saw him. What's the matter?'

'What else? He went to the shop. As usual our boys told him "No sugar". He asked me when the supply would come. You had gone to the temple. I said I did not know anything. He is waiting to ask you.'

Saying nothing, Vaiyapuri stroked his moustache with a self-satisfied smile.

'What are you going to tell him?'

'That the stock has not come yet.'

'I don't like what you are doing.'

'It is all for you, Meena. The stock is becoming costlier. I've set myself a week's time. If I sell it after that, I'll get a profit of a hundred rupees per bag. For thirty bags, three thousand. In this time of shortage, won't everyone buy at whatever rate I quote?'

'One day or the other you are going to get caught, surely.'

'That will happen only if I exceed my limits. I'm not greedy. Do you know what every garbage man and vegetable vendor does? They buy sugar from the ration shop[7] at the control rate of 1.75 rupees per kg and sell it for 3–4 rupees. If you look at that daylight robbery, I'm not doing anything wrong.'

Meena was silent, then asked, 'You said it's all for me, what is that?'

'I'm going to buy diamond studs for you for Rs 2,500 out of the Rs 3,000.'

'The balance?'

'Perform a *kalyana seva*[8] for Tirupathi Balaji. It will be *punyam*,[9] right?'

'Yes,' Meena said and touched her cheeks devoutly. 'Do what you have to, you know what to do. Breakfast is getting cold, come. Should you not go to the shop afterwards?'

'Coming, I'm so tired. Burning sun … such heat.'

'No rain. It looks as if even the raindrop is afraid to hit the earth.'

'How will it rain? Sins have multiplied everywhere. Today when I was returning from the temple, that shameless creature who is roaming around here approached from the opposite direction. How will it rain with such sinful creatures around?'

'Why do you talk about her? Wash your mouth. So what if such wretches exist, shouldn't it rain for a pious person like you who is devoted to temples and dedicated to performing kalyana seva even for Him.'

Vaiyapuri resumed his air of humility. It was not easy to control his pride at his own skill at placating the Divine by doing these occasional good deeds.

'You go and prepare the breakfast. I'll send that man home.'

---

[7] The public distribution system. Here, Vaiyapuri procures sugar and hoards and sells it at a high price.

[8] The performance of marriage for the deity, which is a mode of worship.

[9] The fruit of virtuous action.

Though Kannappan argued for a quarter of an hour, Vaiyapuri was unmoved. The words 'No stock now, come next week' were repeated like a multiplication table learnt by rote, effortlessly even though he was questioned and cornered.

Kannappan was the manager of a rich man's estate. He was the manager of all the affairs of his employer ... even the private ones.

'In four days, they are going to celebrate Ayya's child's first birthday. He wants to invite everyone for a feast. He is depending on you for sugar. He is a regular customer, isn't he?'

'That's fine. But what can I do, Mr Kannappan? I'm also expecting stock. We are only retailers. How can we supply without stock?'

Kannappan looked away tactfully and said, 'Ayya asked me to tell you. Don't say no because you don't trust us. Whatever your price may be ... even Rs 5 per kg ... why should you hesitate to say so to a rich man? They can give anything you ask. Why do you insult us saying no, no? Don't you need their goodwill?'

Vaiyapuri looked down as he thought over it. A clever businessman's important qualification is to know the limit beyond which a stretched bargain will break. To indicate his assent, he spoke cheerfully. 'Poor people like us survive only on the goodwill of the rich, Mr Kannappan. The price is nothing. If Ayya chooses he can give even fifty not just five. This is just nothing for him. I am not one to drive a hard bargain like that. Is Ayya well? Come to the store tomorrow. In all probability, I would have received the stock. You may take it.'

Such bargains cannot be made more explicit than this. The man who had looked away from Vaiyapuri understood. Then they exchanged pleasantries and spoke about each others' families and the weather.

'The heat is unbearable,' said Kannappan wiping his perspiring face with his upper cloth.

'Will you have some buttermilk?'

'No, it's getting late. I'll go.'

'Please tell Ayya that I enquired about him.'

'Ayya said you and your family must come for the feast.'

'Of course! Don't we know Ayya's large heartedness? Lord Muruga will see to it that Ayya lacks for nothing!'

Kannappan stepped into the street flicking his umbrella open. The sky held the pallor of anaemia. It was naked with not a cloud for cover. As soon as he stepped into the street, the heat fell on him from all sides, piercing the cover of the umbrella, and tearing into him like wild beasts springing forth from bushes.

In five minutes his shirt was soaking wet. The outlines of the vest inside, which had appeared like a line drawing, now looked as well defined as a sculpture. His tongue was parched. Though he was very thirsty, he didn't want to drink buttermilk in Vaiyapuri's house. Though he worked for a sinner, and consequently transacted with several sinners, and though he had also paved the way for other sins, he showed his loyalty to his protesting conscience and assuaged it by acts like refusing to quench his thirst in this house.

Appappa, what heat, does it seem like Aippasi?

Is there no room for honesty in this world? The omnipresent fraud and selfishness, the aridness in the hearts of people had spread outside too. Was there not a single honest person anywhere? For whom will it rain if this world is full of people like his master and Vaiyapuri? Master! Rage erupted from Kannappan's insides. His employer had entrusted him with one more task. 'Chee ... and I work for him shamelessly.'

Here! Here was the other person he had come to meet ... walking towards him purely by chance. Or else he would have had to set foot inside another sinner's house.

He clapped to draw her attention. Thangam stopped and raised her eyebrows as if to ask what the matter was. She was returning from the place she had been proceeding to when Vaiyapuri had met her in the morning.

Kannappan took her to an isolated place and somehow managed to convey the message. He was sick with himself and felt like throwing up.

Thangam was not surprised. She had guessed what the matter was by some indications from the rich man. She smiled gently. 'Not possible today,' she said calmly.

'Ayya will be busy from tomorrow because of the function, and on the same day he's leaving town. That's why he wanted this to be arranged.' Though he spoke turning his face away, he felt diminished and disgusted. The perspiration that sprang all over now was not caused by the heat.

'My apologies to him. I have another customer tonight.'

Kannappan felt as if she had slapped him. He had never heard anyone speak so openly of such matters. Had she no sense of shame? For a moment he had forgotten that it was he who had proposed the shameful matter.

'There was no rice at home this morning. There was nothing. I had gone somewhere to get some money. Only a while ago I arranged a meeting with a man tonight. Because my children and I are hungry, he gave me my fee in advance. Who will do that?'

'How much?'

'Fifteen rupees.'

'Pooh! That's nothing. My Ayya will give a hundred times more. Throw that money in that man's face and come with me.'

'Should one also throw away one's words?' What was that something which shone in her face weary with heat and poverty. Had her face taken on the gold of her name?[10]

'Once you agree, should you not honour your commitment? My word is important to me. I took the money from him,

[10] Thangam means gold.

promising him that he is my customer for tonight. Mine is a profession too. I will not commit fraud in my profession. If your master has stacks of hundred-rupee notes, let him lock them up safely in his cupboard.'

Thangam moved away with the notes tucked at her waist to a grocery shop other than Vaiyapuri's since she hated him.

Kannappan's eyes followed her. Now he felt no disgust. Some other emotion choked his heart.

It started to rain that day.

Kannappan was not surprised.

The newspapers said that there was a depression in the Bay of Bengal causing rain and fierce winds.

But he knew that it was not the depression which had brought the rains.[11]

___

[11] It is believed that it will rain for the sake of a single good person or a good deed.

A Rainbow in Her Hands*

*S*ome children were playing on the dusty road under a cloud which looked as if someone had hung a huge wave that had risen from the sea hissing and foaming.

The rear view of one among them. Khaki shorts, no shirt. The X of the straps of the shorts. Two long dusty brown plaits hanging down on either side of the X. A blue ribbon at the end of one plait. No ribbon on the other. Was that a girl in shorts or a boy in plaits? Neither in the voice nor in the face was there anything to mark the gender. Just the plain form of childhood. This half nakedness amidst the other children was a distinct island.

The row of shops in the narrow street of Chintadripet stood adjacent to tiny residences. It was in front of a cycle shop (really the pavement) that these children were playing. The young owner of the shop looked up from his work every now and then and smiled at the children. These evening games were a ritual.

* Originally titled 'Neela Ribbonum Vaanavillum', the story was published in 1981, and later appeared in *Nagalinga Maram* in 2010 (pp. 153–60).

A girl holding the hem of her frock primly with the tips of her fingers and thus hiding the torn patches announced stylishly, 'I am Sridevi.'[1]

'But yesterday you said you were Sripriya,' said the shop-keeper.

'That was yesterday.'

In that young world, today was a lifetime away from yesterday.

A boy picked up a squashed beedi butt, threw it up in the air, and trying to catch it with his mouth said, 'This is Rajini style.' He was Kamal yesterday.

The waves in the sky had disappeared and now trees and human faces appeared. Darkness spread suddenly. The air grew chill. A rolling boom was heard out there in the sky as if crackers were being burst. Was it going to rain?

The children were playing hide and seek and *sadu-gudu*.[2] They played unconcerned by the risk to their lives amidst the heavy traffic, uncaring of becoming grubby from playing on the dirty road. Some, by their happiness, made their tattered clothes giggle, and others, by their memory movements, transformed the dusty road into a dance platform.

A regular customer stood in front of a paan shop, placed a Rs 5 note on the stool, told the elderly shop owner 'Scented *paakku*,[3] as usual fifty grams', and offered a *namaskaram* to the picture of Gajalakshmi hung on the wall, which had a dried garland draped over it.

'Here you are.'

The scented paakku in the plastic bag, and the balance change beside it. 'What is this? You have to return 3 rupees and 25 paise … you've given me only 3?' a shocked question.

---

[1] Sridevi, Sripriya, Rajini, Kamal are all Indian film stars.

[2] A national Indian sport also known as kabaddi.

[3] Betelnut powder.

'The price of everything has risen. Will paakku alone trail behind? Now 50 grams costs 2 rupees.'

'Daylight robbery,' muttering under the breath. 'Nowadays only shopkeepers can survive', an irritated comment and a smile. The customer's eyes roamed over the street on the road. A ten-year-old boy was carrying two glasses of coffee on a tray. Probably the errand boy who carries what is ordered at Geeta Café at the corner of the street. The boy paused for a moment. He picked up one glass and sipped the coffee. Eyes wide, he licked his lips. Then he replaced that glass, and picked up the second one and did likewise and enjoyed the sip. Then he wiped his mouth and looking serious, rushed with a laden tray.

'Everyone is a cheat, a fraud,' said the customer, with the satisfaction that he could at least openly abuse someone. His eyes stretched across two shops where the children were playing. Old but colourful shirts, frocks, skirts, shorts … A cinematic title 'Colours on the floor' came to his mind. He suddenly noticed the khaki island amidst the sea of colours.

'Aha! Shorts and plaits? Is that a boy or a girl?'

The paakku shopowner craned his neck. Not to identify who it was since the description was sufficient. Just for the joy of staring together.

'Boy. Name Ulaganathan. A vow to offer his hair at Tiruttani. Poor thing. Sad case, sir. The father died when this one was still in the womb. He was a shopowner here like me. Snuff shop. Chinnan Snuff Shop was well known in the locality. Even people who drove motor cars would come to buy it. One day a sudden heart attack. Hmmmmh! Their lifestyle too died with him. The mother does some coolie work to half fill their stomachs, or some other work now and then, and takes care of the boy. She would often say that she lives only for this little mite. She has this desire to take him to Tiruttani for a tonsure.'

Ulaganathan's untied plait had come undone during the game. The dull brown hair hung in strands, interfering with his game by getting into his eyes.

From time to time the boy would grumble and move his hair away with his left hand.

'Hey! *Ardhanariswarar*![4] What happened to the other ribbon?' The paakku man shouted.

'My name is not Ardhanariswarar,' he corrected him and then said, 'Amma did not tie it.'

'Annachi, she would not have had time. After four days of starvation, only today she found some work at a construction site. The person in the third house told me so. Will she have the time to beautify this boy with a ribbon?' the cycle shop-owner said.

'If she had the time to tie one ribbon, why not the other? Hey, Ardhanari, isn't there another ribbon in your house? Why don't you wear a single plait? Will Tiruttani *sami*[5] object? Why this two-plait style?'

'My name is not Ardhanari. There was another ribbon. But Amma didn't like it and she said "No".'

'A big maharani, your mother. When survival itself is a struggle, what is this preference for one ribbon over another?'

'Hey, Poongothai,' cried a woman's voice from the street and from the bunch of children, an irritated call, 'What is it, Amma?'

'Where did you disappear when I needed you? Shouldn't you draw water from the well in the big house? Looks like it will rain. Won't they close the door? Then where will we go for water? Come, come, take a bucket and run.'

'Let me play another round ...'

---

[4] The icon of the Divine as half Devi and half Siva.

[5] The colloquial form of Swami, or God. The deity in Tiruttani is Subrahmanya.

'No more round or sound! Will you come at once or not? Look I'm picking up the broom. Hey mule, Poongothai, it's you I'm calling.'

Reluctantly Sridevi became Poongothai. 'Coming, Amma,' she said and walked to her house, looking regretfully at her playmates and ignoring the shopowner's comment, 'Who is it going to be tomorrow ... Srividya?'

'*Chee*, this wretched hair always comes loose.' Ulaganathan glared at his hair that had come undone, holding it with the left hand. The rusty brown hair glared back.

'Why couldn't your mother have tied the hair with that ribbon? Now it is a big bother. Why, Ardhanari, don't you know how to tie it?' asked the paakku man.

The boy did not answer.

'Hey, I'm talking to you and you stand there mum? Insolence?'

'I won't answer you if you call me Ardhanari.'

'Ha! So you've become such a big man? Okay, let that be. Ulagu, don't you know how to tie your hair?'

'No. Amma won't listen if I ask her to chop off this Shani[6] thing.'

'No, no, it's an offering to God. You mustn't say *Shani-kini* and all that. You will lose your sight. Think of God and say sorry?'

Scared, Ulaganathan tried to think of God. Wasn't so easy in the middle of sadu-gudu. Suddenly God appeared just as Mahatma Gandhi promised and he stood still.

A young couple came out of the Geeta Café after a Double Seven, holding a bag full of *murukkus*.[7] When they saw these children, they gave each a murukku. In a minute the game stopped, and the eyes widened as excited hands stretched. One

[6] Literally, Saturn, but used here to say 'this wretched thing' because Saturn is supposed to exert a malign influence on people.

[7] A savoury delicacy made especially in Tamil Nadu.

girl tasted a bit of the murukku and folded the remaining carefully into her gown. Another girl pushed the murukku with her
dirty and sweaty hand into her mouth, finished it in two bites,
and stretched out her hand for more. One boy wiped his hand
on the back of his dirty shorts after eating his murukku. Today's
Rajini broke the murukku, tossed it in the air, and ate it in the
same Rajini style as he had tossed the beedi butt.

Ulaganathan's mouth watered. Yet he hid his hand behind
and firmly said, 'I don't want it.'

The couple persuaded him, 'Why, my boy? The murukku
will be good. Aren't they all eating it? You too take one.'

Ulaganathan shook his head firmly. His eyes watered when
he saw the murukku. His nose dripped too. He sniffed it back.
He controlled his empty stomach, which felt as if it would come
out of his body and reach for the murukku.

'Don't want.'

'Why?'

'Amma has told me not to take anything from strangers.
Today she has gone to work and has promised me a bun.'

'Big fuss pot. Come let's go.' The couple left.

'Why this fuss? When did you become so arrogant? Who
can change what's written in your destiny. Starve! Won't take
anything, is it? Big zamindar family you think you are from?
Isn't that so, Mr Ardhanari, sorry, Mr Ulaganathan?' the paakku
man asked with pain and anger and returned to his business.
That customer had left and others had come. The game was
constantly changing in the street. One by one the children were
leaving the group. The rain remained a drizzle and did not
intensify. A rainbow appeared in the clouds because far away
somewhere it was raining hard.

'Rainbow!'

'Rainbow!'

'Look there!'

'It is the setting sun which is colourful, not a rainbow.'

'No, no, it is a rainbow!'
'You can see the bands and the curve. Can't you see? There is green colour too. It is a rainbow.'

Some persons were talking. Ulaganathan didn't notice anything. All that he could see was that murukku. The sounds of biting into the murukku *kaduk-muduk* echoed in his ears. He stubbornly spat out the saliva that rose in his mouth.

The scent of damp earth wafted up. Rain which ceases after a light drizzle will surely increase the humidity. But at this moment, the cool breeze that blew felt lovely. There was joy in this fleeting chill. Ulaganathan pressed his arms tightly across his bare chest. He tried to remove the hair which blew into his eyes by jerking his head back. Then he asked the cycle shop man, 'May I sit here on the steps until my mother returns?'

'Sure'

He sat on the edge of the steps. He looked up at the sky. If you stare at the colours and wonder if it is orange or red, blue or green, even as you are wondering, the colours blend into each other and deceive the eyes. All the colours wove a magic within the small semicircle. As the evening deepened, the sky picked up its bow and started fading away.

'Hey, Ulagu. Have you gone to sleep sitting up? My dear one! Are you so hungry that you've become drowsy?'

Only then did Ulaganathan realize that his eyes had shut by themselves. His face blossomed when he looked up.

'Amma!'

'Shall we go? But before we do, eat this.' She handed over a paper bag and a leaf parcel. Inside he found a bun and three idlis.

'Idli mma!' he shouted with joy.

'They are for you—eat.'

'For you, Amma?'

'I had tea just now. I have here a bun too. That's enough. There's some more money. We'll buy something for the night.'

The boy started eating eagerly. She enjoyed the scene with a smile. This smile was her only adornment. A bony frame, a protruding jaw, dirty clothes, pieces of small twigs in her ear holes, bare neck, glass bangles. The weariness in the eyes was not born of a single day's exertion; it was the weariness of bearing life's burden. Truth to say, today had been one of her lucky days. She had got some work and food to eat.

She wiped her face and neck with the *munthanai* of her sweat-laden saree. 'Your hair has come loose because there is no ribbon, no?' she said and combed his hair with her fingers and plaited it. Then joyfully, she took out of the knot in her munthanai end, a foot-long blue ribbon.

'I tied one blue ribbon. The other ribbon at home is black, isn't it? How can I tie that? It won't match this blue. Won't it look ugly if you tie two different coloured ribbons? That is why I bought a matching blue ribbon with the money I had,' she said, and tied the other plait with the new ribbon. She looked at the ribboned plaits again and again, with sparkling eyes.

'Only now it looks nice. Only now they match.'

The paakku shopowner who was getting ready to shut his shop, was riveted by this sight. The boy with two plaits tied with two blue ribbons, behind him the mother and the radiance in her sunken eyes as she looked at the matching ribbons.

He looked at the sight for a while, then looked at the sky above. The rainbow was no longer there. A rainbow comes just like a lightning flash for a fraction of a moment, but it turns the sky beautiful.

He looked at Ulaganathan's mother again. She examined with satisfaction the second plait she had just tied. The rainbow had descended into her hands in the form of a blue ribbon.

Does Anyone Care?*

*T*wo boys were playing in the garden in front of the house.
A boy stood, bat in hand, in front of a coconut tree at the base
of which stumps had been drawn in chalk. Another boy was
running up to another coconut tree at the far end to bowl to
him. The ball, struck by the bat, rose high and then began to
fall. Before the batsman could take a run, the bowler had run
across, fallen to the ground, rolled over, and caught the ball.
Both of them laughed so hard that their midriffs, visible above
the shorts, quivered. The boy who had been 'caught out' was
not sad, the bat and the ball exchanged hands and he went to
the other end. Youthful enthusiasm bubbled in them both,
warming their cheeks and making them glow. The one who
had bowled before hitched up his shorts and stood in front of
the coconut tree on which stumps had been drawn, held the bat
and focused on the ball.

The man who was watching this scene did not know him. He
was the new son-in-law of the house. And the young bowler was
his brother-in-law Mani. Pointing to the batsman, who had got
him out, and was now facing the ball, he asked casually, 'Mani,
is he your schoolmate?'

* Originally titled 'Thozhamai', the story was published in 1978,
and later appeared in *Nagalinga Maram* in 2010 (pp. 108–19).

Mani's friend's face changed as soon as he heard this question. His childish joy disappeared. He threw down the bat, shook his hair back, and, looking up at the gentleman, said with an adult pride shining in his eyes, 'I am working, sir.'

The man who asked the question was embarrassed.

Now walking along the street, with an empty cloth bag in one hand and the tip of the dhoti in the other, Jaggu wondered, 'Was I truly that boy?'

At twenty-four, he had the same scrawny frame and could have worn shorts now as he had when he was sixteen.

A heaviness and a weight, not quite physical, oppressed him. With just two or three breaths, a feeling of old age had entered him. He felt that that sixteen-year-old boy was some stranger who had lived long, long ago, in a different time.

This is something truly strange. Only if your life has been eventful and happy, you feel that you have lived a long life, isn't it? But it is strange to feel this passage of time in a life lived like an automaton, from the time he was sixteen, a life that had been routine, work-laden, and monotonous. No difference between one day and another, any two days taken at random were just like twins. Some days when he had woken up, he would wonder, 'Is it today, yesterday, or tomorrow?' He could sense the passage of time only by looking at his younger brothers and sisters who had grown up, completed their education, and made progress right before his eyes.

The face perspired in the rising heat and the thought that 'I must come again tomorrow' made the empty bag feel heavy. That wretched store ... couldn't they have sold the sugar today? Standing in a queue, as long as Hanuman's[1] tail, he had inched forward to reach the third place, when suddenly there was

---

[1] The monkey God in Hindu mythology.

confusion and commotion. A customer accused the controller at the counter that the scales were not accurate. The shopkeeper stoutly denied it. The other customers joined rank and entered the fray. The situation worsened resulting in an exchange of blows and stone-throwing. The police arrived and the shop was closed for the day. There is no knowing whether the shop would open the next day. If not for one's immediate need, one had to buy at least half a kilo of sugar from the open market. Even then the family would expect only him to get it in the black market. Whatever work had to be done always fell on his lot. *Chey!*

When he entered the house, Murali had just then got up and was drinking coffee. The clock on the hall stand showed 9.

'*Tiruppalli ezhuchi*[2] only now?' he snapped at Murali and then called aloud, 'Ammaaaa!' Drawing the limp sweat-soggy ration card out from his shirt pocket, he handed it to his mother who had come out of the kitchen. 'Keep it safe. How many times do I have to ask you to wrap it in plastic so that it does not get torn by frequent handling and dampness?'

'I keep forgetting, da. Have I nothing else to do? Can't you do it?'

'Yes, it will be me, even for that.'

'Okay ... okay. Did you get the sugar?'

Jaggu told her what had happened.

'*Ramachandra!*[3] What is this? Wherever you go there is dishonesty in this country. Will we get it at least tomorrow?'

'Who knows? I have no hope considering what happened today. We will know only tomorrow.'

'Better go early tomorrow. There will be a huge crowd,' Murali suggested as he put down the empty coffee tumbler.

[2] The special verses in Tamil used in the early morning ritual at temples for waking the Deity.

[3] Sri Rama's name is used here as an exclamation indicating frustration.

Jaggu turned to him sharply and irritably, 'Why? Can't you go?'

'Tomorrow is Monday. If I stand in the ration queue,[4] who will go to work?'

'Am I then jobless? I have been earning since I was fifteen.'

'That is why you've got used to doing your work and the household chores ... not me! Amma, where is the paper? Has Susi taken it away?'

How contemptuously he speaks of my work! Jaggu fumed.

It was just three months after he had turned fifteen. As soon as he wrote his SSLC,[5] he had desperately wanted to get a job, without waiting for his results. His father's friend gave him a job at his cycle factory. 'For the time being, I will give you a salary I can afford and take you on as my "assistant". You are not old enough for me to recommend you to others. You work here and learn typing and shorthand. I will get you a place somewhere or the other as a clerk or a steno.'

He had kept his word, and so Jaggu was now a clerk in a commercial establishment. Did he not want a comfortable life too? How casually had this brother dismissed the fact that he had sacrificed everything with a smile. Now, Murali, a graduate, worked as a clerk in a bank. If he passes the bank examination, he would become an officer. It was that arrogance.

'I don't know about that. I stood in the queue till my feet hurt. You must go tomorrow.'

Jaggu threw down the bag on the floor.

'I won't.'

'Nor will I.'

'Then?'

'Why ask me? Am I the only person here?'

---

[4] The public distribution system.

[5] Secondary School Leaving Certificate, the certificate given after completing the secondary-school board examination.

'If you don't go, let Susi go.'

'I don't care who goes. I am not going that's all!'

'Why are you brothers squabbling like this? With the two of you around, why should a grown-up girl stand in the queue among strangers? Have you no sense?' Amma shouted.

'If a grown-up girl can't go, send the younger ones,' said Jaggu.

'Why are you talking like this ... Jaggu, so unlike you? You are the one who always goes.'

'Is that the law? Tomorrow, Murali should go.'

'You know he won't go.'

'Oh! His lordship won't go? You always support him, I know, Amma.'

Murali yawned and cracked his fingers. 'Where has that Susi taken the papers? There's nothing even in the magazine section for her to read. Susee, Susee!'

'She's not home. She said she was going to some morning show with her friends,' Amma said.

'It is okay to stand in queue for tickets to watch a movie. But she can't stand in queue for TUCS[6] sugar. Right, Amma?' said Jaggu.

'Girls will get married soon and go away, and after that who knows what her life will be like? I thought why spoil her enjoyment now and so....' Though Amma gave excuses, Jaggu felt her tone had softened.

'Okay, okay, Amma. Let her enjoy herself, who asks her not to? I alone have to slog like a bullock both at home and outside without enjoying anything, while others will do as they please, right?'

---

[6] Triplicane Urban Cooperative Society, the first consumer cooperative society in the state of Tamil Nadu, offering products at competitive prices.

'I can't stand this self-pity discourse. I'm going.' Murali went out. He was tall just like Appa. Jaggu felt that even now he was deliberately humiliating him.

'Self-pity? Who?' Drying his hair with the towel, Appa emerged shining after his shower. Amma went in to wash his clothes.

'Who else? Your first-born,' said Murali.

'Why? What now?'

'Nothing new. Same old sob story. He works like a bullock. He has not enjoyed anything.'

Appa's smile showed his still-firm shining teeth. 'This is what I don't like about Jaggu. Always pitying himself. Che! Che! What have you done that others have not? In struggling families, isn't it usual for the first-born to start earning early, to put the younger ones through their education and bring them up? What is so special about this?'

Jaggu said nothing and tightened his lips.

'You must not dwell on your own problems all the time. It is true you are not living like a king. But how many in this world live a hand-to-mouth existence? Just remember that.'

Our misery is our Truth. How is the lame one concerned with the problems of the one who cannot see? Without a word Jaggu went in, drank some water, and sat on the steps to the backyard. The shade of the tamarind tree was comforting in the heat.

The old hurt that his father had never sympathized with him rankled as usual. He was always first in class, exemplifying the meaning of the word 'education'. He had dreamt quite achievable dreams of pursuing higher studies and scientific research, and making a name among the best brains in the country. He brushed aside all those dreams one day and told his father, 'Appa, as soon as I complete my SSLC, please arrange for a job for me.'

Without an agitated 'Why, my child?' nor an affectionate 'I will somehow see that you pursue higher studies, why should you at this age sacrifice yourself?' how easily Appa had said 'Yes'! He had not shown any concern. Jaggu's only disappointment was that Appa had not once understood what he had done for the family. He himself had never regretted that decision. The incident which had ignited that decision in his young heart was deeply engraved in his memory.

He was fourteen then ... the eldest brother with four sisters and a brother. With his father's income as a country doctor, the family had always been in a state of semi-starvation. But he hadn't minded that since the words of appreciation from his teachers made up for it.

That day, he had returned home from school as usual and had entered the house with the joyful cry, 'I'm first in class in this test too,' but had stopped short, unable to move forward. In the inner room, Appa was beating Amma violently on her back and on her face. Unable to bear the pain, she had fallen and was weeping and pleading, when he started kicking her with his legs.

'Why do you go there to make *murukku*? What about my prestige? Won't everyone think I'm keeping you in such an impoverished state that you have to go around for these few rupees? Even if we starve to death, you must remain at home. Do you know what will happen if you humiliate me again by going out?'

The kicks continued. Amma trembled on the floor, her face red with tears, her mouth quivering unable to articulate the words 'For our children, for our children'. The anaemic, emaciated shoulder peered out of the torn blouse. The young boy who stood shocked, transfixed like a stone pillar, came to life at the sight of the torn blouse as if in that sight all the horrors of this world had converged. He thought no one who wore such tattered clothes should be beaten like this.

'Appaaaa!' he shouted. 'Stop hitting her. If you hit my Amma again, I won't spare you. I will beat you lifeless. No point then saying that Jaggu is a wicked boy.'

Both the parents had stared at him. Appa looked for a moment at the firm ferocity of the young boy who stood at his shoulder height, with skinny legs below his shorts, his appearance a total mismatch to the words spoken. Appa had walked away silently.

That day a young boy became an old man. The old man bid farewell to the young boy's dreams. A boy who had resolved to secure not less than five-hundred marks in the school finals, studied just enough to secure pass marks. How did it matter what marks he got when he was not going to study further after the school finals? He must start earning at once, his brothers and sisters should not starve.

But above all, Amma should never be beaten again.

'Look at your food when you eat,' Amma's voice brought him back to this world. He realized that he had just touched his food, while all the others except Susi were eating.

Amma stood there with the ladle and vessel in hand. 'See if you want more *kuzhambu*.[7] You have scooped the rice for it. Shall I pour some more?'

'Mmm, just a bit.'

Amma's blouses had no tears in them now. Why, all the family members wore good clothes today. Though they were not very affluent, their lifestyle had surely improved. Murali, a graduate, had started earning. Susila was in the final year BA. Usha would finish school this year. The next two girls were in their respective classes. This positive change became possible because a young boy had buried himself alive so that no one died of suffocation.

Who thinks of that now?

---

[7] A dish that is an accompaniment for rice.

'We should get Jaggu married. What do you say?' Appa asked Amma.

'Very nice indeed ... when we have a daughter of marriageable age! First Susi must get married, only then the son,' said Amma.

'Where will we get the money for her marriage? That's why I say we will first get Jaggu married. With the dowry we get for him, we can perform the daughter's marriage. Similarly, we will get Murali married and with that we can perform Usha's marriage. We will get more dowry for Murali than for Jaggu. He is a graduate, so more income; because he is a bank employee he will soon become an officer.'

Jaggu got up and left the room.

When he rinsed his hands and came into the hall, he heard Amma saying, 'Susi will come from the cinema now and she will be tired. Heat her food, Usha.' There was only a wall between the hall and the kitchen. What was said there could be heard here.

She is respected because she is a college-going girl, so she will be tired after watching a movie. Who cares how much he worked till he was overcome by fatigue? Who remembers that it is months since he went to a movie or to a play? Who respects him in this house?

'Amma, as soon as Susi arrives, tell her that if Murali does not go to buy sugar, she must go,' shouted Jaggu and lay down on the bench with a pillow under his head.

'What is this, Jaggu, even after I have told you so many times? Please go.'

'No, Amma. If you don't have the heart to send your daughter, you go, or send Appa.' He turned to the wall.

'Anna,' he heard Usha's voice.

'What?'

'Why do you bark like this?'

'If you can't let me rest for a while after a meal ...'

'Don't get angry. I wanted to tell you something. If you feel bothered now, I will tell you later.'

Why is she 'softening' me up like this? He turned over and lay facing her.

'Just tell me.'

'Hmm, you get angry for everything,' she said in an ingratiating tone as she sat near his feet.

'Anna, I saw a foreign nylon saree at my friend Nalini's house. Very pretty, smuggled goods it seems,' she stopped, looking at his face.

'So what?'

'She wants to sell it. Will you buy it for me?'

'Can't you survive without a nylon saree? First study properly. Go, go.'

'Please, Anna, it is just 110 or so. The actual price is 250, do you know? We are getting it cheap.'

'Would you find the 110 rupees on trees? You all think I'm a milch cow?'

'Please, Anna'

'No.'

'Why, Anna?'

'I won't means I won't. Now get up I want to sleep.'

'But you got a wrist watch for Susi.'

'So I've bought that as my share. You ask Murali to get you the nylon saree. He is also an Anna? That too an officer-to-be Anna.'

'It seems he's going to get some new trousers stitched. So he says no money for my saree.'

'Oh! That big shot will enjoy all the money himself without sharing with others. But I must work selflessly for others, no?'

'Why don't you tell me point blank you don't want to buy a saree for me?'

'Understood that, right? Now go.'

'Susi is your *chella*[8] sister.'

'No *chellam* or *vellam*.'[9]

'Vellam reminds me. I remember, Amma said that there is no jaggery at home. When you go tomorrow to buy sugar, get jaggery too.'

'Tell that to the one who will be going to buy sugar.'

He closed his eyes. After some moments of quiet, he heard her walking away. Jaggu lay motionless, eyes closed. An emptiness tortured him, a distaste filled his heart. The familiar feeling of aging within, a fatigue as if he had been living for ever.

Why should I continue to work for this ungrateful family? Murali has started earning. Now he can take care of them. He, Jaggu, must go away, far away. He must go somewhere free, without care, without these family ties, and chase this fatigue away. He must rise to the top by becoming a graduate studying at least by correspondence. He must enjoy all the pleasures of life, spending whatever he earns on himself. He must do as he pleased—go to movies and hotels with friends, and have by his side a beautiful woman. He stubbornly continued to dream for a while. This was a right that all the worries of life cannot snatch from us. The dream of freedom is the permanent possession of any prisoner.

The intoxication of that stage dissolved and reality grasped his throat. An unbearable loneliness assailed him. Who really cared for him in this house? No one cares. All of them cared nothing for him, whatever he did was taken for granted and as a matter of course.

He heard the sound of slippers. Though he heard Susila's laughter, her cheerful farewells to her friends, he lay with his

[8] Favourite.

[9] The word 'vellam' meaning jaggery is used here only to rhyme with 'chellam'.

eyes closed. Even the jokes like 'Sleeping like a Kumbakarna[10] in broad daylight' did not make him react.

Susila went in, ate the food that Amma served, while reviewing the movie, and then she said, 'Amma, if I pass my BA in first class, I want to study MA in my own college. All the friends with whom I went to the movie tell me that I will definitely get admission and that I must study.'

'Why study more? My concern is about your marriage.'

'Go on, Amma, I want to study. Won't you be proud if I study MA? What is the hurry to get me married? What have all these married persons achieved?'

'I don't like it. Then it's your wish. You must ask your father and your brothers if you want to study.'

'Appa has already said I can do as I wish. I don't think Murali will object.'

'What does Jaggu say?'

'What can Jaggu say? Murali is the one who has studied more, who earns more, and who can advise and guide me. If he says yes, who is Jaggu to object?'

'What did you say?' Amma's eyes pierced Susila. 'Say it again, come on.'

'Wwww ... what Amma?'

'Just say it once more and I will disown you forever,' Amma said clearly.

Susila was shaken. 'What is this, Amma? What have I said for you to speak like this?'

'Just try insulting Jaggu again. What do you think? Who knows what you would have done if my child had thought of his own future and gone ahead that day. Your BA, MA, and everything else is the alms thrown to you by him. Remember that.'

---

[10] In Ramayanam, he is the younger brother of Ravana. He is cursed to be sleeping all the time.

After Amma washed the dishes and left them to dry, she closed the kitchen and came to the hall and saw him lying on the bench. She approached and gently placed her hand on his forehead.

Jaggu opened his eyes and looked at her. He touched the hand she held to his forehead and smiled softly at her.

'Did I wake you up?' Amma asked gently.

'I wasn't sleeping, Amma.'

'But you never lie down like this. So I thought you were not well. All the others have gone out with your father. You sleep peacefully for some time.'

'Yes, Amma,' he smiled again. Amma slowly released her hand and ruffled his hair and left when he said, 'Amma, don't worry, I'll go to the ration shop tomorrow,' and closed his eyes.

Woman in the Dark*

And Vanaja stood there. She too had come.

'What a beauty she is ... even in grief!' was Hema's first reaction when she recognized her, followed immediately by 'Amma must not see her.'

Amma was not in the hall. Probably last night she had wept her heart out, alone beside Appa's body. Now she would be seated, head bowed, in the room beyond the hall. She would not have even noticed the visitors entering or leaving. Can Vanaja go indoors like all the others and offer her condolences? Amma had a *tali*[1] round her neck ... soon to be removed. Vanaja did not. Apart from this difference, the grief they felt was the same. Who could offer her condolence to the other? Anyway who will permit Vanaja to even enter—including those who were now looking at her with shocked interest?

Hema wondered whether the grief the two felt was indeed the same. Amma's grief had social acceptance. She could enter the hall, fall on her husband's body, and wail aloud. The crowd

---

* Originally titled 'Iruttil Irundhaval', the story was published in *Kalki* in 1990, and later appeared in *Nagalinga Maram* in 2010 (pp. 235–40).

[1] The Tamil word for mangalsutra, a sanctified symbol of marriage worn by married women.

which had gathered would approve, sympathize, and console. Vanaja cannot do that. Though the relationship between her and Appa was a well-known secret, it could not proceed even the slightest bit beyond the limit of being a well-known secret. Hema felt like rushing up to her and saying something to console her.

Fifteen years ago, when she was a fifteen-year-old girl, she had met Vanaja on two occasions, again once when she was twenty, and then again at her wedding. She need not hesitate to say 'I'm Hema' even if, for some reason, Vanaja did not recognize this thirty-year-old woman. They had liked each other instantly during those meetings in the past. When they had first met, Vanaja had praised her to Appa, 'Your daughter is like you ... good-looking!' That first meeting was when Hema was returning home after visiting her schoolmate and had seen her father with a strange woman. When Appa asked 'Hi Hema, are you returning after meeting a friend?' the stranger had looked agitated. But Appa continued, 'What? Are you afraid, Vanaja? This is Hema, my daughter. She is very broad-minded. She will surely accept you. Hemukkutti, this is Vanaja, my friend,' and laughed.

It was when Hema had stood transfixed, looking at a radiant Vanaja, who seemed as if a single ray of the golden sun had taken the form of a woman, that Vanaja herself relaxed and told Appa with a smile, 'Your daughter is like you ... good-looking!' Hema had floated with pride. To be praised like that, and that too by a movie-star-like beauty! At fifteen, it was intoxicating. When Appa hugged Hema's shoulders and said 'It is not right to call her my daughter; she is my son' and Vanaja had blossomed into laughter saying 'Looks like she is truly Father's pet', Hema had felt like embracing them both. Amma would also call her 'Father's pet', but not as praise. She would scold her,

'You are getting thoroughly spoilt because he keeps indulging you. You don't attend to anything at home. You don't listen to me.' What a contrast!

The second time she had met Vanaja was an opportunity created by Appa himself. When he took his daughter to a four-star hotel, she found Vanaja waiting there for them. Appa led both of them to the Family Room. Delicious Bombay cuisine, even more delicious conversation ... about art. To Appa, that he was an amateur artist meant more than his position in a private company. He had held a few exhibitions. Gradually, his name was being mentioned in the list of the talented artists in Chennai. Vanaja was an art teacher in a school. That must have been how they first met, thought Hema.

When Hema sat silently like a devotee, looking at them and listening to their sparkling discussion about the pulse of art from different angles—Indian, Western, traditional methods, and modern trends—she had thought, 'Pity! Appa should have married someone like her!' Not only in the matter of art and taste, but even in looks, intelligence, and everything else they were a perfectly matched pair. As for Amma ... a dull-complexioned, ordinary-looking woman, ignorant of anything but the kitchen! 'If only Vanaja had been my mother.' The regret hit her sharply in that fifteenth year.

Hastily, she left the hall and reached Vanaja at the gate. She faced her, but could not speak. Then with an effort, in a low voice, she said, 'I'm Hema ...'

The third time she met her, Vanaja was at her wedding. Vanaja, it seemed, had wanted to see her in her bridal dress. Hema still remembered the arguments between her parents at that time. On the wedding day, Amma's eyes were red with weeping. It made her face look even worse and Hema smiled back at the beauty who stood far away in the wedding hall looking at her with a smile.

Now there was no smile on Vanaja's face. Her eyes were red. But unlike Amma's, Vanaja's reddened eyes looked beautiful. She must be more or less Amma's age. But while Amma looked old, Vanaja had not lost her youth. There was not much change in the person she had seen ten years ago at her wedding.

'Hema, I know. How are you?'

'I am fine.' Do I ask her in response how she is?

On this occasion?

'Aren't you in Delhi now? Is your child six years old? Boy, isn't it?'

'Yes.'

There was no need to ask her how she knew; Appa would have told her everything.

'When did you arrive?'

'The day before yesterday morning. Amma sent a telegram as soon as his diabetes worsened and he went into a coma.'

Vanaja did not speak. She stood with her head bowed. Hema felt uncomfortable. What could she say? How did one console her? She should not have rushed out to talk to her. Meaningless act. She should have left her to return alone with her grief.

Vanaja looked up at her. She shook her head, her lips twitched ... was she smiling or crying ... and she walked away quickly.

When Hema turned back to return home, she saw her mother's face at the window upstairs. She must have seen her talking to Vanaja. That blankness on the face was a good screen to hide the emotions.

Appa's obsequies ended with a kinsman performing the last rites as he had died without a son.

Hema could not sleep even though all the relatives, who were at home, had gone to sleep. After tossing and turning for a while, she sat up. In the dark, she saw the silhouette of her mother seated in the easy chair outside the room on the balcony. She got up and went to her.

'Haven't you slept yet, Amma?'

'I will.'

She knew Amma had been weeping because her voice sounded heavy as if she had a cold. Shall I touch and comfort her? But she had never been close to her mother. It was only with Appa that she had been that way, holding his hands, resting her head on his knees, talking to him fondly ... she controlled the sob that threatened to burst at the thought of Appa.

'You are sitting in the dark, Amma, shall I switch the light on?'

'No.'

She went and sat on the floor near Amma.

After a while, 'Go to sleep, Hema.'

'I can't sleep.'

'True. Weren't you and Appa very close? It will take a long time for your grief to heal.'

'What about you?'

'My case is different.'

'Oh don't say that. Your voice gives you away. Weren't you crying in the dark?'

Amma did not speak.

'Tell me the truth, Amma.'

'Yes.'

'Then?'

'But I did not cry for your father.'

'What are you saying, Amma. Do you think I will believe this?'

'Why should I cry for your father? What did he lack? He was happy as long as he lived. He fulfilled all his desires. He did not give up anything for anyone. When the time came he left. Why should I grieve for him?'

Hema was silent. She looked up at her mother's face. Even though it was dark, the moonlight clearly showed Amma's ordinary face and the resignation that had fallen and hardened there.

This Amma is a wife. The husband–wife relationship is a proper one, a traditional one. So it holds no fascination, there is no romance. The world's attention is always on the lover. Even when it criticizes and accuses her, the focus is on her. The lover's adoration, beauty, the sacrifice which the world sees in her giving herself to the man without social approval—aren't these that are magnified and lit up? Isn't this the stuff of poetry and literature?

I too, fascinated by Vanaja in my childhood, had extolled her and Appa as a good match ...

In her immature dream-world state, she had been unaware of the betrayed heart which was suffering behind a screen, having none of the glitter of attraction and arousal that went with this transgression of tradition. The awareness came later, very slowly, as she grew older as she gradually understood the tragedy of unromantic tears.

Once in Delhi her friend said, 'Hey, Hema, I saw your husband yesterday evening outside a cinema hall with another woman.' Only after her husband later explained that he had dropped his friend and his wife at the cinema and had waited outside with his friend's wife while the friend went in to buy tickets, had her tumultuous heart calmed down. That day she had thought of her mother for a long time and wept.

Again Hema looked up at Amma's face. It was turned away.

Did Amma want to be alone?

Is she saying 'Aren't you your father's daughter? What is your concern about me?'

Hema stood up slowly. 'Then I will go and sleep, Amma.' She took two steps, hesitated, looked at the shadow figure which was sitting in the dark, in solitude. A certain heaviness in her heart. As never before, she stretched out and gently touched Amma's shoulder.

Amma covered the hand on her shoulder with her hand, without turning her head, as if she sensed the bridge in that silent message, which said, 'I understand.'

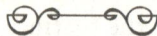

The Visitor*

Once more Mukundan came visiting.

Kasturi was restless. Mukundan had been coming often to see Sudha. But Sudha was not at home when he arrived.

'Please sit down,' she welcomed him with a smile.

'Thanks.' But he did not sit down. Kasturi thought that his dignity blended with the simple decor of her drawing room. It was indeed her daughter's good fortune that he would marry her.

'Please sit down,' she repeated.

'But you are standing.'

Kasturi pulled the *munthanai* of her saree over her shoulder and sat on the chair in the corner. Only then did he sit facing her.

'Sudha was invited to tea by a friend, she will be back soon.'

'That's all right. I've brought a book, Mrs Rajan.'

* Originally titled 'Adikadi Varugiraan', the story was published in *India Today* in 1997, and later appeared in *Nagalinga Maram* in 2010 (pp. 306–14).

Mukundan pulled a book out of its wrapper and placed it on the table in front of her. The title *Poetic Elegance in Tiruppavai* on the cover in red letters against a background of gold caught her eye.

'The other day you said you wanted to read it.'

'That one?' Forgetting even to thank him, she grabbed the book.

The last time Mukundan had come home was on Koodaraivelli,[1] almost the end of Margazhi. The conversation had naturally veered towards Aandaal's *Tiruppavai*.[2] Sudha was praising the Bhakti element in *Tiruppavai*. In fact, she had not even read it; she was just repeating what she had heard others say. All this to impress Mukundan, Kasturi secretly smiled to herself, but casually remarked that apart from the Bhakti, Aandaal's poetic skills were worthy of praise and she cited some examples. She was a well-read woman.

'There is a new book on this subject, Mrs Rajan,' Mukundan had mentioned.

'I know ... by Pulavar, *Karvannan*. I read the review in the papers. I want to read it, but I could not get it.' Kasturi had said, offering her future son-in-law *sakkaraipongal*[3] and coffee. She had left the room leaving the young ones alone saying, 'I

[1] Tiruppavai is the Tamil month roughly between 15 December and 15 January. Koodaraivelli is celebrated on the 27th day of Margazhi. Aandaal and her friends practise a ritual discipline for twenty-six days giving up rich food and adornments and flowers, improper conduct, and bad speech so that they may reach the Divine. On Koodaraivelli, they celebrate by wearing rich clothes and adornments and eating rich food cooked in ghee.

[2] The thirty songs composed by the poet Aandaal, one of the twelve Aalwaars, or Vaishnvaite saints.

[3] A dish of sweetened rice.

have some work, you carry on.' When she returned after a while
she was surprised to see Sudha sitting alone.

'Where is Mukund, Sudha?'

'He left long ago saying he had to meet a friend.'

Only the sakkaraipongal and the coffee remained where
Mukundan had sat.

He had brought the book today remembering what she had
said that day! Oh! Oh! I have not thanked him yet …

'Thank you very much, Mukund.'

'Welcome.'

What a fine boy! Tall and striking. Though not fair-skinned,
he had a smiling face and sharp features. An officer in a bank.
Her future son-in-law … It sometimes sounded strange even to
her. At just forty-three, it sounded odd to call someone 'son-in-
law'. It was more natural to call him Mukund. In fact, it was his
own suggestion. When she had hesitated how to address him,
he had said casually, 'Please call me Mukund.' But he always
referred to her respectfully as Mrs Rajan.

Mrs Rajan—the appellation that had stuck to her from the
time she was eighteen. A wife at eighteen, a mother at twenty,
a widow at thirty. This last name stayed with her when Rajan
died suddenly of meningitis.

She was now forty-three. But who would say so? Her slender
figure, her dark hair, and bright eyes proclaimed that she was
not even thirty. She had given up wearing flowers and the *tali*,
but wore the *tilakam*[4] on the forehead.

When an elderly woman, who knew her family well, had said
sadly, 'Hmmm … you look as if you could get married today',
her lips had curved … to smile …?

It is not easy to be an old woman at thirty. Particularly when
one's own body and mind were enemies, victory had not come

[4] The customary red dot on the forehead which widows did not
wear.

easily. But she had won, holding fast to her child. She resolved that her only aim in life was to raise Sudha and to educate her. Even though her husband had not left behind much wealth, it was sufficient to provide their basic requirements and some small comforts. She had lived a simple life. Now, Sudha at twenty-three was a postgraduate and efforts were on to get her married. And now it was decided who she would marry.

'Will you have coffee?'

'No, thanks.'

This Mukundan and his parents had come last month to meet Sudha formally. They had not indicated their decision, and did they need to? Was it not clear in these frequent visits to see Sudha?

'I don't know what to do with this Sudha, Mukund. Ever since she finished her MA, she has been out every day with her friends visiting some exhibition or whatever. Please don't misunderstand.'

'What's there to misunderstand in this, Mrs Rajan? All these days she would have been engrossed in her studies, now there is a sense of freedom. It could also be because she thinks that after she gets married, it will not be possible.'

'You're so understanding,' Kasturi laughed. 'I'm sure that like her, you too are thinking of the wedding all the time.'

'Before me, you considered another alliance, didn't you?'

'How do you know?'

She was taken aback.

'Your brother told me.'

When his parents had come to see her daughter, she had requested a cousin to be present because it was preferable to have a man around on such occasions. He must have spoken to Mukund. On the previous occasion too, at the time of the other possibility, she had asked the same cousin to be present.

'Yes. We did look at another alliance. Though I had indicated to them even earlier the limits of what I could afford, they gave a list of things that totalled Rs 8 lakhs, and then a lakh in cash. They spoke about the expenses to send their son abroad to study and then a decent wedding ceremony according to one's wish, and then this and that and that ...'

She was bursting with anger when she had heard these demands. She had stood like a spire of rising flames.

'Are you human beings? Go ... go tie the tali round an airplane and fix an auspicious day to bring the golden palace home.'

Today... today when she looked inside herself and that memory, she could feel the heat of her rage.

Slowly she came back to herself. Mukundan was gazing at her.

'Tie the tali on an airplane and bring the golden palace home, right?' Mukund smilingly asked.

She looked at him astonished and blushed. Did her cousin have to tell him all this?

But on that day, her daughter's response did not echo her anger. Sudha looked disappointed.

'What, Sudha? You think what I said was wrong?' Kasturi asked in surprise after they had left.

'No, Amma. But you'll be relieved if I get married, no?'

'But where will I find so much money? What "relief" if your wedding brings debts and leaves me poor?'

'No one wants you to be poor! I don't want to get married at all ... ever! You be happy.'

Sudha flounced out of the room in a sulk. It took some time for Kasturi to get over her shock. Did this girl want to get married so desperately? It is not as if she, her mother, was not on the lookout for a groom.

She followed her daughter.

'What is this, Sudhamma? Don't you understand my difficulty? This alliance is beyond our reach. Did you like that boy so much?'

'Nothing like that, Amma.'

After a long silence she said in a low voice, 'We went for a walk last evening, isn't it? I think my friend Malathi's mother saw us. Today when I went to their house, she asked me if you were my elder sister. Many people ask me the same question.'

Kasturi was broken when she learnt the reason for her daughter wanting to leave her. What is the solution for this? Shall I wear *vibhuti*[5] on my forehead instead of tilakam? Shall I wear only dull shades hereafter? Shall I tuck the saree munthanai like an elderly lady does? Is there some white hair dye like the black one?

'Just wait and see, soon people will begin to ask me if you are my younger sister?' Sudha joked and tried to change the topic.

Kasturi intensified her search. Finally, through the help of a marriage broker she got to know about this good alliance. Good in the sense, good people who would not demand a list of things or cash in hand or a 'decent wedding'.

'Forget it, Mukund. Why should we think of him now? It is Sudha's good fortune that you and your parents came to see her. If your family gives me a good date in the month of Thai,[6] the marriage can be celebrated, okay? If you think it is better that my cousin asks your parents formally, I will send him. Otherwise you let me know on your next visit.'

---

[5] Sacred ash. Traditionally, the widow cannot wear *kumkumam* or vermilion and hence wears this on her forehead.

[6] The Tamil month corresponding to 14 January–14 February. This month is considered auspicious for weddings.

'Finish this book before I come here next. It is very interesting. We will discuss it.'

A sudden discordance ...

'I bought this book for you. You don't have to return it.'

Just as a little spark of anger lit up inside her, she heard the sound of footsteps outside and Sudha entered dressed in a churidar kameez.

'Amma, yummy food in Vasanthi's house. Oh! Mr Mukundan! Good evening. When did you come? A long time back?'

'Stop this interrogation. Sudha, sit down. He arrived the moment you left. At least now sit down and talk to him.'

'What is this, Amma? I had told him when he came last time that I won't be home today and that there is a party at Vasanthi's place. Right, Mr Mukund?'

Kasturi turned towards him sharply when he asked, 'Sudha, you said you had yummy food, you did not tell us what.'

'Oh that ... butter masala dosa, cashew pakoda, chocolate cake, orange custard ...'

Sudha had traces of Kasturi—the height and the form were surely inherited. But somewhere she fell short. What sprang as a radiance had shrunk, dimmed, and vanished as a dot. One might ask if they were sisters. But surely this one could never have said 'Go tie a tali on an airplane.'

'My stomach feels full just listening to the list, isn't it? Amma, what I have eaten today will last me for three days. I won't have anything for dinner. Mr Mukundan, just wait for few minutes. After eating so much, I feel very thirsty, I'll have some water and be back.'

'I'm leaving too. Some other time.' Mukundan stood up.

'Sit down, Mukund. Sudha go, bring some coffee; he hasn't had coffee yet.' As soon as Kasturi said this, Sudha looked up at her and went in. Kasturi was silent for a few seconds.

'Mukund, did you come here only because you knew Sudha wouldn't be in?' She asked after a while, looking at the wall behind him.

'Yes.'

'Tell me the truth without playing a cat-and-mouse game.' She now looked straight at him, gathering her courage.

'Your decision about the marriage is not a favourable one, is it? Is that why you visit knowing she will be away, not wanting to say it in front of her?'

'The decision is positive, but the marriage is not between me and Sudha. I have a close friend, Dinakar, who works with me in the bank. A very good person, handsomer than I am. He is also firm that he will not demand a dowry. Tomorrow itself I will tell the broker about him to initiate the proposal. Sudha will be married happily to him. Don't worry.'

He stopped. If that was all, the matter was over, why didn't he leave?

He did not. He did not take his eyes off her, as if the conversation was not over. Now what remained? Hadn't he said all that had to be said? He had rejected her daughter. A mother's hurt burst out.

'You will recommend someone else for my daughter, but will not marry her, right? What's wrong with my Sudha?'

'Nothing wrong with her. Sudha is a good, educated, beautiful girl.'

'Then?'

'I can't think of her as my wife.'

'Then why did you come with your parents to see her?'

'At that time I had no clear thoughts on the matter. This is a decision I took later.'

'If this was a decision taken later, why did you come again and again to see Sudha?'

'I came here again and again but not to see Sudha.'

She gasped and her hands involuntarily went to her mouth. She went pale, then turned red. In that shocked wonder, she could not say anything.

Then as her anger peaked, she started to tremble. Her eyes flashing she spat the words.

'How ... dare ... you?'

'Only in our country, all this fuss and anger. It is not a problem at all in the West.'

'Get out rascal before I slap you!'

For a long moment Mukund stared at her as if trying to imprint her face in his heart. His voice and eyes fell on her like soft flowers.

'I will leave right away. I will never return. But I will never forget you Kasturi, as long as I live.'

When Sudha came in with the coffee, Kasturi was standing near the window, a solitary figure.

'Where is Mr Mukundan, Amma? You asked me to get him coffee ...'

Kasturi turned around, her face a study in rage.

'What Mister? What Mukundan? The fellow does not deserve any respect.'

She flung the book on the floor with force.

'Bringing a book indeed, the blackguard!'

'What happened, Amma? Why are you so angry?'

'Arrogant chap! The words he said ... shouldn't he know what to say to whom?' Her breasts heaved.

'What was it that he said?'

'Some rubbish ... forget it. Bring the coffee here, we will drink it and celebrate.'

'Celeb ...'

'You had a narrow escape from a rogue, that's what ... that rascal! Don't worry, Sudhamma. I will find a much better bridegroom for you. Are there no other boys in the world?

His comments ... Chop his tongue, that's what I should have done.'

Sudha placed the coffee tumbler on the table and left the room. She understood just one thing from her mother's remarks, this time too no wedding for her.

As Kasturi continued to stand, still trembling, her chest felt as if it would burst. She stood like that for a long while.

Her eyes moved and fixed on the book that lay on the floor face down in a mess.

Poor book! What did it do? A book is Saraswathi ... cannot insult Her!

She slowly knelt down and kept looking at the book. Her eyes stung. Her lips quivered.

She softly picked up the book and went to the chair, sat down, held the book in her lap, and stroked it gently.

Gradually, darkness shrouded her. She did not switch on the light, but sat there with the darkness for company.

Something in her fluttered.

Kasturi closed her overflowing eyes.

She didn't realize that her lips were smiling.

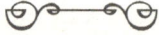

Doors Closed Forever*

My vision dimmed. Like a blob seen through a screen of fog, Amma's face, as she lay there, looked unclear, as it would look when the optician dilates the eyes with eye drops.

I wiped my eyes.

Were these tears only for my mother who lay there unconscious with some pneumonia fever raging in her, breathing through the oxygen tubes?

They were for me too.

When we cry for others, we cry for ourselves, for failing in our duties to them, for not being sympathetic enough, and for not understanding them.

This high fever had darkened Amma's normally wheatish complexion. The fever glistening on her now-dark face. White hair framed both sides of her forehead along the parting, as though she wore a *thalaisamaan*[1] on her dark hair. The forehead bare, there was no *tilakam*. The forehead that had been so for as long as I could remember.

---

* Originally titled 'Iruga Moodiya Kadhavugal', the story was published in *Kalki* in June 1988, and later appeared in *Nagalinga Maram* in 2010 (pp. 219–27).

[1] A piece of traditional jewellery worn on the forehead framing it.

The doctor was not hopeful and he had said so. That is, he said, 'Let us see, Mr Kesavan, we are trying our best. God is great.'

There was some movement near the door and I turned swiftly, but it was only my wife. Did I look disappointed? She must have sensed it.

'Who are you expecting?'

'Mm? No one.'

'You know that at this time it would only be me.'

'Yes.'

'Then?'

'Then? Nothing.'

'I have been watching you in the last four days, both at home and here. You keep looking at the door frequently. Can't I know whom you are expecting?'

Her voice was a bit sharp. When one is right, there is bound to be indignation. A loving wife who looks after my mother uncomplainingly. Does she not have the right to know whom I am expecting and to whom I had written about my mother's health? But if that interferes with Amma's right? Doesn't everyone have a right to privacy?

'No one important, Neela.' I lied.

'Even so you can tell me. Who is it?'

'An old family friend of ours. Very close to Appa. Since we do not have many people as our family, I wrote to him that Amma is seriously ill, regarding him as family. That is all,' I said as if disinterested.

Only last month I accidentally came to know that Mr Chellappa was in this city. Ever since, thoughts of telling Amma about it and the desire to invite him home have been nagging me. The young Chellappa of my memories had gone away on transfer, and now the aged Chellappa had returned to Chennai as the head of his department. Would his hair have turned white, or maybe he would have gone bald and was carrying a walking stick? No, no, no, he will not be more than fifty-five or fifty-six years old. One sees people in their fifties with their upright frame, swift movements and dark hair, who do not look a day more than forty. It is silly to imagine that a person of the previous generation must be decrepit and old. Only to a child's eyes does thirty seem old, but at my age too?

I had not invited him home. I had not even told Amma about it. Ever since she fell ill with acute pneumonia, I had been thinking that I should tell her.

I sat looking at Amma's face. The tongue has not the words to speak all the emotions the heart feels, but the eyes can. When feelings come flooding in, only the eyes speak. The faculties shift their locus.

'Why are you just sitting like this? I am here now, you get up and go home,' said Neela.

I got up slowly.

'*Appappa*, I was fed up by the time I sent the two brats to school. Loud protests that "Appa has taken a holiday from work, why shouldn't we?" When they return in the evening, scold them a bit, cajole and advise them, give them tiffin, and make them study.'

'Even yesterday Arun said that he wanted to see Paatti. Shall I bring him in the evening? He can see Amma and return with you, no?'

She thought for a minute. 'Why? Why now? He is a young child. He will get scared if he sees all these oxygen tubes. Let's decide after four days. Athai may get better and the doctor may remove the oxygen tube, isn't it?'

It is true that the oxygen might be removed. But it may not be because she gets better. We did not acknowledge even to each other the other possibility, which hid behind our silence with a thousand tongues.

Neela had eaten her lunch. She placed the book she had brought with her and the flask containing the afternoon coffee on the corner table. Then she went to the cot and bending down, stared at the motionless figure for a few moments.

There was no change in the patient's condition. This was the message we exchanged, when our eyes met.

'Then I'll go, Neela.'

'Mmh. Sister has given her the injection?'

'Yes. It seems the doctor will come at 12.'

'I'll take care.'

I stepped down into the street. The forenoon sun stung sharply. When I reached home it was 10:30. The hospital was just within walking distance from home. I bathed, ate what Neela had packed into the hot flask, and lay down exhausted. This exhaustion was because of the heat, because I was going back and forth between the house and the hospital having applied for five days' leave. It was because of worrying about Amma ... and it was because of the heart's burden.

Since I had stayed awake all night sitting beside Amma, my eyes burnt now. I closed my eyes. Sleep came in snatches and in that sleep came distorted images which you can't call dreams. Amma's face fading and reappearing, and there, alongside it, an eight-year-old boy. For a minute I opened my eyes and closed them again. Did I sleep again? Now another face appeared—a fair, long face, pleasant smile, a deep look in the bright eyes, wavy hair. While I was looking at it, the face too slipped away. I woke up with a start.

I turned over and fell into a half-sleep state again. And my mother's face reappeared young. It expressed a kind of eagerness. The lips speak and there is shock in the boy's eyes. The head moving from left to right to indicate refusal. I woke up again. I was drenched in perspiration. I did not feel rested at all because my sleep had not been deep and undisturbed. I sat up and looked at the clock. It was 3 pm. I got up and washed my face, turned the gas stove on, boiled the milk, and made *upma*.[2]

The doorbell rang. I rushed to the door and opened it. It was the postman with an invitation for a wedding.

Will the person I am waiting for never come? I had written to him about Amma's illness and all the other details so that he could see her face before she died. Will I not be granted the satisfaction of making possible this small act? I can't convey the message in person because when he is home in the morning and evening, I am with Amma in the hospital. When I have all the time during the day, he is at work. I can't ask Neela because she does not know the significance of this and I am also hesitant to explain to her. Why can't I ask one of the evening nurses to remain in the room for a while, so that I could go and tell him myself? The doctor's face had indicated that there was not much time left. If I waited two more days for a Sunday, it may be too late.

At 4:30, the children Padma and Arun came home from school. I gave them coffee and tiffin. I too ate after setting some aside for Neela.

'How is Paatti today, Appa?' asked Arun.

'Just the same, nothing new.'

'I will come to the hospital and see Paatti, Appa.'

'If Anna comes, so will I.'

'Both of you need not come now, my darling.' I lifted Padma onto my lap. 'After one or two days, we will see how Paatti is and then I myself will take you.'

'Now, in a short while, you will go. After that, both of us have to be alone, no?'

---

[2] A quick light dish made with semolina (rava/sooji) eaten either at breakfast or tea time.

'Why alone? You will be with the next-door aunty for half an hour. Then Amma will return from hospital, fetch you, and bring you home.'

'Appa, when will you again spend the night at home and tell me stories?' Padma snuggled next to me.

I stroked her hair and kissed her.

'Until Paatti comes home, should I not be with her in the hospital, my dear? The doctors say that some family member must be with her all the time. That is why Amma and I take turns to be with Paatti.'

'Mmhmm. *You* must only be here. *You* must not go to the hospital ...'

I pacified the crying child. 'You must not cry, darling. You are a good girl, no? Suppose Paatti wakes up in the night, she mustn't feel sad thinking "*Ayyo*, my son is not here", isn't it? When Paatti comes home, I will come too. After that I will be here at home all the time. I will tell Padma new new stories every night ...'

Won't it be cruel and unfair if I listen to this child and do not go to the hospital? What do children know? It is the adults who should have the wisdom and clarity to decide whether their remarks deserved to be considered.

Why did Amma listen to that eight-year-old boy's words?

I was back again in the hospital in the evening, back beside my unconscious Amma.

'Did the doctor come, Neela?'

'Mmh ...'

'Did he say anything new?'

'Mmhmm, medicine, injection, oxygen, God is great, everything as usual.'

Hesitantly, I asked. 'Did he come? That's what. The one that I sent word to. That man.'

'No one came.' Her keen look said, 'Are you so anxious about someone unimportant? And you want me to believe it?'

I looked away. Indeed I owed Neela an explanation, but she is a very conservative woman. Suppose she thinks the less of Amma?

'Then shall I go home?'

'Mmh yes. The children will be expecting you.'

After she left, I sat next to Amma.

Amma lay motionless. With artificial respiration, there were none of the moans of illness. Her chest rose and fell evenly. Was she living in some other time in her subconscious mind, behind the screen of unconsciousness?

I saw the lines on her forehead, life's tracks. On one such track stands Amma. A young Amma. An apprehensive but happy Amma who looked transformed as if filled with radiance, and an eight-year-old boy in her embrace.

'Do you like Chellappa uncle, Kesav?'

'Oh! I like him very much.'

'I ... I too like him very much, Kanna!'

'He is a nice uncle.'

'Shall I make that nice uncle your father?'

An uncomprehending expression on the boy's face—like a hurdle—and a hesitation on Amma's face.

'What, Amma?'

'Shall I marry him?'

The son had now turned into a figure of shock.

'Mmmhmm. No. It is wrong.'

'You will get an Appa, Kanna!'

'My Appa is dead. You are my mother. Mothers must not do anything wrong ...'

The son had shaken his head in refusal.

That young boy would not know that in that shake of the head, he had firmly sealed the door of another's life. But now I know, I know, I understand, I repent, I am ashamed, and I weep.

The world of children starts in the self and ends in the self. They can see everything and anything only with reference to themselves. *My* mother, *my* father, *my* brother, *my* friend, *my* teacher.

How can a child perceive persons as individuals? As far as he was concerned, Amma was an adult, *his* Amma, *his* guardian, *his* protective background.

How can a child have the insight to look at something objectively and the maturity to identify the mother as a thirty-year-old young woman, filled with expectations, looking at her whole life stretching ahead?

Why did you listen to that child's words, Amma? Why did you listen to that child who could not think of anything beyond his mother? Why did you listen to the child who was a product of a traditional society which thinks that widow remarriage is wrong? First of all, isn't it wrong to ask a child for advice? If you had treated the child as only a child and gone ahead on the path shown by your heart, the child may have protested first. But later I would have understood and rejoiced. I would not have suffered this burden of guilt these many years for ruining the happiness of two people.

If everything had happened differently!

Kumkumam on Amma's forehead, joy in her smile, radiance on her face. Old age and death come to all. But this loneliness would not have been there. To what extent can the son—the next generation—who grows up day by day and branches off to make his own life, however affectionate he may be, be his mother's companion?

I stroked Amma's hair, touched her softly, and grasped her hand. There was no response to anything.

Amma, Amma, how will I reach you? I want to tell you so many things, but my tongue does not stir. Even if I speak, you cannot hear me. But does your heart sense it? Do you understand my love, my grief, my remorse which are unspoken? Do you understand that the silent sobs that shake me now are not only for you, but for myself too, Amma? Do you understand and forgive me?

I think a long time had passed. I lifted my head, sniffed, and wiped my eyes. I went to the bathroom and washed my face with a little water from the bucket.

It was nearing 8. I'll ask a nurse to come and sit beside Amma and go to Mr Chellappa's house myself ...

I had not reached the end of that thought when my eyes identified the person standing outside the door.

There were some wrinkles now on the long fair-skinned face, a grey here and a grey there in the wavy hair. Yet I could recognize the fineness in that face, the pleasant smile, the bright eyes, the father's friend familiar to that eight-year-old boy.

Not knowing what to say, I stood just looking at him. He has come, he has come, he has come.

'Kesav, Kesavan, isn't it? I am Chellappa.'

Even that voice had not changed.

'I know,' I said somewhat falteringly.

'I was not in town for two weeks. I returned only this evening. I saw you ... your letter. I came at once.'

His eyes moved and focussed on the figure lying on the bed. I saw his lips twitch. The feelings of an entire lifetime broke loose in that one look. In a moment he was alone with my mother. This moment belonged to those two. A tiny last symbol of the many years that should have been theirs.

'Come in and sit down, sir. I'll be back soon.' I said and left the room.

Neelayathakshi at Sixty[*]

*L*ooking into the mirror, she plucked out the single white hair, gripping it between the tips of her thumb and index finger. That small white strand which was on her chin was now between her finger tips.

She stared at it. Just four days ago she had cleaned up the hair on her chin and upper lip with Anne French. So soon a new sprout, and a white one at that! It was only after her menopause that this new trouble had started: The frequent locking of her room to remove the fuzz on her upper lip and chin with a depilatory cream. Previously she would lock the door only to dye her graying hair. After menopause, this additional chore. 'Shaving!' she told herself angrily. Marks of the male, in the aging female.

'*Cha*!' she cursed silently and got up suddenly. Just then her knees creaked. It hurt. Arthritis. Sixty years. A whole circle

---

* Originally titled 'Neelayathakshi Ammal: Arupathu Vayadhu', the story was published in *Kanaiyazhi Kalanjium, August Malar*, in 1986, and later appeared in *Nagalinga Maram* in 2010 (pp. 194– 204).

of sixty years starting from *Prabhava*, *Vibhava*, and ending with *Akshaya*.[1]

She went to the windows, opened them, and looked out. The outside was a blur.

Was she losing her vision? A chill hit her stomach.

Then she understood. When she had peered into the mirror, she had been wearing her reading glasses. She now removed them and put on her distance vision spectacles and everything looked as clear as if a veil had been removed from a picture—the street, people, vehicles, tree tops in the distance, houses capped by TV antennae.

Bifocals were an option. But it would proclaim to everyone '*Kizham! Kizham!*'[2]

Everyone was seated in the hall watching TV.

'Paatti, are you comfortable?'

'Come and sit here on the sofa, Paatti, more convenient to rest your back.'

'Sure, sure. But this chair is quite convenient. Do you think I can't sit up straight? Are you all ready to "lay me out in the open on the ground"?'[3]

The puzzled expression on the youngsters' faces indicated at the same time that they didn't understand what she had said, and that the phrase was such an archaic expression, deepening the chill within her for a while.

---

[1] The sixty-year cycle according to the Hindu almanac.

[2] This is a derogatory term for an aged person.

[3] The Tamil phrase *Rezhiyil thooki poduvadhu* is a euphemism for placing a dying person on the ground in anticipation of the end.

'*Oliyum Oliyum*'[4]—young lovers rolled over and over. The grandson and granddaughter were very excited, whispering exchanges, laughing softly, singing along when the songs were familiar, and their fingers or feet tapping with the rhythm. Their parents were in a quandary ... a state of confusion, questioning themselves if they should let the youngsters see these scenes, and, at the same time, justifying to themselves the difficulty of insulating children from the trend of the times.

But she alone was boiling with rage. What nonsense was this? Designed to corrupt young minds ... how wrong to stuff the facts of life down these young minds prematurely instead of allowing them to mature gradually!

'They did show love scenes in the films of olden times. But this? Today's movies are partially responsible for the social degradation we see. As if what is shown on the television and in the movies is not enough, now we have day-long videos like *akhanda bhajanai*.'[5]

The children smiled to themselves at her outburst. 'Poor, Paatti, she has grown old.'

How avidly had this same Paatti, who now frowned at the screen, watched during a recent re-telecast of a movie from forty-five years ago!

Theatrical acting, a song for every frame, lovers who spoke romantic lines positioned two feet from each other, sarees draped to completely hide the figure, fighting adversaries halting their combat to deliver fiery dialogues only to resume their struggle.

The youngsters were not interested. They left for a friend's home to watch a new movie on the video. The parents were also quite bored, but they concealed their impatience. But while

---

[4] A very popular programme on the Tamil TV channel in the 1970s and the 1980s which consisted of song sequences from Tamil movies.

[5] Non-stop chanting. The reference is to hiring of video movies and screening them for a private audience especially at homes.

they watched the movie, they discussed other things that worried them: The monthly visit to the ration shop is due; will we get palm oil at least this month; the clerical staff in the office may go on strike this month; and so forth.

Neelayathakshi alone was completely immersed in the movie. Was it good? That was immaterial. What she saw was not just the movie, she was reliving her youth. She remembered watching this film when she was fifteen years old, seated between Appa and Amma. 'Isn't that button-puff-sleeves jacket nice? We'll make one for our Neela,' said Amma. During the interval, she had bought the book containing the lyrics of the film's songs. Appa had bought a cold drink for her. She sat between her parents feeling completely and comfortingly protected.

Was this the reason old memories were so sweet? Not because the parents now dead were then alive, but for the feeling of being protected. This is what parents create for their children. The child encircled by parents. No responsibilities, no worries. Youth is really not the absence of wrinkles and grey hair. It is the absence of worries and responsibilities. It is the certainty that when I wake up tomorrow, my world will be secure like it is today.

To her own surprise, the tune and the words of the song played on the TV awoke in her memory. She hummed softly with the song. She did not notice her son and daughter-in-law turning to look at her with astonishment. She thought she would not remember the next words of the song, but she found herself recalling every word and as each line unfolded in her memory, she sang the whole *charanam*.[6] And as she remembered that time, forty-five years ago, when she heard the song on screen ... the memories of Amma asking her in a soft voice ... bending towards her, 'Do you know what *ragam* this

---

[6] The last piece in a musical composition—pallavi, anupallavi, and charanam.

is?' her reply '*Simhendra Madyamam*', and Appa praising her '*Shabash*, Neelu!' all jolted her for a moment. For a moment, Time flipped backwards and her world stood on its head. While watching this movie on the TV in 1986 in one of the new urban colonies, in a mosaic-floored concrete construction, seated in an air-conditioned room, she was flung forty-five years back in time, back into the girl in a half saree who had travelled with her parents in a train to watch this same movie in Broadway Talkies. Thinking she would either go mad or her head would shatter, she shouted in panic, 'Turn it off! Turn it off!' When she saw the concerned expressions of the others rushing towards her, she covered her face.

'I will also play with you.'

'This is cards, Paatti, Not *dayakattai*[7] or *pallan kozhi*.'[8]

'Not pallan kozhi, *pallan kuzhi*,' the mother corrected.

'I pronounced it the way I've heard it, how do I know all your old-fashioned games,' the words brimmed with the pride of youth, ignorant of earlier days.

A new feeling now plagued her: An unknown jealousy and a feeling of alienation.

'I know cards. I have won at 304,[9] making 10 over the bid even without a supporting Jack.'

'Go, Paatti. God alone knows what game that is. We are playing Rummy. Do you know Rummy?'

'Rummy gummy. Can you play Bridge? My father was a champion Bridge player. He taught me, and Appa, Amma, and I would play. You know what happened one day … Appa bid three spades, I had five spades in my hand.'

---

[7] An Indian board game resembling Ludo.

[8] Palan kuzhi is a traditional south Indian game.

[9] A card game.

'Don't bore us, Paatti.'

The grandchildren continued to play as if she was not there. After some hesitation, the parents also gradually enjoyed the game.

I am boring them! These kids play mere Rummy; just matching sets and they are insolent to a person who once played an intellectual game like Bridge. It's all because I'm old. Even the other day, I was telling them about a funny incident that happened at my wedding. Both of them looked so lost. Looking at their watches every now and then, yawning, finally they ran away saying, 'We have to study.' After a while I peeped into their room and what did I see? Both of them were discussing world cinema. I shouted angrily, 'This is how you study, is it?' They laughed in my face.

She stood up holding her knee and came into the verandah and sat on a high chair. For a while now she had had this difficulty in rising briskly from a chair. She needed a higher chair, to be able to sit down and get up with ease.

Sometimes, just the weight of memories scared her. If memory could go back ... so many years ... so many years? Was she so old? Those persons and events familiar to her seemed as strange as fiction to the youngsters. 'Oh ... yes I remember it faintly like a dream. I must have been a very young boy,' says her own son half astonished. It was like a stab. Old age ... and then?

For a moment there was a blackout.

I am still alive. I am still with you in this life. Don't exclude me. I will also play Rummy with you.

Her son peeped in. The eyes under her wrinkled forehead were wet.

'Amma, why are you sitting here? Are you crying?' A slight irritation. 'Are you crying because of what the kids said? Forget them. Immature brats. Today's children and their blunt words. Don't make too much of them. Why do you have anything to do with these kids? If you feel bored read *Thevaram, Thiruvachagam,* or *Tiruppugazh!*[10]

'Venu, was I born as a sixty year old? Don't you remember me as a young woman? When that Pankajathamma comes next time, ask her. She and I are the same age. We played together ... she has known me since I was your daughter's age. Me a young girl like a little bird ...'

'Amma, Amma, what is all this? Hungry? Old people can't bear hunger, a pity. Kamalam ... take Amma in and give her something to eat. Go to sleep soon, Amma.'

Don't exclude me.

Something rough on the chin. Grown again. The usual four–five strands of hair and like a jack in the box that white one.

Again doors closed, again apply cream. Are there more wrinkles on the body and face than before? More grey hair? If one could keep tally of grey hair and wrinkles then how good it would be.

But thank God one can't.

It is raining outside. But inside the hall, bright lights, new clothes, loud chatter—the guests had arrived.

She sat a little away feeling the rain in her bones. In her hands too, a tumbler of coffee.

The young ones sat in the middle, the centre of attraction.

'How are your studies?'

'And what sports are you interested in?'

[10] Tamil religious poetical works. *Thevaram* and *Tiruvachagam*, by Saivaite saints, are about Siva; and *Tiruppugazh*, by Arunagirinatha, is about Muruga.

'What Latha? Have you already decided that you are going to become a computer scientist?'

'Rajesh? What are you going to do to match your sister?'

'If you let him, he'll join the movies right away.'

Laughter ... jokes. From her corner, she too smiled showing her teeth.

She was a little vain about her teeth, they were all her own.

When it was time to go, the guests patted the young on their backs warmly. Exchanging small talk with the parents, they neared the door. Then as if they suddenly remembered her they came near, smiling falsely and with raised voices (If one is old does it mean one is hard of hearing?) 'Bye, Amma, take care,' they said. When they arrived they asked, 'Are you all right? Keeping good health?' These were about the only two sentences they said to her. What is 'wrong' with her that they should enquire about her health. Just arthritis. Whoever met her asked the same questions. Was she about to die? Maybe she looked like that to others.

'It is a great support to have an elderly person at home,' the guests told the hosts.

The coffee in her tumbler had gone cold.

What streamed from the sky was not rain, but arrows of fear.

When I get up in the morning, my joints are stiff, but slowly as the sun rises, I wait to make peace with my age-related ailment as my bones are released from the prison of immobility. Do I fear old age?

The systems of Hindu religion, worship youth as divinity in the form of Kaumaram.[11]

[11] The worship of Kumara (Subrahmanya). The six systems are Souram (Sun), Gaanapathyam (Ganapati), Kaumaram (Subrahmanya), Saivam (Siva), Saktham (Devi), and Vaishnavam (Vishnu).

The world of stories and advertisements belongs to youth.

So are the elderly then aliens? *Che*! Old age is also a stage of life. Every stage has its beauty, its value ...

The sound of slippers at the door. Was someone entering the house?

She hastily started to apply dye on her hair.

Her head spun. Was it the regular use of hair dye, or perhaps a stroke? Will my limbs be paralysed?

For a second she was still. Then her hand slowly started applying the dye.

This dark hair did not deceive anyone. Who cares for her black hair? Who bothered to speak to her?

And yet....

Was this heaven?

A vision ... an explanation without any explanation.

She saw her parents. 'Appa, Amma, I am dead,' she informed them.

'Appa? Amma? We had only one child. A girl, Neelayathakshi. Aren't you a man?'

Only then she saw. Her long white beard touched the floor.

The obituary columns elicit three kinds of reactions in her. If the person was seventy and above, 'Ripe age. Has gone after enjoying life fully. Good life.' If the person was young, 'Poor thing. Died early. What to do? That is fate.' Both are distant from her. But if the death was of a person fifty-five to sixty ... Her arthritis hurt her more that day, she felt chilled and sleep eluded her for a long time.

'Hey, Latha, Rajesh. You are just striding ahead. Paatti is struggling to walk on the beach. Shouldn't you hold her hand?'

'Go on, Appa. Must we look after Paatti even here on the beach?'

'Are you coming here or not?'

The youngsters came up with a frown.

At this moment I'm a nuisance to them, my age is an unwanted burden, 'No, no, I don't want anyone to hold my hand. I will come along slowly. Children, you go on.'

With that permission, without giving their father a chance to say anything else, the children ran happily to the sea.

'Hey, Venu. Do you remember? When Latha was a baby, one day we came here ...'

'Yes, Ma. Be careful. Remove your slippers.'

'It was full moon. I brought the food and we all ate here. Appa was with us then.'

The slipper caught in the edge of the saree. Her son and daughter-in-law rushed forward and held her before she fell headlong.

'Careful, Athai. Give me your slippers.' Turning to her husband, she said. 'Do tell her yourself.'

'Will she listen? Amma, didn't I ask you to remove your slippers? You won't listen and continue to walk in your slippers, chasing away the ones who offer to help. If you fall, who bears the burden? If elderly people are as stubborn as children, what can one do? If you really were a child, we could scold you or give you a whack.'

'Whack me. Why are you beating about the bush? If that's what you want, give me four whacks. Take my slippers and hit me with them. Why ...'

'Amma don't talk rubbish. I'm saying this out of concern. It is I who must slap myself with my slippers.'

She panted. Her lips trembled. Unable to speak, she walked with her son's support. After going a little distance, her son tried to turn her back.

'I want to walk a little more.'

'You'll be walking when you return. That too is a stretch you can walk.'

'I want to go near the sea.'

'You know yourself that you can't walk that far.'

'If my legs hurt, I'll sit down.'

'You know you can't get up if you sit down.'

'I can. Let go of me.'

'Don't be silly, Amma. When we told you we'll bring a chair for you to sit, you said you didn't want it because everyone would look at you. Now if you sit down, everyone will stare at you when I help you up. You won't like that. So we will slowly walk back and sit in the car.'

'Let go of my hand. Can you dictate to me that I can't enjoy the beach air or walk on the sand? Will I die if I walk? If I actually die, first cremate me and then walk away.'

She wrested her hand away and walked fast.

'Amma, Amma, listen to me … stop!'

How many times would she have walked on the sand. Hey, sea breeze … I know you. You are my old dear friend. I am used to this thrill that runs through my mind and body. Walking here is not new to me. It's just not walking, I've run around here, I've played catch with my friends. He blames my legs. I've stood near the waves splashing my feet and *pavadai* all wet. I've stood in a sand pit covering myself up to my thighs.

She panted. Knees hurt. Eyes watered. I can't walk, is it? I'll show them.

But no young person says there is beauty in old age. Only the elderly say that.

She pursed her lips and walked faster. She huffed and puffed and walked. The pain became unbearable. Her feet stumbled in the sand, she staggered.

'Amma, Amma, stop. At least hold my hand and walk.' He ran behind her, holding her slippers.

I'll walk, walk. I can walk without any help. I can walk up to the sea. I can stand in the waves wetting my saree.

'Amma, stop!'

'Aaaaaah ...'

The pain and the pace hit her weak legs and she fell.

'*Ayyo*, Amma!'

The son and daughter-in-law came running and lifted her up before the kids, who came from afar running and shouting 'Paatti', could reach the spot. A small crowd gathered. 'What Amma? What happened?'

'*Adada* old lady, poor thing.'

'How can you let old people go alone?'

Many voices, many more remarks.

Warm blood scorched her body. She didn't raise her head. Fatigue swamped her as she lay limp and unresisting in the grasp of her son and daughter-in-law.

'Stubborn as a child. This is what old age ...' There was no connection between the son's angry murmur and his tender grasp.

Tears kept welling in her eyes. The spectacles dimmed. The hands which held her, slowly guided her back into the car. Even then she did not raise her head. Slowly she wiped her glasses. After wiping them she wore them again.

The wrinkles on her hands were visible to the downcast eyes.

The Couple*

*T*he sound of someone approaching ... Thaatha looked out of the window and retreated hastily into the house. In a short while Srimathi came in search of him.

'Several persons have come. Thaatha.'

'I know.'

'Will you come out?'

'Mmmhm!'

'They have come only to see y ...'

'I don't want see anyone. You just listen to all that they have to say and send them off.'

'Will they go without seeing you?'

'Give them some explanation. Tell them I am not well.'

'They will not believe me.'

'Then tell them I'm dead, just go.'

Srimathi turned away without a word. Her heart felt heavy. How many people had come to see Thaatha, all saying the same phrases as if repeating lessons they had memorized? 'Very sad ... poor thing why do *you* have to suffer so at your age?' 'She was such a blessed soul. She has left this world so auspiciously

---

* Originally titled 'Inaip Paravai', the story was published in 1979, and later appeared in the collection *Nagalinga Maram* in 2010 (pp. 142–52).

with her *tali*, flowers, and *manjal kumkumam*.[1] You must console yourself only with that thought.'

'Your son and daughter-in-law care for you so much. Your grandchildren dote on you. Console yourself with those thoughts.'

'What a blow at *your* age when it cannot be borne!'

Even Srimathi felt that all this was meaningless, lifeless verbal garbage which did not even touch the edge of truth. How would it have seemed to Thaatha ...?

She went out determined to send all the visitors away. But it was of no use. However tactfully she tried to make them understand, one of them, more persistent than the others, went indoors to meet Thaatha.

'What can one say, Mr Chari?'

Thaatha who was standing near the cowshed looking up at the sky stiffened. 'Who is it? Varadan? Come, look at the sky. Doesn't it look as if it will rain?' Thaatha asked without turning around.

The visitor was taken aback and could not say anything immediately.

'Why no reply? It will be a relief for all of us in this water shortage if it rains, won't it?' asked Thaatha and turned to smile at the man.

'You obviously do not think so. That's also correct. A little rain won't settle this drought. It must thunder and pour. What do you think?'

The one who came to offer his condolences collected himself and said, 'I heard the news, Mr Chari. I was not in town then. I had gone on work to Tiruchi. As soon as I returned they told me the news. I felt very sad. I just can't think of what to say to console you.'

---

[1] Tali, flowers, manjal kumkumam are symbolic of a woman whose husband is alive.

'Your second son had attended some interview. What happened?'

'You probably don't want to think about the loss, truly you are detached. If you give way to grief it is difficult to recover. You alone can console yourself. You should not have to face this tragedy at this age. Even though as far as Maami is concerned, it is true she has gone away like a Mahalakshmi.'[2]

'The interview was for a bank job, right? Has he applied to any other company?'

Varadan stared at him. He quelled the flash of doubt that plumed. No, no, it can't be ...

'I have come with some friends. They want to go shopping. Just think of it ... such a big world. Was there no room for Maami in it? But nothing is in our hands, it is His will. We are all mortal. Console yourself. Perumaal[3] must give you strength. Be brave, sir. According to custom, I must not take leave of you on such an occasion.'

'So you are leaving. Well, all right. Come another day at leisure. If you come after sunset, it will be a pleasant walk too,' said Thaatha.

Srimathi heard Varadan telling his friends, 'He was always arrogant. Even now he cannot bring himself to be courteous to others. Wonder how that lady coped with this man! Poor thing!'

Srimathi returned to the backyard.

Thaatha was still staring at the sky. Then he looked at the cowshed, then at the stone on which clothes were washed, and then at the jasmine creepers. It was as if he was gently stroking everything that he saw. Srimathi remembered that her Paatti

[2] Goddess of prosperity. In traditional Hindu society, widows were considered inauspicious. So a woman who died before her husband was thought to be fortunate.

[3] Synonym for God, meaning Great Being.

would mix the cow feed for the cows, then wash her *madi*[4] saree, and tend the jasmine creepers. Thaatha had stared at her lifeless body, unblinking. He did not cry. Neither then, nor later in those two weeks that followed had any one seen him cry. All that he did and continued to do was to caress with his eyes every part of the house and every object in it.

She wanted to return unobtrusively, when Thaatha's eyes accidentally fell on her.

'What? Has someone else come to condole with me?' Srimathi swallowed. When it is the loss of a companion of sixty years, can the word 'loss' be an adequate description? Is there any word with the capacity to contain that feeling? A married life which completed the sixty-year cycle beginning at *Prabhava*, then *Vibhava*, and ending with *Akshaya*. Was it just a sixty-year companionship? He had not even glanced at another woman other than Paatti. How many times Paatti had said with moist eyes 'I am so lucky'? That ecstasy lingered even on her lifeless face. Can the full dimension of the meaning of that word be conveyed in the formal words of condolences? Words sometimes do not know when to be silent.

'I am warning you, I will slipper the next person who comes here to enact a full-scale mourning.'

'All right, Thaatha. I will see that no one enters.'

'Good girl, come here.'

He sat on the topmost stone of the steps leading into the backyard where Paatti usually sat enjoying the fresh air. He made Srimathi sit next to him and held her hand in his. His eyes were again fixed on the jasmine creeper. He said nothing. Srimathi cautiously held this silence, as cautiously as one would hold a brimming vessel taking care not to spill a drop. She was

[4] Literally, ritually pure. Traditionally, people washed their own clothes to maintain ritual purity. While they wore madi clothes, no one was permitted to touch them.

very still, believing that even the slightest glance at Thaatha would be an intrusion. Her hand, entwined in his, felt the tremors that went through him every now and then.

'Appa, shall we eat?'

Was it already night? When Srimathi's father called them, his voice fell like a huge rock into the silence. Srimathi looked at Thaatha anxiously. But he said, 'Mmmm, I'll come, you go in.' He said in a normal tone, letting go of her hand. 'You go and sit down to eat. I will follow you.'

But even when all of them had seated themselves, he was missing.

'Is he still staring into the dark?' asked Srimathi's father.

'I think he's forgotten that he has to join us,' said Srimathi's younger brother. 'If Paatti had been here, he would have heard from her!'

Srimathi's elder brother was eating silently. He was newly married. The bride had not yet moved in.

'This has become a daily "drama",' said Srimathi's mother.

'Poor Appa, sometimes I feel it would be better if he cried out aloud. One must not suffer suppressed grief so silently,' Srimathi's father glanced at his wife.

'What kind of grief is this? If he is really grieving, wouldn't he have shed at least a tear when she died?'

'What are you saying? That Appa did not love Amma?'

'What do I know? All I know is that men are not to be trusted.'

Srimathi got up and left the room hurriedly, 'I will go and fetch Thaatha.'

Thaatha came in to eat. He did not say anything. Srimathi's mother served him respectfully as usual. Every time he looked up, his eyes wandered as if they were searching for something. After a while, he finished eating, went out, and washed his hands.

Srimathi's mother who was about to fill his plate, asked with surprise, 'Maama, you haven't finished ...'

'I have eaten, so I got up,' Thaatha answered.

'You haven't eaten curd rice yet.'

'Oh,' said Thaatha, 'That's all right. I feel full.'

Srimathi's father looked at him sympathetically. 'I understand, Appa! I too feel like that. When grief engulfs us, we don't remember what we are doing. I remember Amma every moment. Wherever I look I expect to see her. I can't believe Amma is not with us anymore.'

'Srimathi has grown up. We must get her married soon,' said Thaatha.

When he left the room, Srimathi's younger brother asked his father, 'Appa, how old was Thaatha when he got married?'

'Is it so important that you should know? Go! You've finished eating! Go and study.'

Srimathi and her brothers left the room. Srimathi's parents looked at each other.

'Appa is really unapproachable,' said Rangan.

'I feel afraid when I look at him,' said Kanakam.

'Why?'

'I wonder how a man can be so devoid of feeling. Your poor mother, she slogged for him. Not a jot of feeling that the companion has gone.'

'What is this sudden love for my mother? You never got along with her while she was alive. Whether scrubbing the cows or washing the clothes ... you never lifted a little finger to help her,' said Rangan laughing.

Kanakam glared at him angrily. 'I can see you have chosen the right time to criticize me. Why didn't you ever ask me to help your mother?'

'Should these things be explicitly said?'

'How can someone sense what is buried in your mind? If I so much as approached her, your mother would leap up and down because her ritual "purity" would be destroyed. Did you know that? You have only seen my faults.'

'Must you criticize her even in death? You staged a *Kurukshetram*[5] every day when she was alive.'

'My God! So much repressed anger. Then you looked like a cat that didn't know how to sip milk. You may say a thousand things, every man is ultimately tied to his mother's apron strings. Nothing the wife does will be appreciated. A deep and special place in the heart is always reserved for the mother.'

'Okay, take it like that. You can also be happy that our Naanu, in spite of loving his wife, will always have a deep and special place for you in his heart. Since he is now married, that comforting thought is very important to you, isn't it? I doubt if any mother will get her son married but for this.'

'I am not like that. I deserve all this and more for supporting your mother,' she turned her face.

Rangan thought to himself, 'Truth stings', but said, 'Don't get angry Kanakam, it was just a joke. Do you think I like Appa's behaviour? Death is an unfamiliar concept. If we give it the respect which is due to it by weeping, then the initial shock will dim a bit. If someone doesn't give it that respect and sits like a stone as you say, it is kind of scary.'

'It is not that. When I see your father not crying for your mother, I wonder if all that the wife toils for amounts to nothing and is an exercise in futility, and that upsets me.' Kanakam's voice broke.

Obviously she had put herself in the dead mother-in-law's place. Does everyone experience everything with the self as the basis, even the deepest mystery that is death? Hmm, as far as man is concerned, the world is small, one need not go to the moon to understand that.

'Kanakam, don't think of all this and feel bad,' Rangan said, patting and comforting her.

[5] In this context, a quarrel. In the Mahabharatam, this was the battlefield where the Kauravas and Pandavas fought.

'Let our daughter-in-law come home. Just see how united we will be,' she said.

Soon after lunch, Srimathi's elder brother left for his in-law's house on his scooter. Vatsala's face blossomed when she saw him.

'What! All of a sudden? You didn't tell me you were coming? Have you had lunch?' she asked.

'Yes,' said Narayanan. Both of them went into Vatsala's room. They had got married just a month ago. The auspicious date had been fixed for her to move in, but Paatti's death had postponed it.

'All day we talk about Paatti at home. Those who mourn Paatti never understood Paatti. If you think of that, I feel that Thaatha's behaviour is correct.'

'It seems your Thaatha never wept. It seems he hasn't uttered a word about Paatti till now. Are all the men in your house stone-hearted?'

'Hey, there may be so many things between a husband and wife. There may be so many reasons why Thaatha is like that. Can others understand that? I'm not referring to that.'

'Then?'

Narayanan's eyes softened.

'My Paatti was a wonderful woman.'

'All of you just adored her. Srimathi told me.'

'No one who knew her will be surprised by that. Even my mother who fought with her ...'

'Ayyo! Mother-in-law–daughter-in-law problem in your house? I am scared. Even Appa said we should move out.'

Narayanan smiled and playfully pinched her ear. 'Silly. What is there to be scared? This mother-in-law–daughter-in-law problem was only a ritual between them. Outside they would quarrel like crazy, but every night Amma would heat the milk with saffron and prepare it just right for Paatti. She wouldn't allow even Srimathi to do it. And Paatti might forget anything, but never Amma's birthday. She would go to the temple and do *archanai*[6] for her.'

'Oh. Like that, is it!'

'What I mean is, anyone who knew Paatti loved her. There was a reason for that.'

'What?'

'Anyone who looked at her would feel a joy that they were alive. She was the personification of Life. She embraced life. When we were young, she would tell us stories—king and queen stories, Purana tales, epics, fairy stories. In everything, the Good would triumph and Evil would be destroyed. But she would go beyond to the basic truth that the Life Principle called Living and Evolution wins, and destruction and death is defeat; and imprint it in us. Why does goodness succeed ... because it is Life; why does evil lose because ... it is Destruction. From her perspective Life was a Huge Carnival. Life was a permanent spring. She did not believe in death. That is why I said if you mourn for her you have not understood her.'

Vatsala was listening to him with wonder. It was as if the ecstasy on her husband's face, the remembered joy in his face had drawn her into a magic circle.

'I now feel sad I didn't know your Paatti,' she said.

'No sadness. A sad heart can never know Paatti. The feeling you have that life is wonderful ... that was my Paatti.'

Both were silent for a while. Narayanan looked at his wife tenderly. 'Let us not mourn, Vatsala, let us celebrate life. We will affirm life. There can be no more beautiful and apt way to show my love for Paatti. That is why I came here.' His arms went around her. 'Do you have any objections, Vatsala?' She put her head on his shoulder.

---

[6] Special prayers.

'Why are you crying?' Srimathi's younger brother asked her and sat next to her. Srimathi wiped her eyes and said, 'I really don't know.'

'Thinking of Paatti? I too feel very bad, Srimathi. The house doesn't look good without Paatti.'

'Yes. But I'm not crying for Paatti, Vasu. Funny, but I'm really crying for Thaatha.'

'Why for him? He hasn't cried at all. Why should you cry for him? You are a fool. That's okay, Srimathi. I have written a poem, want to listen? About Paatti's death.'

'Let's hear it.'

Vasu started reading enthusiastically. He had described the death very movingly. His face lit with the joy of creative writing and the pathos of the poem's subject slowly faded. 'Isn't this part very moving, as if you want to cry?' he asked with a joyous expression.

While he was reading, Srimathi stared at the front of the house. No *kolam*[7] there. No kolam for a whole year.

Thaatha was sitting on a chair in the front verandah. When he was with others, he appeared as if he was alone. But when he was by himself, how is it that he appeared engrossed and as if he was not alone, wondered Srimathi.

Even after her younger brother got up and went away, Thaatha sat just like that. Srimathi approached him slowly. 'Thaatha, not sleepy? Shall I read the Ramayanam for you?'

'No, I'm feeling sleepy. I will go in.' It was a long time after Thaatha, Srimathi, and her younger brother had gone to sleep in the hall. Her brother was asleep. But Srimathi knew that Thaatha had not slept. Thaatha didn't know that, nowadays Srimathi was aware of that fact every night. He did not know she was acutely aware that he was tossing and turning, and that

---

[7] The traditional decoration drawn with rice flour in front of the house, which is discontinued during the year of mourning.

when the whole world was asleep, a pair of old eyes was staring into the night.

She heard the faint sound of him sitting up. She was startled. Shall I ask 'Do you want water?' But she didn't have the courage to touch his privacy.

Thaatha stood up. Thaatha walked ahead and Srimathi followed him in the dark slowly and unseen by him.

Thaatha went round the house into every room. He stood here and there and stared. He stood in front of Paatti's pooja room for a while. Then he opened the rear door. He moved like a sleepwalker. The cattle shed, the stone slab, the jasmine creeper—he went and stood near each of these. He stood hesitantly here and there, sweeping his eyes over the sky and the earth. Then he returned. He staggered and reached the bed. Srimathi wasn't sure if he staggered because of the darkness. Srimathi, who had been following him anxiously, returned with relief and crept into her bed softly like a kitten. She pretended to be asleep, but her eyes were on Thaatha.

Thaatha sat on his bed motionless. Then he lay down. She knew he was not asleep. She knew his eyes were open because she could see them shining. She heard a deep sigh.

The next morning, Thaatha did not wake up.

The Fourth Stage of Life[*]

I looked up to see clusters of clouds. The sky had broken into fragments.

The darkness was looming. Would it rain?

Will Sankari get wet lying in the open?

Have I gone insane? Lying out there in the open, was she a living being? Would it matter to the body, which is to be cremated, even the memory turning to ashes, whether it rains or shines?

I am befuddled because I still haven't got used to the fact that she is dead. I must steady myself. I must drink deep the truth of her death and fill myself.

And the fact is it was I who lit the fire.

Sankari has a son, yet it was I who performed her last rites.

Sankari is dead.

My wife Sankari is dead.

My wife Sankari, who fell down from the third floor, is dead.

Am I building a tomb for her with my word slabs? But could any tomb have really limited her?

* Originally titled 'Naangaam Aasiramam', the story was published in 1972, and later appeared in *Nagalinga Maram* in 2010 (pp. 70–83).

Her expanse, her completeness, her sweep—wasn't hers a maturity that claimed these as its birthright?

Nothing could have imprisoned or fettered her.

She was a free spirit. Liberty and bondage are concepts created by us, right? She was a spirit beyond any shackles.

Is it drizzling?

I looked up. The sky was clearer than before. Whence then, this wetness on my cheeks?

Am I weeping for you, Sankari, or for myself?

For whose sake do I shed these tears?

She died yesterday.

Am I weeping because you did not live happily ever after, Sankari?

No, I am weeping for myself, mourning this huge deprivation of your loss and aching if I will ever see a treasure like this again.

I had really grown selfish. Otherwise would it have come to this end?

Sankari, who was my friend's daughter, later my student, and then my wife, was almost twenty years younger than me. Yet she chose to marry me.

'Sankari, do you realize what you are doing?'

'Of course I do, Professor. I never do anything blindly,' she laughed.

She was thirty-eight then, known to me for many years as my friend's daughter. That form and that smile were familiar to me. Was she a beauty? I do not know what to say. Her beauty depended in the eye of the beholder. It was a beauty that was like a many-layered poem, capable of being interpreted by each according to his view. When she said those words with a smile, I realized that this familiar girl had suddenly become an enigma, a new being, the meaning of all I had searched for, and a totally pure vision. It was really a wonder that I, who was quite content with my single state, found in my fifty-eighth year that I had fallen in love. I think it must have been love because our life together was not an old man's folly born out of time, but the union of two equals in its fullness.

Something choked in my throat, and my legs buckled weakly. Had I set fire to all my strength along with her in Krishnampet?[1] The sky was quite bright, and though it was 11 in the morning, the heat did not sting as it should, for it was the month of Karthigai.[2] Yet sweat burst and trickled down my bald head.

How long had I been walking? Away from the cremation ground? Here I was at Luz and its bustling shops, and I sat in front of a department store, totally exhausted.

My heart was heavy. Why did Sankari, who had flown like a breeze lightly into freedom, weigh so heavily only in my heart?

She always called me 'Professor'.

'Am I not your husband now? Do I continue to be just a professor?'

'You are not just a professor, but my professor for everything,' she had said with a smile, which made me lower my head.

A professor for everything. True, she had known me only as a professor; then she had elevated me so greatly in her esteem and had planted her love firmly in that image she had had of me. This was the basic reason why she had married me. Heedless of the passage of time, we would immerse ourselves deeply and revel in the flavour of intense discussion and exchange of views regarding books, philosophical enquiries, and other such subjects. Sometimes she would just let me go on, listening carefully, and then would praise me, 'Professor, when you explain things, I can easily understand even the subtle views of this philosopher.' She would just melt, 'Do you know how happy I am being with you?'

[1] A cremation ground in the city of Chennai.
[2] The Tamil month of 15 November–15 December.

'Hullo, Professor.'

Startled, I looked at the figure standing in front of me, and then nodded.

'Hullo.'

Moorthi stood there, an officer at the income-tax depart-ment. Though I thought of him as *Avan*, he was nearly fifty years old. Seven years older than Sankari, he had been married to her before me.

'May I sit next to you for a while?'

'Sure.'

He sat down. Even at fifty his youthful appearance had not changed—his thick hair had just begun to turn grey. But now his face was ashen with deep sorrow.

'I came to the cremation ground. As soon as I heard the news, I felt like rushing to your house, but I did not have the courage.'

'Why not? I would have understood.'

'I heard she fell from the third floor.'

'Yes.'

'My heart breaks to think what she would have suffered.'

'She did not suffer; death was instantaneous.'

'Thank God for that, Professor.'

Both of us were silent for a while.

'You may be surprised that I still love Sankari,' said Moorthi.

'Why should I be surprised? Wasn't Sankari worthy of being loved by all?'

'But, yet, I was the one who let her go.'

'One must have courage to let go ... and love too.'

'Professor, I do not know for sure if love was the reason for my letting her go. What did I really feel when she told me she wanted a divorce? Was I angry because she said she wanted to leave me? If I had let her go because of my anger, how can you call it love?'

He continued after a moment of silence.

'That too she said she wanted to marry you, after a life of intimacy with me. You know don't you, Professor, how people described us?'

'Yes, they would call you Rathi and Manmatha.[3] Some sarcastically and some enviously. Yes, I know.'

Moorthi sighed. In truth, Sankari and he had lived in an incomparable union. The couple had exalted the body's divinity to its peak and showed the world that sensuality was the purpose of life.

'After living with me like that, you can imagine how enraged I was when she suddenly decided to divorce me and marry someone twenty years older. You can imagine how jealous I would have been. Maybe that was why I agreed to the divorce, maybe I felt why should I continue to live with this woman who thinks someone else is better than me. That is not love. That is anger ... wounded self-esteem.'

'Maybe it was. At the same time, isn't it possible that your ego was not so hurt because the man she left you for was not a man your age but an old man, and that it was not a real contest.'

'True. Can we really understand ourselves? But this much is true, whatever may have been my feelings when she married you a year after our divorce, till this date a certain love lives on in me. And when I heard she had died, I felt an unbearable sorrow. And the yearning to see that body at the cremation ground at least one last time unseen by others was quite uncontrollable.'

Both of us sat there drowning in our memories.

The salesperson looked at us suspiciously. 'Want to buy something?' The question was loaded with the underlying statement, 'If not, just clear out.'

We walked out.

[3] Rathi and Manmatha are the Goddess and God of love in Hindu mythology.

Moorthi asked, 'Where do you now want to go? Home?'

'No plans. What's the hurry to go home? Who is there now?'

'I too am upset. I feel that it will be a kind of healing, to talk to you about Sankari for a while.'

'Let's do that.'

'Instead of walking around aimlessly, shall we sit for a while in that hotel there? I know we won't feel like eating anything, but they won't chase us out if we place our order and sit talking even if we do not eat, right?'

We went in and sat at a table. When Moorthi ordered some snacks, I did not even register what it was. I wonder if he did either. Plates heaped with food were placed before us and we stared at the emptiness amidst them.

Suddenly Moorthi asked, 'You were her literature professor when she was in college, no? Was she in love with you even then? Is that why in the end she wanted to leave me and marry you?'

'No. When she was my student, she was just that—my student.'

She herself once told me that her heart was drawn to me only later. 'In my college days, I often thought can anyone be like Professor Gnanaskandan? Your intelligence and the way you think made me appreciate you so much. Now so many years later, Professor, I need only those qualities. The qualities which I merely appreciated in the past, I fell in love with, and I have now come to you.'

Moorthi asked, 'Why did she suddenly feel that a man known as her father's friend for years, her professor, and so many years her senior, should now become her husband?'

'I think you never understood her, Mr Moorthy.'

'I really didn't. I still can't understand why she, who had entwined her body and life with mine for so many years, who had borne me two children, should ask for a divorce in the end. What attracted her to you?'

'She could critique a book with me, she could discuss and share with me very serious subjects. Lying in bed as man and woman, we could argue all night if Christ or Nietzsche understood human nature better. Therein lay the attraction, can you understand?'

He stared at me with some amazement for a while and then whistling softly he tapped the table with his fingertips and was lost in thought.

'Now I get it,' he said fully and slowly. 'She had indeed changed even before she asked for the divorce. I would come home from office, hold her hand, and eagerly ask if we could go to a movie. She would reply mentioning the name of some thinker and say, "He is speaking at Adyar at 7 o'clock, let us go there." One night, she came to me with a book in her hand, looking aroused and said, "Read this. It is great literature and so philosophical. At the same time, it seems as if there is some literary beauty in the way some philosophers logically explain their thoughts." I could not appreciate this. I could no longer understand what she was saying. I only understood that our relationship had changed. On many occasions, I felt that while she was physically with me, her mind was elsewhere. This change after the life of intimacy we had shared was too apparent for me to miss. In the past when the moon shone brightly, our bodies would come alive in arousal. But now? Sankari asked, "Man has landed on the moon, a great achievement. But horrors are still committed in this world because of class and racial violence. And when you read about them, you feel they are no different from the horrors that were committed during the Christian crusades so many centuries ago. Then, what is progress? Which of the two reflects the real man? What is progress?"'

'What did you say?'

'I said, "Don't talk rubbish."'

I laughed sadly, I felt sorry for him.

'In the end, one night, I went to her, full of passion. She looked at me and as if she was sharing some important information, said, "They say that God is a sea of compassion. But when I see what happens around us, I think that anyone who is really compassionate at heart cannot believe in the existence of God. What do you think?" How can I explain how enraged I was that day, Professor? I shouted, "If you keep on talking like this, I will admit you in a lunatic asylum!" The look she gave me then! I understand today that with that look she distanced herself from me.'

It was he who celebrated this body's divinity with her, and she had gifted him that bounty. But when she evolved, extending beyond this body, he was unable to travel along as her companion.

Sankari told me, 'Professor, with you beside me, my thought shines and grows like a child.'

'Professor, don't you think Sankara's concept of *jaganmithya*[4] is reflected in the thoughts of this foreign philosopher?'

'Professor, can there be a more beautiful sight in this world than a few persons coming together in happiness and laughing freely? Without understanding this, why should people hurt each other, making this world a hell?' And we would talk about that.

Yet another time, 'Professor, how beautiful is the moon. Don't you think we should read poetry or something equally beautiful to realize the fullness of this moment? Shall we read together?'

'Yes, Sankari.'

Her face would glow with an 'otherworldly' joy.

This man wants to know what had attracted her to me.

'She was a very independent person, Professor.'

---

[4] At the heart of monism is the theory that the world is an illusion.

'Yes.'

'I think she decided to leave me as soon as her heart moved away from me. She did not live with me as my wife after that. Her nature did not allow her to be anything that she could not accept. Nothing could control her. She was a free spirit.'

'Yes.'

'I now understand that it is only thereafter that she made up her mind to marry you. She had the honesty to ask me for the divorce.'

'And you had the magnanimity to give it to her.' I remembered that after he had agreed to file for divorce by mutual consent, they had lived separately for a year to comply with the legal requirement.

'Me ... magnanimous, Professor? Did I visit you at least once after you married her to enquire about her welfare? In the end, what is the difference between the way I behaved just because she had divorced me and married another and the way my children severed all ties and refused even to look at her? By not visiting her at all, have I not behaved as narrow-mindedly as they?'

'Who can call you narrow-minded, Mr Moorthi? If you had been that, would you, in the first place, have married Sankari who was a widow?'

The boy who came to remove the dishes saw that they were untouched and looked at us.

'Server, please bring the coffee after a while, by then these plates will be empty,' I said and he left.

I held my head in my hands, a head heavy with the sadness of Sankari's memory.

'When I married Sankari, it never occurred to me that she was a widow. For the first time now, I am curious about that first marriage. I think you know about it, Professor, don't you?'

Casting the heavy weight aside slowly, I looked up. 'I was her father's close friend. I knew the family very well. I blessed the couple when Sankari married Manoharan. I also blessed you both at *your* wedding.'

Moorthi laughed gently.

'Mr Moorthi, are you laughing at the effect my blessings had on both occasions?'

'No,' he said quickly, indicating clearly that that was what he thought, and then asked eagerly, 'Professor, please tell me about that marriage.'

'Nothing much to say. When she was sixteen, she insisted she was in love with him, and stubbornly got married to him. Before giving his final consent, her father asked me for advice. I was the one who maintained that "The now-awakened new life has only fallen in love with itself. How can you resist it?" I told him to say yes.'

'I don't understand it.'

'She was young, the age when one sees life, world, and existence, with a freshness of feeling as though everything is wonderful and amazing. It is the age when the heart comes awake. It is the age, so new, when everything looks and appears ineffably beautiful and stunning. It is the age of joy which intoxicates and turns every day into a dream. Her love for Manohar was a manifestation of this ecstasy. He was only eighteen. You could see the reflection of her flowering in his eyes. He was in the same season of newness, and in fact the manifestation of her dreams. Actually, she was more in love with life than with Manohar. She was in love with the new radiance that arose from her feelings. Her love was with life and budding youth. It is difficult even to think that when she had married a dream, there was a physical element in her married life with Manohar.'

'That Manohar died very young, didn't he?'

'Yes, it was leukaemia.'

'How old was he, then?'

'Twenty-one.'

'A pity, it was such a short life.'

'If you look at it one way, you must say it was appropriate that he died so young. If he had lived like others and grown old, grey, and feeble, life would have gone off-key after Sankari's first flush of emotion had faded. He would have become meaningless. Dreams should never grow old, Mr Moorthy.'

Silence reigned again between the two aging ex-husbands of a woman whose first husband they had been discussing. The persons in the hotel room, staring curiously at us and at our untouched plates, could not have known that both were sitting there thinking painfully of a woman and grieving with only each other for company.

'Sir, not eaten anything?' asked the waiter who had come with our coffee, raising his eyebrows.

Moorthi collected himself before I did.

'We are not hungry. Please take the dishes away, and just leave the coffee. Don't worry, we will pay.'

The waiter carried the plates away.

'I think we must drink at least the coffee, Professor.'

Moorthi drank the coffee. I too lifted the tumbler to my lips.

Would the body have burnt completely to ashes by now?

I replaced the tumbler. I felt full, swallowing the black grief that curled up from the bottom of my heart.

'Why, Professor?'

'I can't, please forgive me.'

Sankari is dead and I am a living corpse.

It was Moorthi who paid the bill and then we came out of the hotel and walked straight along Luz Church Road.

'Of the three of us—Manoharan, you and I—I think it was with you that she formed the lasting union.' Moorthi said. I could sense a regret in him when he looked up and down my aging frame.

'No,' I said calmly, 'in the end, she wanted to divorce me too.'

He stopped in his tracks.

I had to warn him of the rushing traffic, 'Get on to the pavement.'

Stepping on to the pavement, he stared at me and it took him a while to get over his shock.

'What? She wanted to divorce you too?' There was an unmistakable note of disbelief in his voice.

'Yes.'

'Why? Did she want to marry for the fourth time in her forty-fourth year?' For the first time, contempt curled in his lips.

'You foolish fellow!' I said softly.

'Those are strong words, Professor—why?'

'Then what? You have still not understood her!'

'After so many years, why did she want a divorce?'

'She wanted to be alone.' After a pause, I uttered the words, 'To be herself.'

'I don't understand.'

'Her spirit was ready to attain complete maturity.'

Sankari floated before me. Two wide, deep, calm eyes stared at me unwaveringly from that face with its well-defined bone structure, and her voice sounded strong and clear, with the confidence that I would understand.

'Professor, please divorce me. I want to go away from here. I want to live unshackled. I have attained the maturity that I needed from my bonds, my relationships. Now my independence will reach its fullness only in solitude. I cannot stop midway. Please let me go.'

'Please explain to me, Professor, I still don't get it.'

The heat of the sun stung sharply and inside my shirt I could feel the sweat rolling down my spine.

I spoke slowly from the depths of my thoughts. 'Moorthi, every human being is really alone. Even though there may be relationships out of which one forms oneself and one grows and one matures, in the end, one must distance oneself from them all and only then by being alone, by being oneself, one can reach true liberation. Many do not realize this truth. Sankari did. Gradually she grew and became this complete being by attaining self-fulfilment. At first, it was the season when she went through just emotions and dreams throbbing with life which she spent with Manoharan. Then she went past mere emotions and she lived physically and sensually with you. That was the next stage. Though she lived a normal married life with all the three of us, it is significant that it was only in her life with you that she had children. As a woman, she was now complete physically because she had attained motherhood. Then she went past that stage and when she evolved internally, her wisdom and thoughts expanding, she lived with me. Then she went past that stage too, and she attained that maturity when she could reach her fullness only by being with herself in solitude. It then became necessary for her to free herself of all ties including the marital tie, and a complete soul will naturally reach that point. She asked me to divorce her only to be alone, to be released, since she had left behind everything, no, no she had experienced them all, relationships, bonds, duties, marriage, family, and she had untied herself from everything, outgrown everything, and become free. She wanted to be alone, that is why she asked me to divorce her.'

'Amazing!'

'What is so amazing, Mr Moorthi? Did not our ancestors lay down four ashramas[5] for us, four stages in life, commencing from brahmacharya? This was probably the four stages that a *woman* had to live through. She had completely experienced what she had to from the first three stages. She was ready to graduate to the fourth. She wanted me to give way for that.'

---

[5] The four stages of life, *brahmacharya*, *grihastha*, *vanaprasta*, and *sanyasa* which may be loosely understood as student days, life as a householder, retirement, and renunciation.

'And you said yes, right? You had the intelligence to understand her.'

'What is the use of intelligence?' I replied, but only after a moment's hesitation.

'Why?'

'Moorthi, I became bound to her. She went through every relationship, and after living in it, grew out of it. Whereas I, who found my first relationship at fifty-eight, immersed myself in it fully. It had grown in me. Therefore, though I completely understood her, my greed, my intense love for her, blinded me and prevented me from being mature enough to let her go.'

He stood staring at me.

'Mr Moorthi, I told you earlier, didn't I, that *you* had the magnanimity to let her go? I said it because I am bitter that I was not magnanimous. I did not want to lose her. Moorthi, I did not let her go. I refused to give her the freedom that she desired. I stood in the way of her fulfilment. I told her firmly that I would not divorce her.'

I shrank with shame.

He stood shocked. I think he guessed the rest from my anguished voice and my trembling body. His gaze unmoving, he stood there like a stone. I looked up at him. My heart darkened heavily in sorrow,

'We know, don't we, Moorthi, that she was a free spirit? Nothing could hold her back.'

Moorthi did not speak even now.

'I did not let her go ...'

'So ...?' his voice came from a bottomless abyss.

'Yes. So ... she escaped and left me.'

I did not care to see if he came along.

I walked away.

Loss of a Crest Jewel [*]

She was not unused to physical pain. She had endured a lot in her life and yet when I saw her emaciated body put on a ventilator, I felt she did not deserve this final indignity of clinical imprisonment in an intensive care unit. Sometimes our love for a person makes us do what is advised by doctors as best for them and there is no way this dilemma can be resolved. And I am sure she understood the love and affection that lay beneath these decisions. She was that kind of a person. In this instance also she surrendered herself to whatever medical treatment was given to her with no complaints. When I bent down and called out her name on the day when she was semi-conscious, she opened those soulful eyes of hers and they slowly filled with tears. I knew the tears were for me; for the deep friendship we shared. It was her way of saying, 'Good bye, take care and keep writing.' At least that is what I would like to think for whenever we met, even when she was ill or otherwise busy, she would always ask me what I was writing. She belonged to that era of writers who had great grace and warmth for fellow-writers. My friend, the well-known Tamil writer R. Chudamani, whom I have known

* This article appeared in *The Hindu* on 2 October 2010. It appears here with slight modifications.

for the last forty-five years, breathed her last in the early morning hours of 13 September 2010. Come January she would have been eighty.

Chudamani began to write, encouraged by her artistic mother Kanakavalli, when she was in her twenties. Her first story *Kaveri* was published in 1954. In the year 1957 Chudamani also received the Kalaimagal Silver Jubilee Award to be followed by the Narayanaswami Iyer Memorial Award of Kalaimagal for her novel *Manathukku Iniyaval* (A Woman Close to the Heart). They were four sisters and a brother in the family. While her sisters went to school and later to college, Chudamani studied at home due to her physical disability. Apart from her regular lessons she also learnt to paint. But what she enjoyed most was learning Tamil from the well-known writer who wrote under the pseudonym 'Makaram'. When her first story appeared her mother and her sisters were happy that she had found an avenue for her expression. Her younger sister Rukmini Parthasarathy also began to write later and all the four sisters were particularly close to one another.

In the years following Chudamani remained low-profile but quietly made a place for herself in Tamil fiction writing resisting any bandwagon-climbing, both politically and linguistically. She chose a style of writing which was not loud and proclamatory. The core concern of her stories remained till the very end, human life as it is lived in the present day. Women in her stories emerge as characters bracing the strong winds of life, fighting and resisting and sometimes succumbing. Sometimes it seemed as if her characters had exaggerated emotions, but it was more than made up by the earthiness she gave them, and by the lyrical and poetic language in which she painted them, which caught the subtlest of emotions with ease and dexterity.

I came to Chennai in 1964 for my postgraduation studies in Madras Christian College. I met Chudamani in 1965. Balapriya, a writer in the Children Writers' Association, who

knew Chudamani, offered to introduce me to her. I had also
written some stories and had won the Kannan magazine's prize
for my children's novel. After that first introduction I came on
my own to meet her. Around this time a novel I had written for
the Kalaimagal Novel competition won the second prize. They
had sent me a postcard giving me the news. I took the postcard
with me to Chudamani and as we were talking her elder sister
walked in and Chudamani told her, 'There is some good news.'
'A marriage in the offing?' her elder sister asked. 'For us writers, good news is something else,' Chudamani said and told her
about the prize. It felt good to be counted as a writer by her.

As a young girl I was very possessive about Chudamani and
did not like her to like anyone else. Our meeting had to end
with her standing by the window waving out to me. Whenever
I met her, as soon as the ice-cream vendor came in the afternoon,
she would ask me, 'How about an ice cream?' for she knew I
loved ice cream. So did she. Both of us would discuss stories and
Tamil literature over cups of ice cream. I remember embroider-
ing pillow covers with 'Sweet Dreams' written on them and
presenting them for her birthdays. She would graciously accept
them and put them away. She was down with spinal TB at one
point and had to lie on a hard wooden bed but she would still
lie down and talk to me. Not realizing her pain I once wrote to
her that she had not replied to my letters and that I was upset.
She wrote me a letter lying on her back and told me she won't
be able to do this for a while.

As the years went by the nature of our friendship changed.
She had allowed me to mature in my own way without interfering in any way or trying to mould me in any way. Our lives
became very closely wound together in the years following my
MA when I went to Delhi to do my PhD. I stayed with her
whenever I came to Chennai and shared with her the excitement
of research, new friends, and the ways of a different city. I told
her every little thing that happened in my life and shared with

her my unconventional attitude towards relationships and she never once told me to do anything differently. She eagerly read what I was writing and during the long years of lampooning and cruel criticism that I faced, she stood firmly by me giving me the strength to write what I wanted. I had come to her as an admirer of her stories and later I also began to give her my critical views which she heard very carefully. She was not averse to criticism. In fact, a particular critic who always praised her once told someone, 'I don't want to criticize her because she has a physical disability.' She told me she could have taken severe criticism from him, but that after these words that he spoke, his praise hurt her much more than his criticism would have.

In the later years when I wrote *The Face Behind the Mask* on Tamil women writers, I dedicated the book to her, but I had also critically viewed her stories and even my own early stories. She always told people laughing, 'The book is dedicated to me alright, but she has torn me to bits inside.' We had entered a new phase of our friendship with that. In the later years, SPARROW, the women's archives I am part of, and even my three foster children for whom she became Chudamani Periamma, became a part of her life.

Chudamani's own writing received very good notices and she won several awards. She tackled several layers of human relationships and stories like '*Daktarammavin Arai*' and '*Iravuchudar*' and her play *Iruvar Kandanar*, which has been performed several times, revealed her sensitivity towards unspoken and unrevealed emotions on which everyday life is based. In 2009 Chennai Book Fair she was chosen for the Kalaignar Mu. Karunanidhi Award in the category of fiction.

Much earlier in 1966 she had won the Tamil Nadu Government Award. She did not make much of the awards, but I saw her truly happy when Vasantha Surya translated *Iravuchudar* as *Yamini* in English. She continued to write despite physical problems, but the death of her younger sister Rukmini

Parthasarathy hit her hard and her two other sisters became her emotional support even more than before. After the death of her eldest sister a few years ago and the recent death of her other elder sister Padma, she began to feel isolated and lonely. She had a wonderful friend in Bharathi who continued to visit her and cheer her up and ease the pain of recent ailments. Her nephew Anantha took good care of her, but Chudamani had withdrawn into herself.

As someone who does not believe in final resting places I am not able to say the usual formal words regarding her death. But a good homage to her will be to bring out her Collected Works and to institute an award for short stories in her name which her friends and family must take up. As for me there will never be another one like her.

AMBAI

About the Author and the Translator

The Author

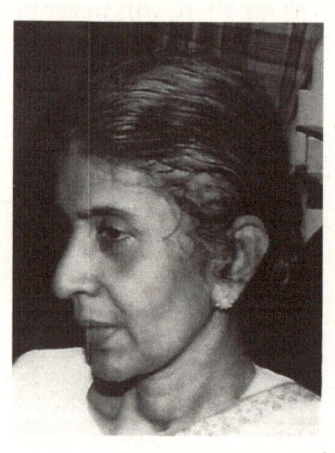

R. Chudamani (1931–2010) was a respected Tamil writer, who has to her credit about 500 short stories. She had no formal education due to frail health. She began publishing in Tamil in 1954 and in English in 1962. She has 32 volumes of fiction to her credit that include short stories, novels, and plays. Her writings are marked by uncommon sensitivity, a laser vision capturing the vibrations in the inner recesses of the human emotional realm, and a subtlety which avoids pronouncements. She lived a life of great nobility and of silent charity. She willed her entire estate to a few deserving institutions involved in humanitarian service. She received the Kalaimagal Silver Jubilee Prize for her story 'Kaveri' (1957), the Narayanasami Aiyar Prize (1959) and the Tamil Nadu Government Prize for her novel *Manathukku Iniyaval* (1966), the Ananda Vikatan Prize for the drama *Iruvar Kandanar* (1961), the Bombay Tamil Sangam Silver

Jubilee Prize for the drama *Arunodayam* (1966), the Ilakkiya Chinthanai Short Story Prize for her story 'Naangaam Aasiramam' (1972), and the Kalaignar Mu. Karunanidhi Award in the category of fiction (2009). Her short stories have been translated into many Indian languages and English.

The Translator

Prabha Sridevan has degrees in literature and law. She was a judge at the Madras High Court (2000–10) and the chairman of the Intellectual Property Appellate Board (2011–13) dealing with patents, trademarks, and geographic indications. She was named by the UK magazine *Managing Intellectual Property* as one of the 50 most influential people in the world of intellectual property for two years consecutively. Her judgements include *The Da Vinci Code* case, the economic worth of a homemaker's work, and the compulsory licence of a cancer drug. She writes regularly in English and Tamil on issues of law and life, and this collection of stories is her first work of translation.